MA

THE WATER'S EDGE

A Selection of Recent Titles by Nicola Thorne

AB		MM	
MA		MN	
MB		MO	
MC		MR	
MD		MT	
ME		MW	
MG			
MH			

THE WATER'S EDGE

Nicola Thorne

MILLS

This first world edition published in Great Britain 2002 by
SEVERN HOUSE PUBLISHERS LTD of
9–15 High Street, Sutton, Surrey SM1 1DF.
This first world edition published in the USA 2002 by
SEVERN HOUSE PUBLISHERS INC of
595 Madison Avenue, New York, N.Y. 10022.

British Library Cataloguing in Publication Data

Thorne,   Nicola
    The water's edge
    1.   Domestic fiction
    I.   Title
    823.9'14 [F]

    ISBN 0-7278-5832-7

Typeset by Hewer Text Ltd.,
Edinburgh, Scotland.
Printed and bound in Great Britain by
MPG Books Ltd., Bodmin, Cornwall.

One

T he wedding would be in the summer after Alan returned from abroad.

Was she sure? Peg Hallam gazed anxiously at her fiancé for a moment, conflicting emotions appearing momentarily to flicker across her face, to be followed by a relaxed, confident smile.

Yes, she was sure. She threw her arms around Alan's neck and kissed him. The onlookers roared their approval as Peg leaned forward and with one tremendous puff blew out the twenty-three candles on the birthday cake. Then, seizing a knife, she cut the first slice with the assurance of one who would shortly do the same thing to a wedding tier while Alan, his arm round her waist, looked on as if sharing her thoughts.

Once again Lord and Lady Ryland had generously allowed the hall at Ryland Castle to be used for the celebration of Peg's birthday and her engagement to Alan Walker, a fellow journalist, whom she had known for three years.

It had not been a straightforward courtship. There had been no doubts on Alan's side but a lot on hers. However, all the family liked Alan and were pleased when, at last, Peg accepted the man who had wooed her for so long. In particular her mother's dying wish was that she and Alan would marry, and in accepting him she felt that she was being true at least to her mother if not to herself.

Peg turned to study his eager face, thrust forward over the

1

cake. There was so much to like about Alan, so much that was good; steady, reliable, straightforward qualities that were so important in one's lifetime companion. What had made her hesitate had been the absence of any feeling of passion on her part, that is until he went away and she realized how much she missed him. Then she was sure. Yes, yes, of course she was sure.

She kissed his cheek again as Mrs Capstick, the cook at the castle whose handiwork the cake had been, moved over to take the knife from Peg's hand and finish cutting the rest.

'Hip, hip,' cried a voice from the back and the crowd took up the resounding response: 'Hooray! . . . Hooray!' Then, as Alan and Peg clasped hands, raising them high above their heads, the crowd broke into a fresh chorus – 'For they are jolly good fellows' – until the rafters echoed.

It was a wonderful way to celebrate a double occasion, a birthday and an engagement: surrounded by her family, who had come from all parts of Dorset, and friends with whom she had been at school.

'Happy birthday, Peg.' The voice came from just behind her, scarcely audible above the crowd, though Peg, recognizing it at once, turned and looked up at the face smiling down at her.

'Oh, Mr Hubert!' she exclaimed shyly, pulling Alan forward.

'We met before.' The Ryland heir warmly shook Alan's hand. 'Many congratulations.'

'Thank you,' Alan said.

'You must be the happiest of men.'

'I am, sir.'

Alan turned as though that was the end of the matter, but Peg's expression scarcely altered. She resisted the tug of Alan's hand as if she was reluctant to move away.

'When is the wedding to be?' Hubert seemed inclined to chat.

'In the summer. Alan has been sent abroad by his paper. He's the European correspondent. I shall be joining him after our marriage.'

'How exciting.' Hubert took out his silver cigarette case and offered it to Peg, but she shook her head as Alan turned away to talk to Hubert's sister Violet, who had joined them.

Just then the band started to play and as couples strolled on to the floor, Hubert, still with a cigarette between the fingers of one hand, lightly placed the other around Peg's waist and began to dance.

'You must be very proud of Alan,' he said as he swept her on to the by now crowded floor.

'Why?' Peg gazed at him challengingly.

'Well, because . . .' Hubert looked nonplussed.

Peg's eyes gleamed 'Because he was given *my* job.'

'Oh, I didn't know that. In that case you must be annoyed with him.'

'Not with Alan, oh no. He couldn't help it. I suggested to my boss, the proprietor of the newspaper, that I should be the European correspondent because so much was happening there, but he said I was too young, inexperienced and, above all . . . a woman.'

'I see you would have been a suffragette.' Hubert looked amused.

'I certainly would. And am. Women have still not got enough rights.'

'You must talk to my sister. I think she is beginning to agree with you.'

'Beginning . . .' Peg snorted.

'Well, you know Violet has led a protected life. Our parents are very conventional. It's the way she was brought up, but now I think she is beginning to change. Since the war, everything has changed.' Hubert's arm tightened around her shoulder and he leaned towards her until their heads were almost touching. 'I'm just sorry I didn't get to know you better before.'

'Excuse me.' Alan, his face as dark as thunder, sharply tapped Hubert on the shoulder and almost wrenched Peg from his arms.

3

'There was no need to do that,' Peg said crossly. 'He meant no harm.'

'I didn't like the way he was looking at you, or holding you.' Alan gazed around at the couples pressed up against them. 'Everyone was staring at you. I felt embarrassed.'

'You forget who he is.' Peg continued to feel angry. 'His father is Frank's employer. I had to be nice to him.'

'Sorry.' Alan held her awkwardly to him and then accidentally trod on her toe. 'Sorry,' he said again, this time more humbly.

Then, rather like an old married couple they continued to dance sedately round the dance floor, not coming too close.

By the time the dance finished Hubert had disappeared. It was cold outside but hot and stuffy in the ballroom. Couples were repairing to an anteroom where there was a bar and table groaning with refreshments. To one side a small crowd was huddled round Violet Ryland, who was talking to Peg's sister Verity and her stepfather, Frank, with whom she'd just had a dance. Violet Ryland was probably the most popular member of her family as she was the most informal and relaxed. She always came to staff parties and behaved in a friendly and unstuffy manner, whereas her parents, though charming and generous, seemed to be on their dignity.

She looked up as Alan and Peg came over, Alan looking hot and uncomfortable, still simmering from the sight of Hubert's familiarity with Peg. The music started again and Violet stood up and extended a hand. 'I think you owe me a dance,' she said. 'You promised.'

Alan blushed violently at the memory of his rash words, uttered while Peg had been talking to Hubert, and shook his head.

'I meant it in fun, Miss Violet. I can't dance.' He turned ruefully to his fiancée. 'Ask Peg.'

'He *is* an awful dancer,' Peg agreed, 'but you're welcome to him if you don't mind getting your feet crushed.'

4

With a gay smile Violet propelled the reluctant Alan on to the dance floor.

'He really can't dance,' Verity said to her sister. 'I was watching you on the dance floor.'

'He's too shy. I'll have to take him in hand,' Peg said, adding, 'after we're married.'

'Why wait that long?'

'Because Alan is going away next week and won't be back until just before the wedding.'

'I didn't realize it was that soon.'

Verity looked gravely after her future brother-in-law then back to her sister. 'You will miss him, Peg.'

Peg nodded. 'But the time will fly past. There is so much to do.'

'I wish you could come home for a while. I do miss you.'

'Oh and I miss you, Ver. But I am needed at work. I have a lot to do. A woman's viewpoint in the male-dominated world of journalism is important. Besides, I want to keep up my journalistic skills. They will become rusty and I'll get out of touch. I don't just want to be a wife when I settle down. I want to be something else as well. Just like you.' She looked at her sister, who was the superintendent midwife in a large Bristol hospital.

The sisters were close. They had lived together in London but after the death of their mother things changed and Verity had moved from London to be nearer her family. There were a younger brother and sister, Ed and Stella, now lost among the crowd here tonight and Addie, who had left her husband to look after her daughter Jenny, both also here but for the moment out of sight. Peg and Verity were also very different: Peg beautiful, impulsive, ebullient; Verity with a strong, handsome face, rather severe, looking older than her years.

A young man with sleeked-back hair, also perspiring from the heat, was leaning towards Peg, nervously fingering the knot in his tie.

'Do you remember me, Peg?'

'Of course.' Peg jumped up. 'Cousin Martin.'

Cousin Martin beamed with pleasure. 'I wondered if we could have this dance?'

'Of course.' Peg smiled at Verity and allowed her cousin to lead her on to the dance floor.

Cousin Martin was one of the many relations on her mother's side, the Swayles, who came from Bournemouth and had attended all the family occasions that had been held in the castle for nearly two decades: the many birthday parties, the wedding reception of middle sister Addie, the reception following their mother's funeral.

After Peg and Martin left her, Verity sat gazing around at the groups of chattering people, the dancers on the floor. She was quite content with her own company, yet nostalgic with her memories of the past. But even on this happy day she felt somehow fearful about the future, wondering what sort of life lay ahead for her darling Peg, who she longed to protect but knew she must lose.

Verity was the eldest, eight years older than Peg. She was loved and respected by her siblings, who were also in awe of her. She was a capable, formidable woman who had lived an adventurous life. The war years were spent as theatre sister in a busy London hospital, and inevitably the effects of that experience had made their mark and now formed part of her personality.

She had been on the verge of marrying a doctor who had jilted her two weeks before the wedding. But Verity had carried on with her life, resolutely concealing her hurt from her family.

Shaking herself from her reverie, Verity got up and wandered round the room, pausing to chat to the many relations and friends who had come to share Peg's happiness, answering the questions they inevitably had about Alan and his adventurous life as the foreign correspondent of a large newspaper, about Peg's good fortune in capturing the heart of a professional man.

The night wore on. As the lights were lowered the dancing

became more intense, couples drawing closer, some openly kissing in the darker recesses of the hall.

Peg danced with a variety of partners and the last waltz she reserved for Alan. They danced quite close together and Peg realized that the next week he would be leaving and she would miss him. He was no Romeo but he had his own unique appeal. He was not wealthy or titled but he had integrity, ability, ideals they both shared and, above all, he was devoted to her. Impulsively again she kissed him.

The following morning, just as dawn was breaking over the nearby hill, Alan, his hands deep in the pockets of his coat, wandered up the road to the castle. It was bitterly cold and he had had very little sleep, conscious of Peg's lingering kiss on the dance floor, her tantalizing presence in the room next to him during the night, so near and yet so far.

He had been introduced to her family at her twenty-first birthday and soon became a favourite of her mother because he was so attentive and polite. He loved leaving his London digs for the warmth and comfort of Peg's Dorset home with her large friendly family, her brother and sisters, her mother and stepfather, Frank. He had been a rather lonely only child from a working-class background in the north of England. He had gone to grammar school and had worked hard to succeed in his chosen profession of journalism. He knew he was clever and ambitious but he lacked confidence in himself as a man. He was tall, thin and bespectacled and he knew he lacked charm. How could Peg, whom he had met when they both worked for a news agency in Fleet Street, fall for someone like him? She was witty, glamorous with a seductive charm. For a long time she had repulsed his advances while maintaining their friendship because they both cared about all the poverty and hardship in the world. They were wedded to the principles of social justice and the equality of man.

It was their strong Socialist beliefs in the gradual emergence of a just and egalitarian society that drew them together, and finally seemed to convince Peg it was a basis for mutual love.

But sometimes he wondered if it was enough. Was it that she was just used to him, like a beloved but well worn coat that one was reluctant to discard?

As he walked along, lost in his thoughts, suddenly a horse loomed out of the early morning mist and, rising on its hind legs, whinnied sharply as it crashed down, its forelegs catching Alan in the chest and pushing him to the ground.

With a startled cry the rider leapt off her steed and, after bringing him under control, threw herself beside the body supine on the ground.

'Oh my God,' Violet Ryland cried, 'what have I done?'

Alan, badly winded, lay looking at the sky, unsure whether or not he was injured. He first wriggled one leg and then another. They both responded. He raised his arms and they too responded. He put a hand on his chest, but there was no blood, just the reassuring feel of the thick material of his winter coat that had undoubtedly saved him.

He was profoundly frightened of horses, and now his fear had been realized. He was shocked, but he didn't think he had in any way been badly injured.

He became aware of the woman beside him but he couldn't speak. Suddenly the bile rose in his mouth and he turned away from her and was violently sick. Embarrassed because of her presence, he attempted to sit up and, producing a handkerchief from his pocket, wiped his mouth.

'I'm terribly sorry, Miss Violet,' he said apologetically. 'I didn't see you.'

'And *I* didn't see you!' she exclaimed, gazing at him anxiously. 'Look, we must get you to the house at once and send for a doctor. You might have injured yourself.'

'No,' Alan said cautiously, wiping his mouth. 'I am quite all right. I can move all my limbs.' With a feeble smile he made an attempt to stand up, but his feet gave way beneath him.

'You're *not* all right,' Violet insisted.

There was a fresh sound of a horse's hooves nearby and Violet got to her feet and frantically waved her arms above her head.

'That will be Hubert. Hubert,' she called through the mist. 'Over here. Quick. There's been a terrible accident.'

Now Hubert, astride an even larger horse, appeared through the swirling vapour and, seeing them, vaulted off his horse. He seized the bridle of Violet's mount, which was still restless, and held it together with his own, at the same time looking incredulously at the figure on the ground.

'Why, it's Peg's fiancé.' He stared at his sister, who had got to her knees beside Alan again. 'What on earth happened?'

'I was trotting along, fairly slowly, waiting for you to catch up when Champion was startled by Mr Walker suddenly appearing out of the mist. He panicked, rose on his hind legs and hit him on the chest.'

'Gracious me!' Hubert stooped to peer anxiously at Alan. 'We must take him at once to the castle and get a doctor.'

'That's what I said.'

'No I . . .' Alan began in a feeble voice, feeling sick again.

'We *insist*.' Hubert handed the reins of the horses to his sister and, bending down, attempted to help Alan to his feet. Alan groggily began to rise and then, to his mortification, was sick again while Hubert nevertheless held firmly on to him. His body sagged as he retched, but Hubert's sturdy grip prevented him from falling.

'Poor chap,' he murmured sympathetically, 'poor old fellow. The castle is only a few yards away. Can you manage it, do you think?'

Too sick to speak, Alan nodded and, preceded by Violet leading the two horses, the two men staggered towards the door of the castle, where a servant, who was polishing the door brasses, threw down his duster and ran over to help them.

'Go and telephone for the doctor,' Hubert instructed Violet. Then, as she obediently went off, to the servant: 'Here, John, help me take this gentleman upstairs. He must lie down immediately.'

Alan was half led, half dragged up the broad staircase of the Ryland ancestral home and along the corridor to a guest room where the bed was already made up although it was extremely cold. He flopped on to the bed fully dressed, still shaken from the force of the impact and the shock.

'John get some wood and coal and light the fire,' Hubert commanded. 'But first go up to my dressing room and find some pyjamas.'

'No, really.' Alan attempted to sit up and then sank back on the bed again. He felt incredibly weak.

'Would you like us to send for Peg?' Hubert enquired solicitously.

'Oh no, not yet. I don't want to alarm her.' Alan lay still for a moment. 'I really think my head is clearing.' His hand then moved to his chest and he prodded it delicately. In fact the force of the horse's hooves appeared to have been taken by his thick winter coat.

'No harm was done,' he went on. 'I'm afraid it was the shock. You see I am very nervous of horses.' He looked apologetically at Hubert, who, he was sure, was a fine horseman. Here was a man he despised because of his aristocratic roots, yet who now surely must despise him?

But Hubert continued to show genuine concern. 'Nevertheless you must stay here until Dr Woolridge has seen you. You must rest. We insist on that.'

'I was supposed to go back to London today,' Alan protested.

'That, I'm afraid, is out of the question,' Hubert said firmly and turned as the door opened and Violet appeared. 'Mr Walker must stay here, mustn't he, Violet?'

'Most definitely,' Violet said. 'The doctor is on his way.'

'No bones broken.' Dr Woolridge, having examined his patient from top to toe, and sounded his chest, put his stethoscope back in his bag and took out a phial of white tablets.

'I don't think there are any internal injuries. It wasn't a very bad blow, was it?' He looked over at Alan.

'What you might call a glancing blow,' Alan replied. 'I think my thick overcoat saved me.'

'He was terribly sick.' Violet still looked anxious.

'I really feel all right now,' Alan assured her.

'Nevertheless a day's rest and a mild sedative is what I prescribe.' Dr Woolridge counted out some of the tablets on to a dish by the bed. 'I'll come and see you again tomorrow. In the meantime I'd like you to stay here, where you will be well looked after, and not move around too much. You may get up this afternoon, if you wish, and try sitting in the chair.' He looked at Hubert and Violet standing side by side. 'Any change in his condition, please tell me immediately.' Then he glanced down at his patient. 'In the meantime as much sleep as possible. Sleep and rest.'

Peg stood at the kitchen door and looked anxiously towards the castle. The morning mist had cleared but there was no sign of Alan. A few minutes before, a car had swept out and Frank, looking out of the window, said he thought it belonged to the doctor.

Peg always rose early and she had tapped on Alan's door, only to find his room empty. She guessed he had gone for a walk – he too was an early riser – but she didn't feel like joining him. It was cold and she had only had a few hours' sleep, so she occupied herself with lighting the fire and making tea for herself and Frank and her sister Addie, who had joined them to huddle, all bleary-eyed, round the kitchen fire.

'It's nearly eight,' Peg said, returning to the warmth of the kitchen. 'I hope nothing's wrong.'

'What could be wrong?' Frank said, spitting on the black shiny boots which he was polishing. He was Lord Ryland's chauffeur, but when he was away he performed other duties on the estate and up at the castle, acting as assistant to the bailiff or the farm manager. Tomorrow was market day and some of the grazing animals had to be sorted out to be sold.

11

Peg went into the hall to get her coat and came back shrugging it on. 'I think I should go and look for him. He may be lost.'

'Lost!' Addie snorted, tying an apron round her waist. 'It would be very hard to get lost round here.' She began to walk towards the larder. 'I'll be getting breakfast.'

'Jenny not up yet?' Frank looked towards the door.

'I'm going to let her sleep,' Addie replied. 'Verity is tired too, and as for Stella, she'll sleep until noon.'

'Alan wants to get a train about noon,' Peg said. 'That's why I'm worried.'

'Plenty of time for that,' Frank reassured her. 'He'll have met someone and stopped to chat. Maybe gone further than he meant to.' He eased on one of his boots and looked up as there was a knock at the door. 'That will be him.'

'No need for him to knock,' Peg said, relief showing in her voice. Hurrying to the door, she flung it open. Her face fell as she saw who was on the other side.

'Why Mr Hubert . . .' she said, backing away. 'Is anything wrong?'

Sensing immediately that such an early visit boded no good, Addie and Frank looked anxiously towards the visitor as he removed his hat and stepped into the kitchen.

'Now there is nothing to worry about,' he said, taking in the worried faces before him. 'Mr Walker has been involved in a slight accident.'

As Peg, ashen-faced, slumped into a chair he went over to her. 'Now really there is *nothing* to worry about. He is perfectly all right, just a little shaken.'

'What happened exactly?' Addie slid into the chair beside her sister and took her hand.

'He was walking along the road towards the castle. It was still almost dark and there was a mist. My sister was starting out on an early morning ride, a little in front of me as it happens, and the sight of Mr Walker appearing through the mist frightened the horse, which reared up and caught him on the chest.'

'Oh!' Peg's hand flew to her mouth.

'Not as bad as you might think,' Hubert hurried on. 'It was a glancing blow. He stumbled and later on he was sick and, of course, very shaken. We called Dr Woolridge who came at once and he has examined him very carefully.'

'I said it was his car.' Frank turned to Peg who still had a hand clasped to her cheek, her face pale with shock.

'Alan is resting in bed at the castle for today and Dr Woolridge will pop in again tomorrow to give him the all clear.' Hubert leaned towards Peg. 'I assure you there is *no* cause for alarm.'

'Can I see him?'

'Of course. He is asleep at the moment, having been given a sedative by the doctor, but as soon as he is awake I will come and fetch you myself.'

Some hours later Alan woke to find Violet sitting by the side of his bed reading. When she saw that he was awake she quickly laid down her book.

'How do you feel?'

Alan blinked and put a hand to his head.

'I think I have a bit of a headache.'

'Oh I do hope . . .' Violet got anxiously to her feet.

'It's nothing. Don't worry.' Alan smiled at her. 'I didn't bang my head. It must be the effect of the drug. I don't like drugs.'

'Neither do I. Would you like a cup of tea?' Violet turned to the bell by the side of the fireplace.

'That would be lovely.' Alan yawned and looked around him at the strange, unfamiliar room. He was in a large, canopied double bed. To one side was a heavy mahogany wardrobe, then a chest of drawers and, in front of the window, a dressing table. The highly polished furniture gleamed in the morning sunshine.

'It's a glorious day,' Violet said, taking her seat again by the bed. 'Pity you're missing it.'

13

Alan lay back and gazed at the ceiling.

'I feel I'm being an awful lot of trouble.'

'Not at all.' Violet put a marker in her book and firmly closed it. 'You could have been killed.'

'No, really?' Alan blinked at her in surprise.

'Yes, really. I mean Champion's blow was very light, but he is a large horse and he was frightened.'

'Not as frightened as I was. I am yellow-livered.'

'Oh, I'm sure you're not.'

Violet smiled at him kindly. She was of medium height, a fair, elegant woman with fashionably cropped hair. She wore quite a lot of make-up, perhaps to hide her natural pallor. She had on a long blue woollen skirt and a cardigan buttoned up to the neck, over which was a single strand of pearls. He thought she was about thirty. He noticed her long hands lying on her lap and a diamond ring on her wedding finger, which he stared at for some time.

'Are you married?' he asked.

'I was engaged to someone who was killed in the war.'

'I'm very sorry.' Alan lowered his eyes. 'I shouldn't have mentioned it.'

'Oh, I don't mind now.' Still, Violet's eyes were sad as she looked towards the window. 'It seems a long time ago. I had a brother who was killed at about the same time, so it did take a long while to get over. My fiancé's name was Ted. Ted Mortimer.' She gave a deep sigh. 'Yes, it's true I miss him.' She looked across at Alan. 'Thank you, by the way, for our dance. I enjoyed it.'

Alan found himself blushing slightly.

'I'm *very* clumsy.'

'Seriously, I did. You should have more confidence in yourself. After all, I understand you're a foreign correspondent. That sounds very brave and responsible to me.'

Alan shifted uneasily in his bed. 'I merely report on the political situation in Europe. No bravery is involved at all. It's not as though there's a war, not yet . . .' He paused.

Violet's large blue eyes widened. 'Oh, don't say that! Surely not another war . . .'

'Well, not at the moment. Maybe never; but sometimes I think things *are* ominous on the Continent. The Peace Settlement was handled so badly.'

'And Peg will join you when you're married?'

'Oh, yes. I can't wait for that.'

'How long have you known her?'

'Three years. You've known her a lot longer, of course.'

Violet nodded. 'Since she was a little girl. We love that family.'

Alan appeared to examine the statement critically.

'But do you really?' he said at last, his head on one side. 'I mean—' he stopped.

Violet raised her eyebrows interrogatively. 'You were saying?'

'I mean . . . well. It's a class thing, isn't it?'

'Not at all. I don't understand you.'

'You don't really think of them as friends. They're servants.'

'I don't think you've got that quite right.' Violet's tone was crisp.

'But you said you loved them. That's patronizing if you don't see them as friends.'

Violet seemed genuinely puzzled, also annoyed, and was framing her reply when the door opened and a maid appeared carrying a tray which she placed on the table by the side of the bed. 'Mrs Capstick says would the gentleman like anything to eat, madam?' she enquired.

Violet looked at Alan. 'A little toast?' she suggested.

'That sounds very nice.' Alan, grateful for the interruption, hauled himself up in bed. 'I think I'm beginning to feel a lot better.'

'I'm sorry I upset your fiancé last night, Peg,' Hubert said contritely as they walked briskly up the hill towards the castle. The mist had cleared and the valley was bathed in the mellow sunlight of midwinter. Up on one of the fells the diminutive figures of Frank and the farm manager could be seen sorting out the sheep for market.

Peg stopped to get her breath and looked at him.

'That's all right. He was just being silly. He *is* a bit touchy.'

Hubert also stopped and gazed at her with undisguised admiration. 'I don't blame him. You're a very attractive young woman. I'm sorry I left it so late.'

His tone seemed half joking, half serious.

'Left what too late?'

'Well you know . . .' His meaning was unmistakable.

'Aren't you married, Mr Hubert?' Peg enquired, a little archly.

'In name only. We married in haste during the war. My brother had just been killed and my father was afraid I might be too, and the family would be left without an heir. The title would die out – a very old title.'

'Oh, you've children?' Peg looked surprised.

'Alas, no. But fortunately I survived, although with an unhappy marriage. My wife and I proved to have nothing in common. Still –' they had reached the castle and Hubert pushed open the door – 'that doesn't mean that I don't wish you and your fiancé every happiness, because I do. He is a very fine chap . . . even if he is afraid of horses,' he added humorously and led the way up the stairs to the door of Alan's room.

'I'll leave you now,' he whispered. 'Violet and I will be downstairs in the drawing room.'

Peg watched him go and then gently tapped on the door and pushed it open. Alan, his face very pale, was lying on the bed and seemed asleep. She crossed the room and stood for a moment looking down at him. Somehow she had expected bruises, but his face was unmarked.

She sat gingerly on the side of the bed and he opened his eyes and immediately reached for her hand.

'You are a silly sausage,' she said, her voice thick with emotion. 'Throwing yourself in front of a horse.'

16

'I did no such thing,' he retorted. Then, after a pause, 'I do love you, Peg. The only thing I thought of after the horse hit me was you. I wondered, as I fell, if I'd ever see you again.'

'Silly sausage,' Peg murmured again, reaching out to crumple his hair. 'Silly old man.'

Two

A lan's departure for his second tour of duty abroad was delayed by two weeks owing to his encounter with the horse at Ryland Castle. He had stayed on for an extra day although his injuries were not considered serious. Perhaps it was because, despite his Socialist principles and his contempt for aristocracy, he rather enjoyed sleeping in a castle and being administered to by the charming and solicitous Miss Violet, whom he had eventually agreed to address by her Christian name. Violet intrigued Alan. The sadness he had perceived, and the cause of which he now knew, added an air of mystery to her dignity, her breeding.

She was the opposite to the outgoing, ebullient Peg and he had never known anyone like her. It seemed to him that they were both rather regretful when he left, that a strange bond had been established of which they were both only dimly aware.

Aroused from his reverie, Alan turned from the window through which he had been gazing, and saw Peg looking at him.

'Penny for them?' she said, going up to him. 'You seemed very far away.'

As if mesmerized Alan stared for a moment at her pinched face, the tip of her nose, slightly pink from the cold. It was freezing inside the house. She wore a red woollen scarf tied loosely around her head, knotted under her chin, and a thick blue overcoat. It was a combination of colours which seemed to enhance her natural beauty. Peg was tall and slim, with a sculpted face, china blue eyes and a pale unblemished complexion. Her hair, which she wore plaited into a soft bun at the nape of her neck, was almost gold with little tendrils escaping across her forehead. Although she was such a modern woman, switched on to everything new, there was a slightly old-fashioned, pre-Raphaelite quality about her appearance which, in Alan's opinion, made her almost unbearably beautiful.

'This time next year we'll be married,' he said with an air of wonder. 'I can hardly believe it. Can you, Peg?'

Peg shook her head but said nothing.

Alan put his hands around her shoulders. 'You still do, Peg, don't you?'

She looked up at him as though she didn't understand. 'Do what?'

'Want to get married.'

'Of course. I wouldn't be looking at this house if I didn't.'

She gazed round at the bright room with dormer windows looking out on to a cherry tree in the small front garden. She remembered what her sister Verity had once told her about how she hadn't been swept off her feet by her fiancé, Rex, but knew that she wanted to marry him and have children, and live in a nice house and . . .

But Peg was very different from Verity. She was ambitious, and somehow the idea of settling down, even in a pretty house like this and having children, failed to appeal. Or maybe it was too premature. Aware of Alan's anxious gaze she said, 'Why did you ask?'

'I wanted to be sure. Sometimes I wonder if you really love me or if . . .' He stopped but she said nothing, her eyes regarding him gravely.

'I wondered if it was because you wanted to go abroad . . .'

'You think I'd marry you just because I wanted to go abroad?' Peg said indignantly.

As soon as he'd spoken Alan knew he'd made a mistake.

'Sorry,' he said immediately, contritely. 'I didn't mean it.'

Peg angrily stamped her foot. 'You're always saying, "Sorry", Alan. Sorry about this, sorry about that. Sometimes I think you don't have *any* confidence at all . . .' She seemed to run out of breath, maybe regretting her intemperance, and stopped abruptly. His expression was so dejected that she knew she had hurt him deeply. He was struggling for words and she felt ashamed of her outburst.

'I don't,' he stammered at last, 'where you are concerned. I don't have *any* confidence.'

Peg, who knew her ability to hurt Alan, now deeply regretted her outburst and clasped his hand. 'You *know* how much I care for you,' she said. 'Look how worried I was when you had your fall. I was beside myself!'

'But is it love?' Alan said, searching her face. 'Is it really love?'

'Yes.' Peg vigorously nodded her head. 'Yes. It is.'

'Then let's get *married* now,' he said urgently. 'We can go to Rome straight away and look for a place when we get back.'

'But don't you like this?' Peg looked round, dismayed. They had spent days looking for a house, and now that they had found one they liked he seemed to have lost interest.

'Yes, I like it. We can still take it.'

'I can't,' Peg said, folding her arms and leaning against the windowsill. It was a cold wintry afternoon and the house was cold. It had carpets and curtains but no furniture and was to let at a reasonable rent. Tucked away in a leafy street just off Highgate Hill, it seemed ideal.

'Why can't you?'

'Because . . .' Peg paused.

'Because you don't love me,' Alan burst out. 'You're playing for time. We could have got married, had the family wedding you wanted. There was plenty of time, but you've been messing about, delaying, making excuses.'

'That is *not* true.' Peg's eyes flashed angrily. 'Why should I delay or procrastinate for no reason?'

'Because you're not sure. You know you're not sure.'

Oliver Moodie employed both Peg and Alan and he valued them equally. He had given Peg her chance on the newspaper and through a fortunate, or unfortunate, circumstance she had achieved almost instant fame. Reporting a political meeting in the East End of London, she had been involved in a fracas which might have cost her her life had not Alan seen her plight and rescued her.

After that both Peg and her family always had a deep sense of obligation to Alan. He became for her a dear familiar, someone who was necessary to her, whom she could not do without, and in time her need for him convinced her that indeed she loved him, and she agreed to marry him.

This feeling seemed particularly strong tonight as they sat in Oliver's splendid dining room at his house in Welbeck Street, which had been the home of his distinguished publishing family for generations. The lights of many glittering candles were reflected in the highly polished mahogany of the Chippendale dining table, on the engraved Queen Anne silver, and they were surrounded by solemn portraits of past Moodies, men and women, many painted by famous artists.

Peg and Alan had often been guests of Oliver Moodie over the past year. To him they were valuable employees. Peg's acerbic articles had increased the circulation of his newspaper, and so had Alan's perceptive despatches and commentaries in depth from the heart of Europe, still reverberating with the aftermath of war.

Usually Oliver entertained several guests to his generous hospitality, but tonight there were just the three of them. The mood at dinner, although relaxed, had been sombre, not only because of the prospect of parting, but because of the growing Fascist threat in Italy where Mussolini had assumed power to rule by decree. For the past six months Alan had been observing the situation in Germany from his base in Berlin. Now he was off to Rome to report on the course of events there.

Peg had a genuinely high regard for their employer, not only because he had believed in her, given her her first chance, unusual for a woman, and promoted her but because he was a genuinely kind man, a man of intelligence, wit and charm.

21

It was true that she had wanted the job of European correspondent and he had given it to Alan, but such was the climate of the time, which was against women working on missions considered dangerous, that she didn't hold it against him, couldn't hold it against him.

'So when is the wedding to be?' Oliver asked as they relaxed over fruit and cheese at the end of a lengthy discussion about events in Europe and their probable course, about which he had closely questioned Alan.

'July,' Peg replied taking an apple from the dish of fruit and beginning to peel it.

'In Dorset?'

'Of course.'

'A big family wedding, I take it?'

'We hope you'll come as a guest?'

'I should love that. I should like to meet your sister Verity, of whom my sister Geraldine is so very fond. Is she happy in her new job?'

'Very happy,' Peg replied woodenly, being the only person in the room who knew that Verity had had a clandestine affair with Geraldine's husband, Philip. Then, 'We saw a house in Highgate the other day. We like it very much and I'm going to move in while Alan is away and get it ready for him.'

'I'd like to get married now,' Alan said quietly, 'but Peg wants to get the house ready.'

'There is so much to do,' Peg murmured. 'At work as well as there.'

'That's good news for me if not for Alan,' Oliver said. 'It means you're going to stay on with me for a while. I shall hate to lose you, Peg.'

'And I hate to go. But I shall also be reporting from the Continent, even if not as official European correspondent,' she added slyly.

'You are both my protégé's,' Oliver continued. 'Two of my great successes. I'm not always so lucky in my judgments about people. I'm very proud of you both and I'm delighted you are going to get married.' Oliver paused thoughtfully. 'And if you would allow me I would like to offer you the house you're interested in as a wedding present.'

'Oh we *couldn't* . . .' Peg looked askance at Alan.

'Possibly accept,' Alan finished for her. 'Besides, it's to rent.'

'Well if you like it very much maybe a purchase could be arranged. I'll make enquiries. Would you like that?'

'It's too generous,' Peg murmured, looking at Oliver. 'I don't know what to say.'

'No need to say anything.' Oliver reached out and pressed her hand. 'Shall we go and have coffee? If Alan's leaving tomorrow you'll want to get to bed early.'

'He really is the kindest man,' Peg said happily as they climbed into the taxi Oliver's butler had called for them. 'I shall miss him terribly. You see I *am* going to marry you.' She smiled and, as the taxi moved away Alan put his arm round Peg's waist and kissed her cheek.

'I'm sorry . . .' he began.

'Don't say it again,' Peg warned, putting a finger firmly against his mouth.

She felt at that moment very close to him. She had been particularly proud of him that evening. He was always at his best with Oliver, articulate and knowledgeable. The breadth of Alan's mind was an essential part of his appeal. She was always impressed by the intensity with which he discussed current political problems, his range, the expression of gravity on his earnest, eager face. He could never be called handsome, but he had a certain kind of attraction when, in the course of intellectual discourse, his face came alive, his features lit up, a lock of hair hanging nonchalantly across his brow, his spectacles gleaming in the candlelight. Watching him perform, Peg had felt proud and mellow, and grew more mellow under the influence of Oliver's excellent food and fine wines.

Alan leaned forward and gave the taxi driver an address, then he sat back and put his arm round Peg's waist again and she cuddled up to him. There was an extraordinary feeling of harmony between them.

'This time tomorrow I'll be on the train,' he murmured.

'Don't!' Peg buried her face in his coat, and they said no more as the cab sped on eastwards through the wet London streets.

Some time before Verity had left London Peg had moved out of the flat they shared in Swiss Cottage and had taken a room in Clerkenwell two streets away from Alan and a relatively short distance from her job in Fleet Street.

All too soon, it seemed, they reached the house where Peg had a bedsit, sharing a bathroom and kitchen with other lodgers.

'It's late,' Peg said as they stopped. 'Let the taxi take you home.'

'No, I'll see you to the door,' Alan insisted, leaning forward to pay the fare, 'as usual.'

'But you're tired. Besides I'll see you tomorrow. I'm coming with you to the station.'

Alan handed the cabbie some coins and opening the door of the cab firmly ushered Peg out and walked her to the front door. She turned to him and he bent to kiss her. She put her arms round him and drew him close, and for some moments as they clung together Peg seemed to see Verity saying goodbye to Rex all those years before and not knowing whether he was going to return.

'I don't want you to go,' she murmured. 'I wish I was coming with you.'

'May I come up for a few minutes?' Alan whispered and she immediately opened the door and they stumbled up the stairs to her room at the top. They paused on the landing to kiss again and then Alan drew away. Peg put on the hall light and opened the door, Alan following her. Once inside the room they embraced again, in the grip of an overpowering sense of physical desire, a heady abandonment which was completely new to them.

As they breathlessly drew apart Alan, his voice thick with emotion, said: 'You don't have to if you don't want to.'

'I want to,' Peg said trembling. 'I want to very much.'

She threw off her coat and he began to unfasten her dress, his hands fumbling with the buttons. 'I'm not very good at this,' he murmured.

'You know I've never done it before,' Peg said shakily.

'Neither have I,' Alan replied as, still only half undressed, they tumbled together clumsily on to the bed.

The lovemaking was very brief and ended abruptly. It was over in fact before it had begun.

Peg and Alan stood on the crowded platform waiting for the boat train to come in, pressed close together because of the volume of people on either side. There were couples like themselves also bidding each other goodbye. Many of them clung to each other, some were openly locked in a prolonged embrace. Peg and Alan faced each other rather awkwardly as though thrown together by force of circumstance rather than desire. He had a hand on her arm, she with fists clenched by her side, unresponsive.

Eventually Peg looked up at him and said: 'Whatever you do, don't say you're sorry.'

'I am.' He rubbed his nose apologetically. 'I hope it hasn't put you off.'

'Of course not,' she said briskly, looking along the railway line and wishing the train would come. She reached up and pecked his cheek. 'Don't let's talk about it.'

'Maybe we should have left it until later? We didn't really have enough time.' His speech was jerky, awkward.

'I told you not to worry.' Peg lightly tapped the tip of his nose. 'Don't worry and don't say you're sorry.' She attempted a brave grin but knew that it was all false.

There was a movement in the crowd and relief surged through her as the train came puffing slowly along the side of the platform, engulfing them in steam.

Propelled along by the swell, Alan seized his small suitcase and, as the doors of the train opened and everyone surged forward, he was swept on to the train as if by a massive wave and was momentarily lost from sight.

Peg ran along the platform, anxiously trying to peer through the windows of the train for sight of him. But he was nowhere to be seen as people gathered in the corridors and the aisles of the train. She didn't even know if he had secured a seat. She stepped back, hands in her pockets, feeling sad and dejected. She thought of Verity and Rex standing on a platform just like this ten years before and wondered what their emotions had been. Regret? Sadness? Thoughts about what might have been?

She felt regret and sadness too, but what might have been *had* happened. They should have waited. She knew that now. It wasn't as if he was going to war. England and the Continent were still at peace.

The guard blew his whistle, the train started slowly to pull out and still she couldn't see Alan. Just the same, she stood watching and waving in case he could see her.

Then as it disappeared from sight dejectedly she turned away, shoulders hunched.

Feeling dispirited, desperately tired, Peg was about to mount the stairs to her room when her landlady popped her head out of a downstairs room. Her name was Mrs Hawkins and she was the sort of person who collected the rent money regularly, dead on time, kept the common parts of the house scrupulously clean but who otherwise kept herself to herself.

'Your sister called you,' she said. 'Verity.'

As she was about to withdraw her head, Peg called out, 'Do you mind if I call her back? It must be something urgent if she rang, because she knows the rules.' Peg thought irritably that she would be glad to move from this place with its rigid rules of 'dos' and 'don'ts', which was why she was so keen to move into the new house.

The use of Mrs Hawkins' telephone, which she kept in her sitting room, was rigidly controlled. Residents were not supposed to receive calls or make them unless it was an emergency, a near-death situation.

'Well, as it's an emergency!' Mrs Hawkins grudgingly opened the door wider.

'Did she say what it was about?' Suddenly Peg felt apprehensive.

Mrs Hawkins shook her head, standing back as Peg went over to the telephone and, mouth pursed in disapproval, pushed a piece of paper forward. 'Said she'd be there.'

Peg looked with surprise at the unfamiliar number, picked up the phone and asked the long distance operator for the number.

'The Antelope Hotel,' an impersonal voice said at the other end of the line.

'Is Miss Verity Carter-Barnes there?'

'One moment.' There was a click and whirring sound and Verity's voice, sounding very distant, crackled on the line.

'Peg?'

'Ver? Is everything all right? Where are you?'

'I'm in Durham, Peg. I was called here early this morning. It's Ed. He's very ill in hospital with meningitis. Peg, I wonder if you could come up?' Suddenly Verity's voice, normally so calm and controlled, sounded desperate and began to crack, 'Peg, I'm so worried about Ed. He really is desperately ill.'

'Ver, I'll be up as soon as I can get a train. Give me the details,' Peg said, her voice also breaking. 'Ver, hang on in there. Stay calm. I'll be with you tomorrow.'

Edgar Hallam had lived most of his life in the shadow of his sisters. As the only brother he had been outnumbered four to one. He was a tall, rather gawky, sensitive young man, bookish and pious, destined for the ministry, which had always been his mother's ambition for him. His mother had had a habit of getting what she wanted, sometimes unwittingly to the detriment of her children.

27

Cathy had been a forceful personality, determined that her children should better themselves, that her daughters should marry professional men. It had been her wish that Peg should marry Alan when such a notion was very far from Peg's mind; and although she had not pushed Addie into her marriage with a schoolmaster she had encouraged it on the basis of what he did rather than on what sort of person he was. In the event it had turned out to be a disaster, and Addie and her husband were now separated.

Ed she had destined for the church, thinking that it would suit his quiet, pious disposition, his lack of interest in girls, his intellectual bent.

Masked and gowned, Peg and Verity now stood by his bed, looking down at his deathly pale face, his figure still and unresponsive.

'It is touch and go,' Verity murmured, taking Peg's hand. 'The next twenty-four hours are crucial.' At that moment the nurse moved towards them and with a smile of encouragement beckoned them out of the ward to which they had only been grudgingly admitted on the grounds that Verity was a nursing sister. The fever ward was well away from the main hospital and visitors were not encouraged.

'Is he any better?' Verity asked as the nurse closed the door behind her, but she only puckered her lips as though she didn't quite know what to say, or how to respond.

Disconsolately the two women left their masks and gowns behind them, resumed their coats and hats and walked slowly out of the hospital.

'How does one *get* meningitis?' Peg asked angrily. 'Above all *why*?'

'It's something you pick up.' Verity shook her head distractedly. 'It's a germ, could strike anybody but usually young people. No one knows why or how. It comes on suddenly and well . . .' Ashen faced she looked over at her sister. 'It *can* be fatal. We must face it, Peg. We should know in a day or two whether he is going to live or die.' And suddenly she fell sobbing

28

on to Peg's shoulder in the middle of the street, with people gawping all round them.

Back at the hotel Peg made Verity lie down and sent for tea and toast. She had come up on an early morning train, not waiting for breakfast. Even now she wasn't hungry. It was not a year since they had lost their mother from TB, and now it seemed too awful to contemplate the same thing happening to Ed.

His gentle character and temperament, his unselfishness and willingness to please endeared him to everyone. He had never been any trouble, adored his mother, loved and respected his sisters, done well at school, sung in the choir, had been an excellent scholar and was also good at games. In a way his shyness made him self-effacing and it was easy not to notice Ed except that now that he was older he had grown so good-looking with the black hair and blue eyes of his father Jack, but without his father's philandering nature which had caused their mother, and other women, so much grief.

The tea and toast was brought to the room they were sharing by a porter. Peg poured and took a cup and a plate of toast over to the bed and sat by her sister.

'Eat something please,' she begged. 'It won't do if you get ill too.'

It was so unlike Verity to collapse that Peg felt at a loss. It was always Verity who took the responsibility, on whom they all leaned, relied on, to whom they went for advice and succour. Peg knew she had not realized how much she loved Ed. He was taken for granted. You never did until you were on the verge of losing a person, and immediately she thought of Alan and how afraid she'd been of losing him.

Verity sat up and sipped her tea. Appreciating its warmth and the cheer it gave her – it was after all the nurse's standby – she heaved herself upright and took the tempting plate of toast Peg offered.

'You're right,' she said briskly. 'It won't help Ed get better if I behave like a silly schoolgirl.' She smiled cheerfully across at Peg. 'It's so good of you to come, darling. I do appreciate it. What with having just seen Alan off you must feel very sad.'

She reached out and squeezed Peg's hand. 'I expect you wished you'd gone with him,' she said as Peg, continuing to look sad, didn't reply.

Suddenly tears began to flow down her cheeks and to her horror she was completely unable to contain them.

Verity flew off the bed and threw her arms round her sister.

'Peg, oh darling. Was it so terrible? Did I say the wrong thing? It was stupid of me.'

'No,' Peg sobbed. 'It was nothing you said. It's not you . . . Oh Ver, I did a very silly thing I—' She stopped and stared desolately at her sister. 'You remember long ago when we talked about you and Rex, you said you didn't . . . you know, that a man didn't *respect* a woman who gave herself too easily. But you didn't know, didn't really know . . .'

'I remember,' Verity said slowly as if the memory still pained her.

'But you said *sometimes* you regretted it, because you thought that *sometimes*, if they did, that is, it made two people love each other more.'

Verity's expressive eyes grew wide.

'Oh *Peg*, you're not pregnant . . .'

Peg shook her head. Her eyes were dry now, but this was a new, horrifying dimension she hadn't thought about.

'I really don't know,' she said, sitting down suddenly. 'It only happened the night before last and was something I never even thought about.' She looked wildly at Verity.

'I didn't enjoy it at all. I had no idea it would be like that. Oh Ver, you're not going to tell me that women have to put up with that sort of thing and pretend to *enjoy* it? Surely you didn't enjoy it, Ver? Or if you did, and other women do, I think there must be something wrong with me. I had thought it was beautiful, an experience to be treasured, but now . . . Surely I *couldn't* have a baby,' she said, and then it was her turn to lean her head against her sister's breast and allow herself to be comforted by her.

'Isn't it funny,' Verity murmured sadly almost to herself, 'how bad things never seem to come singly but in pairs?'

Three

Although everyone saw her as a strong person, Verity knew her weaknesses. The part of herself that she showed to the world was a front to hide these inner insecurities and uncertainties that had dogged her throughout her life, mainly, she felt, because her mother had allowed her to be adopted, had in fact given her away.

This act, which had been forced on her mother through poverty, had in fact been to Verity's benefit. She had received a good education and had flourished and been very happy in the loving and protective care of her aunt and uncle, who had been childless. She loved them and continued to love them and visited them whenever she could; but to her own family she had always seemed remote, the eldest sister whom none of them really felt they knew.

This had changed when she and Peg had shared a flat in London; yet even then the relationship had been a difficult one. She was eight years older than Peg, eleven years older than Edgar, to whom she now seemed not so much a sister as a mother as she watched anxiously over him during the long weeks of his convalescence.

Verity had digs in Bristol, but after Ed returned home she decided to commute, setting off early in the morning to catch the train from Sherborne and returning home from the hospital late at night. So while Addie did the cooking and looked after the house, and saw to the needs of Jenny and Frank, Verity supervised Ed's medical care, and in the course of it the two became much closer and he felt he could confide in her.

Ed had nearly died from a particularly virulent form of meningitis; but he was now on the way to making a full recovery, though still very weak and unable to return to university.

He got up late and read a lot, or went for short walks in the land surrounding the family home, which was the lodge at the gates of Ryland Castle. Sometimes he was accompanied by Addie or Jenny when she came home from school. Sometimes he walked alone or, at the weekends, with Verity. He was thus given the opportunity to think a lot about his life and the illness which had so nearly ended it, and its consequences.

Instead of giving thanks to God it had seemed to drive a wedge between him and his hitherto deeply held Christian beliefs. Or had they really been so strong after all? These and a lot of other questions he re-examined in his mind time and time again. Had he just been trying to please his mother, to do what she wanted him to do?

But this remote, much older sister had become a kind of mother to him now and one day during their walk he told her about his misgivings about entering the priesthood. His wan, thin face deeply troubled, he sat with her on a bench overlooking the lake which lay below the castle. They were both well wrapped up and sat, arms linked, watching the little waves made by the keen March wind upon the surface of the water.

'I wanted to do it to please Mum,' he said. 'Now I'm not so sure.'

'You only wanted to do it to please Mum?' Verity looked at him sharply.

'Well –' he shrugged – 'that and not knowing what I *really* wanted to do.'

'And do you know what you really want to do?' she asked, looking at him closely.

His pale face lit up as he brushed back a lock of his thick black hair. 'It is completely the opposite of being a priest, but I think I'd like to be a soldier.'

'A soldier!' Verity gasped.

'Does it seem so awful?'

'No, not at all. I just never thought you were at all interested in that kind of thing.' Her gaze lingered on him for a long time. 'But then I never knew you very well, did I, Ed? I'm trying to make up for it now.'

'Then what do you think?'

'I think you should give it a bit more thought. Has this idea just come to you?'

'Well, recently.' He shifted uneasily in his seat. 'But I realized I wasn't really interested in divinity studies some time ago.'

'But, Ed, you're in your second year. Why did you say nothing before?' Verity looked at him in surprise.

'Because of Mum. I knew how disappointed she'd be. I didn't want to let her down. Then after her death we were all so upset.'

Verity remembered Ed reading the lesson at their mother's funeral in a fine, sonorous voice and everyone had thought what a fine priest he would make. Did she feel a sense of disappointment too?

'You always seemed so *close* to the Church,' she murmured. 'Sunday school, the choir, always so devoted and strong in your faith. Never missing a Sunday service.'

'Then . . .' Ed hesitated. 'While I was ill I was calling on God, but felt there was no answer. That there was no one there.' He looked gravely at his sister. 'I really wonder if He exists. Don't you, Ver?'

'Oh no!' Verity said fervently. 'I am quite *sure* He exists. And, after all, you did get better, an answer to my prayers. If I did not feel this my life would be empty indeed. Sometimes my religion is the only reality I feel I have to cling on to. And I must believe that one day we will see Mum again and . . . well others who have passed on.'

'Your father perhaps? Do you remember him?' Ed, feeling they had never before talked so intimately, warmed more and more to the sister he had for so long considered a stranger.

'Oh yes,' Verity replied. 'I remember him very well and the terrible day that he had his fatal accident. I was about seven and was sent home from school to help Mum, who was expecting Peg. My father was killed by a runaway horse as he was trying to stop it from bolting. He was a hero really because it could have done a lot of damage, maybe killed someone. Yes, in heaven I will see Dad again.'

'And it was because of that that you were adopted by Aunt Maude and Uncle Stanley?'

'Yes.' Even now the memory seemed painful. 'There was a collection to help Mum, but it didn't amount to much, and she took in washing; but of course none of this was enough to feed four mouths.'

She put her hand gently over Ed's. 'Then what will you do? Go back and resume your studies? You are halfway through your second year.'

Ed shook his head. 'No, I don't want to return to Durham. When I am really well, fit and strong again, I am going to apply to the Army, to do an officer's course, hopefully at Sandhurst.'

Addie stood at the kitchen door feeding the birds. Nostalgically she remembered, as she often did, how Mum used to gather the pieces of bread in her apron and fling them out on to the lawn. It was, she used to say, her quiet time in the morning before the family got up. She would also hang up pieces of fat for the blue tits to eat.

Addie stood for a long time watching the birds and thinking about Mum and her last sad days. Mum had been the strong bough of the tree and they the small branches who were so dependent on her.

Mum had died of tuberculosis nearly a year ago and they never ceased to miss her, particularly Jenny, who was in fact Addie's daughter by an illicit liaison who Mum had brought up as her own.

Addie had married a schoolmaster with exacting moral standards who had refused to give a home to her illegitimate daughter. This attitude, together with a lack of obvious affection on her husband's part, had led to such a deterioration in the marriage that after her mother died Addie had left him to care for Jenny and her widowed stepfather, Frank.

Addie fingered in her pocket the troubling letter she had received that morning from her husband, Harold, and wished so much for her mother's wise advice. Instead she would ask Verity when she returned from her stroll with Ed and, turning back into the kitchen, she busied herself with preparations for lunch. Peg too was expected home any minute and Addie's spirit lifted at the thought of the family all being together again.

Addie loved the freedom of her life at the lodge, caring for Frank, Stella, Jenny and now Ed. It seemed to make the family complete. She had imagined, indeed longed for, a happy family life with Harold and the children they had planned to have. All these dreams had come to nothing. She thought of the letter in her pocket and her heart was suddenly filled with dread.

She prepared the beef and, putting a great dollop of lard on it, popped it into the oven. She had started on the vegetables when she heard the sound of a cart drawing up and she popped her head round the door as a man climbed down from the driving seat and came smilingly towards her.

'Brought you some logs, Addie.'

'So I see,' Addie said, drying her hands on her apron.

'Want them in the usual place?'

'Yes, please, Gilbert, I'll give you a hand.'

She walked over to the cart with Gilbert Youngman, who worked on the home farm and also distributed logs from the estate to the castle and its tenants, and any left over he sold. He had an untidy crop of thick ash-blond hair, a used, weatherbeaten complexion which strongly contrasted with his warm friendly blue eyes, and a massive frame which meant that he towered over everyone. In her mind Addie always compared him to her mental image of a Viking.

Gilbert was a relative newcomer to the estate. On his own admission he was a wanderer who found it hard to settle, finding work where he could and moving on. But he had been given a small cottage on the other side of the castle, worked hard so that he pleased the bailiff and the farm manager, and was generally considered an agreeable and welcome addition to the staff as he was so willing and good-natured.

They began unloading the logs and stacking them in a shed by the side of the house, working companionably and silently together, and when they finished, Addie, slightly out of breath, asked Gilbert if he would like a cup of tea and he said that if she had a glass of beer he'd prefer that as logging was thirsty work.

With his cheerful, engaging smile he followed her into the house, stooping as he crossed the threshold because of his great height.

Addie produced a bottle of beer from the store kept by Frank in the cool larder, removed the stopper and, pouring the contents into a glass, handed it to him.

'Cheers, Addie,' Gilbert said, tossing back almost half the glass at a gulp and then wiping the foam from his lips with the back of his hand.

'Cheers, Gilbert.' Addie leaned against the sink and watched him with the sort of reserved and, she hoped, inconspicuous admiration she felt whenever she saw him. Besides his good looks there was something so robust and straightforward about Gilbert, so honest. You could never imagine him doing anything mean or underhand, shabby or deceitful. He had none of the pretensions that her husband, Harold, had: the lofty manner, the attitude that he was better than his fellows except to his obvious superiors, to whom he was obsequious and deferential. Gilbert was also very good with Jenny, should she happen to be about when he called, which in fact he did quite often on one pretext or another.

'I saw your sister and brother walking up the hill together. He was walking faster than I seed him of late. I reckon he must be on the mend.' Gilbert's West Country accent was not the least attractive thing about him. In fact Addie could find no fault in him at all and she looked forward to his occasional visits, which seemed to have grown more frequent. It seemed to Addie that he deliberately sought her out, and she liked it.

He hardly ever came empty handed, bringing eggs or vegetables or, occasionally, a side of ham or a piece of beef, apart
from the regular delivery of logs.

'My other sister, Peg, is coming today,' Addie said looking
towards the door. 'A real family reunion.'

'That will be nice.' Gilbert drank the rest of the beer and
wiped his mouth again.

'Do you have family?' Addie asked in an offhand manner,
not wanting him to think her too curious.

Gilbert shook his head.

'Not that I know. I was a foundling brought up in an
orphanage.'

Addie's hand flew to her mouth. 'Oh, I'm sorry, I didn't
know that.'

'Nothing to worry about.' Gilbert gave her a confident smile.
'They were very good people. They treated me well and trained
me for farm work, which has enabled me to earn my living ever
since. I have no complaints on that score at all and I have my
freedom to go where I please and do what I wish.'

He finished his beer, stood up and reached for his cap, which
he'd thrown on the table. 'No need to be sorry for me.'

'Well, I hope you won't be leaving again very soon.' Addie
continued to keep her tone deliberately casual. 'We should all
miss you.'

'Should you?' Gilbert stared at her with a curious expression
on his face. 'Well, it's nice of you to say that . . . and I should
miss you too.'

Suddenly the door flew open and Peg ran into the room
followed by Frank, who had met her at the station, carrying her
case.

'Peg!' Addie screamed with delight as the sisters flew into
each other's arms. Peg, face flushed, looked about her, took in
Gilbert standing by the table, cap in hand.

'This is Gilbert,' Addie said. 'Gilbert, my sister Peg.'

'Very pleased to meet you,' Gilbert said, pumping Peg's hand
while she winced slightly in pain. 'I think I know all the family

now.' He nodded amiably at Frank. 'Just brought some logs. Must be off. I'll see you then, Addie.'

'See you, Gilbert,' she said and walked with him to the back door.

'Gilbert seems to be bringing a lot of logs,' Frank observed slyly. 'Soon we shan't have anywhere to put them. If you ask me he's a little sweet on you, Addie.'

'Don't be silly, Frank,' Addie said, flushing, and turned away.

Peg looked quizzically at her sister but Addie, opening the door of the oven, began basting the beef and, looking over her shoulder, said, 'Why don't you take your things upstairs, Peg? Verity and Ed will be back any minute.'

After lunch Ed went upstairs to rest. Frank went off to perform some task or the other and the three sisters, taking advantage of the fact that Jenny and Stella were still at school, and they very seldom had the chance to be alone together, went into the front parlour to chat. After Addie had put a match to the fire laid in the grate, Peg leaned over to warm her hands on the flickering flames.

'I must say he seems rather nice.'

'Who?' Addie, completing her task, looked across at her sister.

'Gilbert.'

'Don't get any ideas,' Addie said with a touch of asperity. 'He is just someone who works on the farm. Besides he's a wanderer. He never stays long anywhere.'

'Oh!' Peg leaned back in her chair and gazed at the ceiling, busy with her own thoughts. Verity, who never liked to be idle, went on with her knitting, which was a jumper for Jenny. Her fingers were busy with the needles and every now and then she paused to gaze at her sisters, happy to be in their company, the two women she loved best in the world now that Mum was gone. She too had noticed how often of late Gilbert's great bulk seemed to be filling up the kitchen, but her thoughts about his

39

suitability as her sister's suitor were as yet unformulated. He was so unlike Harold, not quite what Mum would have wished for Addie. But immediately, Verity knew it was a snobbish thought, unworthy of her, and though Mum might have been ambitious for her children she was a woman of the working classes and most definitely not a snob. She would have wanted her daughter to be happy no matter with whom, but it was quite a leap from Addie's romance with the heir to Lord Ryland and subsequent marriage to Harold the headmaster, to an itinerant labourer, however engaging, attractive, and true he might be.

But this was speculation.

Addie, meanwhile, was groping for something in her pocket and finally produced a crumpled envelope, which she proceeded to straighten thoughtfully in her lap. She was still sitting in front of the fire.

'I had a letter from Harold today,' she said, extracting several closely written pages from the envelope. She smoothed them out and stared at them, as if seeing and yet not seeing.

Verity put down her knitting and Peg, who had been nodding off, opened her eyes wide.

'He wants me to go back to him,' Addie went on mechanically continuing to smooth the pages. 'He says he will take Jenny and wants us to begin again. He even says he is sorry for the past and his lack of understanding. It couldn't be a nicer letter, and yet . . .' Then she faltered and remained looking dejectedly at the pages in front of her.

'And how do you feel?' Verity asked, gently, anxiously leaning forward.

'I . . .' Addie's face contorted as if she was trying to control some deeply felt emotions and her attempts to smooth the crumpled pages, which had obviously been read and re-read, seemed to grow even more frantic. 'I . . .' Then she burst into tears and the two other sisters sprang from their seats and sat on either side of her, attempting to comfort her.

'I don't want to go back to him,' Addie mumbled when the storm had finally subsided. 'I hate him. Besides, I've been away from him for so long, nearly a year, that I can't bear the thought of living with him again. He is like a stranger to me and his letter is full of phrases like how much "better" it would look if I came back and we could resume normal family life again, though how he would attempt to explain Jenny to these people who matter so much to him parents, school governors and the like – I really don't know and he doesn't say. What people "thought" mattered so much to Harold,' she concluded with a gesture of contempt, 'and I think that that is what is really behind the sentiments in this letter, not love or affection for me.'

The tears having subsided, Peg and Verity resumed their seats again and Addie sat on the sofa beside Verity, who thoughtfully picked up her knitting and consulted her pattern.

'What do you think, Ver?' Addie ventured timidly.

'Well you can't go back to someone you hate, if you really *do* hate him?' Verity examined Addie's face carefully. 'You were never really in love with him, were you? Mum was so keen on the idea of you marrying a schoolmaster, a professional man.'

'Oh no. But I did like him,' Addie protested loyally. 'I mean I respected him, but he wasn't Lydd. That was the trouble. Harold wasn't Lydd, or remotely like him.'

Lydney Ryland, the father of Jenny, had been killed in the war. The affair had been brief, very secretive and Lydney's parents to this day remained in ignorance of the fact that he had left them with a granddaughter.

'I think you should meet Harold and talk it over.' Peg put her hands behind her head, gazing thoughtfully at the ceiling. 'I'll come with you if you like.'

But Addie continued to shake her head. 'What's the point?'

'I agree,' Verity said, cursing silently to herself as she dropped a stitch. 'There is no point at all in going back to a man you not only don't love but actually seem to hate. You should ask him for a divorce, saying that you want to start your life all over again.'

'Talking of weddings,' Peg murmured, 'Alan wants to bring

ours forward. He says he can get leave in late spring, or we shall
have to leave it until the autumn. Oliver wants him to go to
Egypt, which is a big challenge, and he thought we could make
it a sort of honeymoon.'

'Oh, that sounds *lovely*!' Addie exclaimed wistfully. 'Isn't
that lovely, Ver?'

'Sounds blissful.' Verity frowned. 'Only, if it *is* to be in the
spring we shall have to get our skates on. How late in the spring,
Peg?'

'May,' Peg said woodenly.

'Well you don't sound very enthusiastic.' Verity looked
sharply at her sister. 'Don't say *you* want to change your mind?'

'Oh no, I don't want to change it at all.' Peg's tone, however,
was unenthusiastic. 'But I think the spring is too soon.'

'We *could* manage it. We've got almost three months. A May
wedding would be nice.' Verity's tone was brisk, positive.

'And a honeymoon in Egypt . . .' Addie joined her hands,
eyes shining, remembering, perhaps, that the best part of her
marriage to Harold had been their summer honeymoon on the
Continent.

'We could manage it, but with difficulty,' Peg said firmly.
'Let's face it, Ver, there is a lot to do and we still have to look
after Ed.'

'Ed is no problem,' Verity assured her. 'He is very much
better. I have persuaded him to go back to university and at
least finish his course while he makes his plans to join the Army.
As a graduate he will have a much better chance of being
accepted at Sandhurst.'

Peg sat up and blinked. 'What new surprise is this? Ed wants
to join the Army? I thought he was destined for the ministry?'

'I haven't had time to mention it. He told me during our walk
today that he felt he had no vocation. He said he knew how
much Mum wanted it, and that it wasn't until after her death he
gave any real thought to the matter. He is also having problems
of faith – you know, whether or not he really believes in God. I
think most adolescents go through crises like this. I'm sure he'll

42

come out of it and, who knows, after a period of reflection he may decide that the Army was a passing phase and he wants to enter the Church after all?'

'Well you do surprise me.' Peg looked around at the other two. 'You know, none of us ever really knew Ed properly. This illness has made all the difference. But still I think I'll write back and tell Alan it will have to be September or October. It's the sort of thing you can't be hurried into, not if you want to do it properly.'

'You *are* sure, aren't you?' Addie said softly. 'I mean, after me and Harold. We don't want the same mistake made twice.'

But before Peg could reply, and perhaps to her relief, there was the sound of light running footsteps in the hall and Jenny, waving a drawing she'd done at school, burst in and, ignoring her aunts, flung herself in Addie's arms.

'Mummy! Mummy! Look what I drawed. You and me and Uncle Frank. Teacher said it was the best drawing in the class. Oh, Mummy, I am *so* happy.'

And as Addie hugged her daughter closely her eyes filled with tears and she looked beyond Jenny's shiny head towards her sisters, silently mouthing the words, 'I am never, ever going back to Harold again.'

Four

'Read the *British Worker*, the official organ of the working classes . . .' Peg, standing on the corner of Eccleston Square, the headquarters of the Trades Union Congress and the Labour Party, tried to thrust a copy of the paper into the hands of a passerby, who ignored her. She smiled wryly at her companion, a student from the university, who had been on the street corner with her since the edition had appeared.

'The *British Worker*,' Peg cried in ringing tones. 'The *British Worker*. The organ of the striking masses . . .'

She ceased abruptly as a man in a bowler hat stopped, raised his rolled umbrella and shook it in her face.

'You should be ashamed of yourself, young woman. The General Strike is a national disgrace and its leaders should be locked up.'

'Have you read today's issue, sir?' Peg asked sweetly. 'It might help you to change your mind.'

With an angry exclamation and final shake of his umbrella the man walked away. Peg's companion grinned at her.

'You were lucky. He nearly stuck it in your eye.'

'Any sacrifice is worth it for the cause,' Peg said cheerily. 'Down with the ruling classes.'

Clearly she was enjoying herself, cheeks pink, eyes shining with excitement. They had been heady days. The General Strike had been called by the TUC on 3 May in support of the miners. The immediate cause was the report of a Royal

Commission (the Samuel Report) on the coal mining industry which recommended a cut in wages. Led by their leader, Arthur Cook, the miners rose up in revolt and persuaded a reluctant Trades Union Congress to call out workers in all the major industries to strike in support of the miners. His slogan, 'Not a penny off the pay, not a minute on the day', occasioned wide support.

Peg had written a strong article criticizing the Commission. For this she had been severely reprimanded by Oliver Moodie, who had banned the article from later editions of the paper and warned her to stop her agitation.

By now the effects of the strike were beginning to bite. Over two million workers had come out and shortages were already being felt. In London transport was crippled. Only fifteen out of 115 tube trains were running; 300 out of a fleet of 4400 buses remained on the street and nine out of 2000 tramcars. Instead London had been invaded by the families of the urban and middle classes offering their services to ferry people round the capital.

Picket lines were set up by the strikers and their supporters, among whom students and the enlightened middle classes were heavily represented. Families were divided. Scuffles broke out between those supporting and those opposing the strike and national chaos was forecast by, among others, the Chancellor of the Exchequer Winston Churchill, who accused the miners of being led by the nose in 'a shocking manner' and challenging the State. He produced the *British Gazette* with the purpose of disseminating information against the strike.

To Mr Moodie's fury the print workers of his paper, the *South London Gazette*, readily joined their colleagues at the *Daily Mail*, who were among the first to come out on strike. The rest of his work force, the journalists and administrative staff, sat around idly with little to do but read the wires and catch up with their filing. Nevertheless they were expected to put in a full day's work.

Several actively sided with the strike breakers and were

allowed to join the opposition, especially if they had the transport to convey the citizens of London around the capital.

The only known supporter of the strike who had openly nailed her colours to the mast was Peg, and she was expected to join her colleagues sitting around idly in the news room. Some went out to write up stories which would be kept on file in case they were needed. No one thought the strike would last long, due to the opposition of the Government, the vigour with which the population was trying to defeat the strike and the half-hearted support of the TUC, which had come reluctantly into the fray.

Peg had almost run out of her supply of papers and was about to make her way back to the office to replenish them when a sleek black Rolls Royce drew silently alongside, the window was wound down and a familiar face appeared.

'Mr Moodie!' Peg gasped guiltily as a finger appeared at the window beckoning to her. 'I was just about to come to the office,' she added.

'Can I give you a lift, Peg?' the proprietor asked in silken tones. His chauffeur, who had got out of the car, opened the door for Peg as she thrust the rest of her papers in the arms of her companion hissing, 'My boss!' and then climbed in, stumbling in her confusion and nearly missing the step. Revolutionary she might have been, but to be caught red-handed by her boss when she was supposed to be covering a story was a disaster.

She flopped into the back seat next to Mr Moodie, who tapped the window dividing him from his chauffeur, ordering him to drive on.

He then looked straight ahead, hands on a silver-topped cane. He wore morning dress and a black top hat and his expression was one of extreme severity. Finally he turned and looked at her as if from a great height and even Peg quailed beneath the hostility of his gaze.

'I take it that wasn't the *British Gazette* you were distributing, Peg?'

'No, Mr Moodie.'

'It was the *British Worker*, I presume?'

'Yes, Mr Moodie.'

'I have just come from the House of Commons, where the Chancellor called a meeting of newspaper proprietors on ways to accelerate the defeat of the strike. We all promised our cooperation. I dare not venture to think what Winston's reaction would be if he knew that one of my staff was standing on a street corner distributing copies of that worthless rag.'

'It is actually very well written and put together, Mr Moodie,' Peg said quietly. 'I suspect that you haven't even looked at it.'

Oliver fell silent again, appearing lost in thought as the car made its way across Trafalgar Square towards Fleet Street.

As it drew up outside the building housing his paper, a crowd of men picketing it surged forward. Moodie quickly told his chauffeur to go round the block and stop at the back of the building, but it was too late. One of the workers seized the handle of the car, threw the door open and, as Oliver rose to remonstrate with the man, caught hold of his coat papers and pulled him from the car.

Horrified, Peg tumbled out after him and as other members of the picket surged forward, she began to argue with them in an effort to protect her boss.

'Don't be so *foolish*,' she shouted as they suddenly fell silent. 'If you harm this man, that is how you get yourself and the movement a bad name. No one wants to support violence – above all, your sympathizers. *I* am a sympathizer. Now let him go into the building and behave yourselves. The workers' movement is in favour of peaceful protest, not violence.' The burly print worker, who still hung fast to the coat of the hapless Oliver, stared at Peg in amazement and then, as a crowd of his fellow workers gathered round him, he released his captive and stood back while a path was cleared to the door with lines of surly, angry men on either side.

Looking neither to right nor left, but visibly shaken, Moodie

47

entered the building while Peg followed, but just in front of the door she stopped.

'Thank you,' she said to the ringleader. 'Mr Moodie is a very powerful and influential man. He has just come from a meeting with the Chancellor of the Exchequer at the House of Commons.' At the mention of the hated name the men started murmuring ominously again and, massing together, closed the path they had created to the door, so that Peg, standing on the steps, was addressing them from a superior height.

'I am with you fellow workers,' she proclaimed. 'I work as a journalist on this paper and wrote an article condemning the Samuel Report when it first appeared. I want justice not only for miners but for *all* workers. If you like I will try and arrange a meeting for you with the proprietor, Mr Moodie, so that you can explain your case. I don't promise to be successful but I'll try. In the meantime you can best make your point if you picket peacefully without intimidation.'

'Good lass,' a man shouted from the crowd who had listened carefully to her. 'Up the working classes!'

'Long live the revolution,' cried another.

'I'll see what I can do,' Peg said and as the men began to clap her she entered the building where an astonished group of colleagues awaited her, but of Mr Moodie there was no sign.

Later that day he sent for her. She had spent the time in the newsroom writing up an account of her meeting, trying once again to put the case for the workers. It was true that a small proportion of the population lived well, even luxuriously, while a very much larger proportion were in poverty. The General Strike in England, almost unprecedented, was being monitored closely on the Continent where it was being compared to the Syndicalist and other revolutionary movements. Peg felt that there was little sympathy for her in the newsroom, and she was being isolated by men who had homes and families to support and who feared for their jobs. It was true that many of them had resented her, not only because she was a woman but because she was seen as the proprietor's protégée, his pet. Furthermore Alan, her fiancé, had been wooed from another paper and promoted over the heads of all the ambitious journalists as a foreign correspondent.

It was also well known that she and Alan dined at the proprietor's house, a privilege that would never have been extended to anyone else, even the news editor. So she had few friends around her that afternoon as she attempted to make something positive of her adventure early on in the day. Meanwhile the crowd that was gathered on the pavement outside began to dwindle, disappointed, as hope of seeing the proprietor faded.

'Mr Moodie would like to see you, Miss Hallam,' a voice murmured at her side. It was Mr Moodie's secretary and Peg followed her out of the newsroom to the next floor, neither women exchanging a word. Peg was sure that the secretary had had a full account of the morning's events and disapproved of her too. Her lips pursed, her gaze unfriendly, she threw open Mr Moodie's door for Peg to enter.

Mr Moodie sat at his desk looking considerably calmer than he had a few hours before, his dignity and *amour propre* fully restored. However, he did not rise as she came in and his expression remained cold and forbidding.

She wondered whether to sit down or not, but he didn't point to a chair, so she remained standing.

He joined his hands on the desk and cleared his throat.

'Thank you for your intervention today, Peg. Once again you showed disregard for your own safety in what you did for me. The mood of those ruffians was very angry indeed and they could have harmed us both.'

'Oh, I don't think so, Mr Moodie!' Peg had bridled at the word 'ruffian' and her eyes blazed with anger.

'That is where we differ, as about much else,' Moodie said loftily. 'And why, though I'm most grateful for your intervention, I'm afraid I cannot allow a member of my staff to side so blatantly with a movement that is intent on destroying this country.'

As Peg tried to speak he raised his hand. 'Oh, please don't try and defend yourself, or them. I fought in a war to preserve democracy and a decent way of life and these people are out to wreck it. I am one hundred per cent behind the Government and against being brought to my knees by a gang of unprincipled Socialists and anarchists. I have already lost a lot of money as a result of my own workers striking in the print room and I shall be very reluctant to reinstate the leaders, even if they beg me to take them back. There are plenty of people wanting work and there will be more when this is over. We must defeat the strike and punish the wrongdoers.'

Moodie paused and tapped his fingers on the polished surface of his desk. 'You have disappointed me, Peg. I liked you, befriended you. I gave you a chance . . .'

'For which I am very grateful.'

'And is this, *this* how you show your gratitude? I invited you to my house and now you have betrayed me. By siding with forces trying to bring down the elected government of this country . . .'

'Mr Moodie you know that is not so.' Still standing, Peg stamped her foot in anger. 'Nor is it just. It is *most* unjust. The wages of these miners were cut by thirteen per cent and the number of working hours increased. It is disgusting, backbreaking work they do in terrible conditions. The mine owners meanwhile live in large houses and they were the first to cut wages, yet I think that none are anywhere near the poverty line . . .'

Mr Moodie stood up, his fingers thrust in the pockets of his waistcoat. 'That is enough, Peg. I have had quite enough. I see you are not in the least bit contrite or persuaded of the error of your ways. I am therefore suspending you for the duration of the strike. Please clear your desk and leave the building at once and do not attempt to re-enter until you have my express permission. But for my respect for your husband-to-be I would not hesitate to dismiss you here and now. What does *he* think of your position, I'd like to know?' Without waiting for a reply, he continued: 'You have shown nothing but ingratitude for all I have done for you; made you one of the few women journalists in the country. If and when my anger has cooled a little I will decide what to do with you, and if I do decide to dismiss you I will make sure that you never find work on Fleet Street again. What happens now is entirely up to you, but if you take any further action in this affair, like disseminating vicious propaganda on street corners, it is over. Completely over. You may go.'

Breathing heavily, Mr Moodie turned his back on her to gaze out of the window, from which it was just possible to see the great dome of the cathedral of Saint Paul, that ancient symbol of defiance and fortitude, of steadfastness in adversity, shining like a beacon on the crest of Ludgate Hill.

Peg wandered round the house into which she had so recently moved, bought for them as a wedding present by Oliver Moodie. It had been carpeted, curtained, but as yet there was very little furniture; a bed, some chests of drawers, two chairs and a dining table. Being there was rather like camping. She wondered whether Oliver Moodie would regret his gift now, perhaps even withdraw it? It had been an extraordinarily generous gesture and maybe she hadn't been sufficiently grateful, considering it, perhaps, a little too patronizing, an attempt to bribe their loyalty and affection. Possibly that was why he had been so angry with her? The sparsity of the furnishings was because she had had so little time since the completion of the purchase of the house, and the growing prospect of industrial rest which became inevitable after the publication of Sir Herbert Samuel's report on the coal mining industry which had so inflamed the workers.

Peg had written to Alan saying that she couldn't bring forward the wedding. There had been so much to do, so much unrest growing in the country with the result that she had a great many meetings to attend and report on for the paper. There were also so many in-depth articles attempting a fair

51

analysis of the situation, but inevitably seen from the miners' point of view, which were turned down by the news editor under the watchful eye of Oliver Moodie.

If he was regretting his gift he had not said so, especially not at yesterday's dreadful meeting when he had ordered her out of the building.

Peg had also told Alan she would try and join him in Italy sometime in late spring before he went to Egypt, but now it seemed increasingly unlikely if industrial chaos was to paralyse the country for the foreseeable future.

Peg tried not to ask herself too often what her *real* feelings were about Alan, how much she wanted to see him or be with him or even if she still really wanted to marry him. She tried to keep herself busy so as not to allow herself too much time to think.

It was a dear little house in a leafy lane near the Heath. The beautiful waxy flowers on the magnolia tree, which almost filled the front garden, was in full bloom and the borders were packed with daffodils and hyacinths.

But inevitably all her other activities had meant that preparations for the wedding were dilatory and left largely to her sisters in Dorset: Verity diligently sewing her trousseau, Addie making preparations for the great day itself, though that was now postponed to October.

Before then she would see Alan in Rome. What would he have to say to her about the situation now? That she had been suspended from a paper, which would inevitably cast a shadow over their whole future. If she got the sack what excuse would she have for not joining him abroad? Or would he be angry that she had gone so far and maybe jeopardized not only her relationship with the proprietor of their paper but his too?

On the other hand Alan was the one who had set her on the road to Socialism. He was more left-wing than she was and he had certainly approved of her attitude to the developing situation. His views were the same as hers. Only they did not influence his reports from Fascist-run Italy. His lack of bias and objectivity were admirable, much as he deplored Fascism and its leaders.

Peg looked at her watch. She was due to get a lift from the young student with whom she had been distributing papers when Oliver Moodie had picked her up and who lived a few streets away. She stood looking out of the window, contemplating her future, when she saw the car draw up outside and Peter Snowden jumped out, looking towards the house. Peg waved to him and, taking her prepared banner from its place in the hall (WORKING CLASSES UNITE AGAINST THE EVILS OF CAPITALISM! WE HAVE NOTHING TO LOSE BUT OUR CHAINS!), hurried out of the front door.

'Sorry I'm late,' Peter said, opening the car door for her. 'I had difficulty getting the car from my father. He thinks I'm taking it to college. He would have a fit if he knew we were picketing.'

'What does he do?'

Peter grinned apologetically 'He's a banker but he's staying home until the strike is over. He's afraid of being caught up in the chaos.'

Peter glanced at her conspiratorially and jumped into the seat beside her. He was a tousle-headed, freckled-face cheery young man who was studying Classics and looked like a pillar of the established order not an agitator bent on sedition and the overthrow of the state. 'How did it go yesterday with your boss?'

'Awful!' Peg said. 'I have been suspended from my job.'

'Oh, I say!' Peter gazed at her in dismay. 'What will you do?'

'Carry on demonstrating.'

'You're very brave,' Peter said admiringly.

'When it's over he might reinstate me. My fiancé is the paper's foreign correspondent: Alan Walker.'

Peter was impressed. 'Your fiancé is Alan Walker? I always read his column. He's very good.'

'He is good,' Peg agreed.

'When are you getting married?'

'October. It was to be earlier but he is being sent to Egypt sometime in the summer.'

'I'd like to meet him,' Peter said as they drove down Haverstock Hill.

'One day you will.'

As they approached the outskirts of the City the traffic got thicker. There was almost a festive atmosphere with crowds of mostly young people perched at precarious angles on a variety of vehicles scattering in all directions with little thought for the rules of the road.

Their destination was the Bank of England, the bastion of British capitalism. Peter parked his car in a street some distance away and, taking their banners from the car, they walked towards their goal.

A crowd had already gathered in front of the Bank's entrance in Threadneedle Street, with large banners and placards bearing slogans denouncing the capitalist system. People trying to enter the bank were escorted by the police who were there in great numbers to keep the peace, and none of the strikers actively tried to stop them.

Several of the demonstrators knew and welcomed Peg with a rousing cheer as she held her banner aloft and greeted them with a wave. It was a bright May morning and the generally festive atmosphere seemed to penetrate even the grey walls of the City. In the absence of buses and most forms of public transport, crowds thronged the pavement while the steady drift of vehicles for or against the strike – though almost every one proclaimed allegiance – jostled around the Bank, up Threadneedle Street and on into the peripheries of the City and Aldgate to the East End. From there a solid phalanx of protesters made their way westwards to support the strikers, the pavements gay with different coloured banners, each with their distinctive slogans.

'Justice to the workers! Justice to the workers!' chanted Peg in chorus with the rest, who had taken up the theme. She was standing on the edge of the pavement, almost on the road, when a large black Rolls-Royce drove sedately past, about six or seven people crammed into its interior, but it was the figure at the wheel who grabbed Peg's attention. At that moment the car stopped almost abreast of her, held up by the traffic in front, and Peg gasped: 'Frank.'

Startled, Frank, dressed in his chauffeur's uniform, peaked cap at the correct angle, looked at her and his mouth sagged open.

'*Peg*! What are you doing here?'

'*And* what are *you* doing *there*?' Peg demanded.

'His lordship ordered me to help drive people to work. They are staying at their house in South Audley Street.'

'Oh, *are* they?' Peg snorted. 'And I suppose when asked to break the strike you didn't *dare* say no.'

'Peg, I *couldn't*.' Frank looked dejected and unhappy. 'I am only an employee. I am under orders.'

'Under *orders*!' Peg stormed. 'You are a disgrace to my mother's memory, Frank Carpenter. She would turn in her grave if she could see you now.'

The traffic jam seemed to be getting worse and cars tried to criss-cross the streets as the police frantically endeavoured to move the traffic on. At that moment Peg was aware of a tall, fair man with a trilby at a rakish angle approaching the car from the far side and, apparently not seeing her, he said anxiously to Frank: 'What seems to be the matter, Frank? The traffic isn't moving.'

'There is some confusion, Mr Hubert.' Frank glanced anxiously at Peg.

'There's a lorry stuck at right angles just past the Bank. Some scab getting his just desserts,' Peg said, crossing to Hubert and sticking her banner almost in his face. 'Good morning, Mr Hubert. I see you are a strike breaker too. I suppose it's because you are a member of the ruling class?'

'Really, Peg, you *mustn't* speak like that to Mr Ryland,' Frank cried in dismay. 'Your mother wouldn't like that either, *I* can tell you.'

'Good gracious!' Hubert finally identified the face behind the flag and looked at her with an expression that was a mixture of dismay and amused disbelief. 'If it isn't Miss Hallam,' and he stared at the banner in her hand.

'I am part of this picket,' Peg said defiantly, 'and *you* and the likes of *you* are strike breakers.'

'Well, I don't know.' Hubert looked from her to Frank and back again. 'Did you know this young lady had Socialist views, Frank?'

'Er . . .' Frank began, but Hubert went on admiringly. 'What a plucky young woman you are.'

'Really, Mr Hubert,' Frank said disapprovingly, 'I don't know what his lordship would say if he knew.'

'He would have a fit,' Hubert said merrily, putting a hand to his mouth in an effort to stifle his laughter. 'He is a dyed-in-the-wool old Tory, but I swear I shan't say a word.' He was about to continue when the traffic started to edge forward. A policeman ordered Peg away from the road and Hubert Ryland raced back to his car, which was behind the Rolls and likewise was full of bowler-hatted men on their way to work in the City.

'You said you'd look me up in London,' Hubert bawled at her as his car crawled past, 'and you haven't kept your promise.'

Unnerved, Peg stepped back and then, falteringly, recommenced her chant – 'Not a penny off the pay, not a minute on the day' – but with less enthusiasm than before.

Somehow the day seemed to have gone sour and she didn't quite know why.

Just before three, feeling tired and hungry, Peg decided to call it a day. Peter said he had to go to college for a lecture and offered to take her with him and then drive her home, but she said that after standing around so much she preferred to walk. Peter was concerned that it was a long way, but Peg assured him she was used to walking and the exercise would do her good.

The picketing had been successful and had attracted a lot of attention, mostly hostile, from Conservative-minded City workers, who deplored the behaviour of the militants.

Peg and Peter walked slowly back to his car, talking over the events of the day, and when they reached it Peter took Peg's banner, stowed it away and they arranged to meet the following day to picket outside the Mansion House, the official seat of the Lord Mayor of London, another bastion of the Establishment.

'I'll pick you up at the same time,' he said as he got into his car. 'Are you sure you'll be all right?'

'I'll be fine,' Peg assured him with a smile and stood back, waving as he drove off. It was a fine afternoon, the sun shining, and it was with a light step that she started to walk away from the City in the direction of home.

The streets still teemed with people, crowded motor cars, a few horses and carts, some riders on horseback. Peg dug her hands in her pockets determined to keep up a brisk pace. As she walked she recalled the many times she and Alan had walked back to Hampstead when she lived there with Verity and the rapport and affection that had developed between them. But was it love?

She realized that by continuing to join the picket lines she had almost certainly said 'goodbye' to her job. But after the wedding she would have left anyway; there were just a few months left between that event and now.

But she did want to continue working and she knew that the static life of a wife and, perhaps, motherhood would never be enough to satisfy her.

Peg had almost reached Clerkenwell, where she used to live, when she was aware of a car abreast of her which slowed down. Aware of a little prickle of fear, regretting that she had refused Peter's offer of a lift, she looked up and the driver, poking his head out of the window, waved at her cheerily.

'We meet again,' Hubert Ryland called out. 'What an *amazing* coincidence.'

Peg stopped and smiled at him, conscious of a feeling of relief.

'Is it *really* a coincidence?' she said, head on one side.

'Of *course* it is!' Hubert sounded indignant. 'Did you think I was hanging round waiting to see you?'

Peg blushed self-consciously. 'Of course not.'

'Hop in,' Hubert said, indicating the seat next to him. 'Tell me where you live and I'll give you a lift home.'

'Well . . .' Hands still stuffed in her coat pockets, Peg looked at him doubtfully. 'I don't know if I should accept a lift from a scab . . .'

'What's a scab, for God's sake?' Hubert looked puzzled.

'Someone who breaks the picket lines.'

'But I wasn't breaking any picket line. I was organizing lifts.'

'True.' Peg still regarded him gravely. 'But you and I don't share the same political beliefs.'

'Goodness me,' Hubert exclaimed, 'does that mean I can't give a lift to a young woman I've known most of my life? Besides how do you know what my political beliefs are?'

'Well, I shouldn't think they're Socialist for a start.'

'They're not anything,' Hubert said airily. 'I don't give a stuff for politics. Dad asked me to help out and I did. I thought it was a bit of a lark. If you like I'll come and picket with you. What can I say fairer than that?'

Suppressing a smile, Peg went round to the far door and climbed in, aware that she was succumbing once again to Hubert's undoubted charm.

'Actually this is rather nice,' she murmured. 'I was wondering just how long it would take me to get home.'

'Tell me where you live,' Hubert said, eagerly putting the car into gear.

'Hampstead.'

'That's just the direction in which I was going. I live in St John's Wood.'

'Well I can easily walk from there.'

'I wouldn't *hear* of it,' Hubert protested. 'You'll be taken straight to your door.' He glanced down at her finger. 'Are you married yet?'

She shook her head. 'October. We had to postpone the wedding. It was to be in the summer, but Alan is being sent to Egypt.'

'And what does he think of your politics?'

'He approves. Wishes he was here.'

'I see.' Hubert stared thoughtfully in front of him. 'I suppose there will be a big party in the hall?'

'I suppose so.' Peg gave an involuntary sigh.

'You don't sound very happy about it.'

'Of course I'm happy,' Peg said defensively. 'It is just that I would prefer to get married quietly somewhere, but the family so like to party.'

'I hope I'm to be invited.'

'I'm sure you will be, that is if your parents allow a militant Socialist to have a wedding party there at all.'

'You're joking of course.'

'Of course.' They exchanged glances.

She thought what a fascinating man he was, a strong personality, a tease. There was a lot more to him than met the eye. She felt vaguely uncomfortable in his presence now that they were alone and so close.

'What turned you into a militant Socialist?' Hubert enquired.

'Alan. He made me see the error of my ways. Like you I never thought about politics before I met him.'

'Maybe you'll change me too?'

'Maybe I will.'

The atmosphere was charged, flirtatious. Her unease grew, yet with it a curious sense of excitement.

'Poor Frank was very upset.' Hubert looked at her reproachfully. 'I don't know what upset him more, to see you with a banner in your hand or the way you spoke to him.'

Peg felt chastened. 'I *was* a little unfair. It was just spontaneous. I know he is under orders and has to do as he's told.'

'And I was doing as I was told or, rather, requested by my pa,' Hubert confessed. 'Frankly I have no strong feelings one way or the other. I just consider the whole thing a gas.'

He slowed down as he came to the top of Haverstock Hill. 'Now you must tell me which way.'

Peg directed him to the tree-lined street near the Heath and he stopped outside the house, immediately admiring the magnolia tree.

'So this is where you live?' he said. 'What a dear little house.'

Peg made a movement to get out. 'Thank you so much for the lift . . . Hubert.'

'Oh you remembered,' Hubert looked at her slyly, 'to drop the "mister".'

'Well we're both equal now,' Peg said, only half joking, and then paused on the verge of jumping on to the pavement as he put a hand over hers, leaning towards her until their faces were almost touching.

'I say Peg,' he murmured, 'do you think I could see you again?'

Five

June 1926

T he cart bowled along the road between Sherborne and
Sturminster Newton with Gilbert holding the reins and
Jenny sitting between him and Addie. The perfect family in a
way, Addie thought, her arm tightly round her happy daughter.
Gilbert seemed to sense her thoughts — as indeed he might have,
so attuned were they to each other – and looking sideways at
her, past Jenny, gave her a big smile.

Gilbert's smile always melted Addie's heart. It was intimate,
personal, radiant. She was deeply in love with him because he
was so much what Harold wasn't – warm, open, loving,
impulsive, generous and full of spontaneous gestures, little
trips, gifts, tokens of his affection. The fact that he was not
very well educated and couldn't have found his way through
Baedecker to save his life counted for very little. For how many
weary hours had Addie spent in the past listening to Harold's
monotonous intonation from the celebrated guide as they
toured the historic cathedrals, churches, castles or ancient
monuments of the Continent?

Harold had a university degree and a teacher's diploma.
Graham had nothing but an honesty and a way of life that
Addie found simple, charming and which suited her to a T.

Every Sunday if the weather was fine, and sometimes even if
it wasn't, Gilbert took them out for the day. Addie made a
picnic and they went up to Bulbarrow or Brackett's Coppice
and sat on the grass and ate their food and talked while Jenny

played. Gilbert had a dog called Crust which Jenny adored. He was a little mongrel whom Gilbert had rescued from an owner who ill treated him and he remained permanently grateful for any kindness. He was quite a young dog and he loved romping with Jenny while Gilbert and Addie sat and held hands and occasionally, if Jenny was out of sight, they would kiss.

It was a long trek up Bulbarrow, a steep climb, and the horse was tired by the time they reached the top. Every now and then they would pause to admire the view stretching right across Dorset as far as Somerset and the Quantocks. The landscape resembled nothing so much as a great patchwork quilt: hamlets and villages, brown, green and yellow fields, interspersed with lakes and ponds, copses and hills.

At the top of Bulbarrow a long stretch of woodland ran all the way down to Milton Abbey. In the spring it was covered like a gigantic carpet with bluebells, wild garlic lining the roadside. Gilbert turned down a path through the wood and stopped at a clearing beyond which was a vista of fields bathed in sunlight with fat sheep grazing on the slopes.

Addie shaded her eyes in delight at the scene, though it was not their first visit. It was a favourite spot, isolated from the main thoroughfare and shaded by the trees beneath which she threw a rug while Gilbert carried food baskets from the trap, having given his pony a sackful of hay. Jenny rushed off with Crust, her mother anxiously calling out to her to be careful and not go too far.

Addie had freshly baked bread, thick slices of home-cured ham, tomatoes, pickled onions, hard-boiled eggs, custard tarts, Dorset apple-cake, cheese and fruit. There were several bottles of beer and one of lemonade. Gilbert flopped down on the rug, taking the top off one of the bottles and tossing it back to slake his thirst. Having drained almost half of it he wiped his mouth on the back of his hand and grinned at Addie, who was spreading butter on pieces of bread and putting ham and tomatoes between them.

'This is the life,' Gilbert murmured contentedly.

'Isn't it?' Addie paused in her task to smile at him as he opened another bottle of beer, this time pouring the contents into a glass and handing it to Addie. Like him she drank thirstily because it was warm in the sun.

Gilbert then lay on his back looking at the sky and, reaching up a hand, took one of Addie's. He looked at her and she smiled tenderly down at him, then, after making sure that Jenny was out of sight, leaned over and kissed him. He put his arms round her neck and drew her down beside him. Their arms entwined, their lips met in a long, passionate embrace.

Finally, fearing Jenny might return, Addie righted herself, straightened her skirt, rearranged her hair and adjusted her bodice. Then she continued buttering the bread but felt too agitated, too sexually aroused, to concentrate on her task and kept on glancing at Gilbert, who had his eyes closed and looked as though he was sleeping.

Suddenly he opened his eyes wide. They were the same colour as the sky, and Addie thought how handsome he was with his suntanned skin and almost bleached hair. She knew she was not beautiful, not like Peg, but that she possessed a strange power to attract men. It was not that she was plain, but she knew she had to make an effort or she could look frumpish, school-marmish, as she was when she met Harold. Yet before Harold, Lydney Ryland had found her attractive, loved her, although sometimes in her heart of hearts she wondered if he had or if it was that he wanted a woman before he returned to the war. But she banished these doubts because he was Jenny's father and it was important that Jenny had been conceived in love, which there certainly had been on her part.

Suddenly Gilbert sat up, finished his beer, wiped his mouth again and gazed at her steadily.

'I think we should get wed, Addie, don't you? We suit.'

Addie's hand suddenly shook and she dropped her knife with a clatter.

'Don't you think we should, Addie?' he pleaded, but she was looking at the fallen knife on the ground and said nothing.

He put a hand on her arm and then she looked up straight at him, her eyes glinting through tears.

'Addie,' he said, gently putting out a finger to brush them away, 'have I upset you? Don't you think we suit?'

'Yes, I do,' Addie said in a faltering voice. 'Of course I do. I think we suit very well.'

'I love you, Addie,' Gilbert said, his voice breaking. 'As I breathe, I've never told a woman that before. I love you and . . .' he looked way down the field to where Jenny was romping with Crust, 'I love little Jenny. I know Frank is good and like a father to her, but I want to be her real father and, perhaps –' he lowered his eyes – 'perhaps there could be more.'

'Oh, Gilbert,' Addie whispered, 'you *know* I love you but I'm already married.'

'I know that,' Gilbert said testily, 'but he can't expect you to stay married to him, surely.'

'He wants to have me back.' Addie twisted and untwisted her fingers. 'He wrote to tell me so.'

'And what did you say to him?'

'I never replied.' She hung her head. 'I didn't know what to say.'

'And *do* you want to go back to him, Addie?'

'Of course I don't and won't.'

'Then tell him. Tell him you love someone else and want to divorce him. Tell him, Addie. You know you belong to me not him.'

The General Strike had ended very quickly on May 12th. The TUC, which had always been a reluctant participant, climbed down and left the miners in the lurch. Oliver Moodie climbed down too and decided not to dismiss Peg. Instead, in a painful interview he told her that while her behaviour had been unacceptable it was to some extent understandable. He knew her to be an emotional, principled person. He also remembered that she had intervened to rescue him from a crowd of hostile pickets, and he had some admiration for her bravery, disregard for herself and single-mindedness as, indeed, he had always had. Her fearlessness and enterprise had led him to offer her a job in the first place. But Peg knew that probably the real reason was his reluctance to lose his star foreign correspondent, Alan her husband-to-be, who was filing such successful and concise reports from overseas.

Besides Peg was popular among the readers of his newspaper. She was a personality who had an established core of admirers. Her perceptive and well thought-out articles never toed the party line and controversy helped sell papers, especially when it was written by a female journalist, still a rare breed, who was pretty as well as clever. This helped not only to sell the paper but also to raise its prestige in Fleet Street, where it enjoyed a local rather than a national status.

It was a balmy evening and Peg and Hubert sat in his car at the side of the Spaniards' Road overlooking the Heath. Below them were the myriad of magical twinkling lights that formed the great metropolis of London. Hubert had his arm round the back of Peg's seat and he was smoking, in appearance utterly peaceful and content.

They had dined at a small restaurant in Hampstead and he suggested a stroll before taking her home. The atmosphere between them was charged with expectation.

It was not their first date. The day after he drove her home from the City during the strike he had telephoned her. She had seen him daily since, or almost daily. Their rapport was so perfect that she felt she had known him all her life, as indeed she had, from being a very small girl, though it was not an acquaintanceship of equals, however democratic the Ryland family might appear to have been. Her stepfather was a servant to Lord Ryland and their place had always been below stairs, to meet the Ryland family on a social but never equal basis at functions in the castle two or three times a year, or to see them individually around the estate in the course of a day's work when instructions were given and obeyed.

Now the Ryland heir was sitting with his arm around her seat and she knew that he wanted their intimacy to deepen. But a word or a sign from her and they would be lovers.

However, the pleasure of Hubert's company was also guilt-ridden because Peg knew that she was falling in love with him in a way she had never loved Alan: a feeling that was passionate, intense, not based on anything in common, any interests such as she and Alan shared but on a strong sense of physical attraction.

People said that that sort of thing never lasted. Besides he was married and she engaged. Even now, her fiancé was patiently awaiting her visit before he left Rome.

She gave a deep sigh and Hubert turned to her and gently stroked her cheek.

'Penny for them?'

'You know,' she said, taking his hand and putting it to her lips.

'We're falling in love, aren't we, Peg?'

She nodded and rested her head on his shoulder.

'I think I've loved you for a very long time,' he murmured. 'I noticed you years ago and I wondered what you'd be like when you grew up. Now I know.' He leaned over and kissed her. It was a wonderfully melting moment. She knew that sex would be different with him, and yet she was still afraid of that final act of commitment in case it disappointed her again.

Their kiss lasted several moments and when they parted they were both breathing heavily.

'Tonight?' he asked looking at her. 'We can't go on like this.' He had tried before but she had refused. To go that final step was risking everything.

Inwardly she trembled.

'Are you cold, darling?' He reached in the back for a rug and wrapped it round her shoulder.

'I'm afraid,' she whispered.

'But why?'

'It's so final. We can't go back and we are both . . . well, we're both involved with other people.'

'Oh!' Hubert drew away, sat back and lit a fresh cigarette. 'So that's it.'

'It *is* important, Hubert.'

'Not to me. Ida is not at all important to me, nor I to her. It is a marriage in name only. She pursues her own way and I pursue mine.'

'But you still like to be together?'

'We share a house.'

'And a bed?'

There was a long pause before he nodded.

'We do share a bed. I can't deny it. It's a habit that's hard to break. You see –' he turned to her – 'I want to be honest with you, Peg. It's not just a mere affair between you and me . . .'

'Well what *is* it then?'

'I think it's love. Don't you? Do you love Alan the way you love me?'

She didn't reply but sat staring out into the darkness.

'You don't, do you? I can tell you don't.'

'It would hurt him so much. He is such a nice person. A *good* person. A good –' she paused to emphasize the word – 'a good man. It would break his heart. He has waited for me so long.'

'So have I.' Hubert's lips brushed against her cheek.

'Not in the same way.'

'Yes, in a way, I waited for you to grow up.'

He threw his cigarette out of the window and let in the clutch. He drove on for a while, then turned the car round and went down the High Street before turning into the maze of small roads that led to Peg's house. He switched off the engine and she was aware of his gaze in the inky blackness. He took hold of her hand.

'Aren't you going to ask me in?' he murmured in her ear.

Peg lay listening to the song of the blackbird from its perch on a branch high up the magnolia tree in the garden. It reminded her so much of home. To her it was a symbol of luck, of good fortune. She had always been lucky. Some people would have called her blessed. Without undue vanity she knew she was good-looking. She liked people and they liked her. She had been well educated and had followed a profession which she loved and in which she had rapidly achieved an early and unexpected success.

Now she had two men who loved her. And which one did she love?

She stretched in her bed and her fingers wandered along the sheet to the spot which Hubert had so recently vacated. She wondered what he'd told Ida about where he'd been. Lady Ida. His wife was an aristocrat, the daughter of an earl. Hubert must have been a good match, the son of a peer, the heir to the family fortune and estates, equal to her in every respect. They had been married for ten years.

Peg put her head on the pillow where Hubert had rested his and she could smell his haircream. Inhaling it deeply, she lay on her stomach, pressing the pillow close to her face. Tears filled her eyes.

Their lovemaking had been so different from her experience with Alan: it had been sensuous and passionate; there had been no sense of time passing except for the gentle rhythm of their bodies in perfect harmony until that moment of completion which was the first time she had experienced ecstasy. She knew it would never be like that with Alan and that was perhaps why it was the reason for her tears: from sorrow as well as happiness, from elation as well as grief.

Rome, the most romantic of romantic cities, with a city within a city: the Vatican and the great Basilica of St Peter. Rome, city of emperors, popes, statesmen, great artists and musicians. The city of the Spanish Steps, the baths of Caraculla, the Villa Borghese with its beautiful gardens, the Palatine hills, the Trevi Fountain, the Appian way, the Via del Corso, the Colosseum where so many had perished in cruel sports in front of the Roman emperors. A beloved English poet, Keats, had spent his last days in Rome and was buried there.

It had been fought over and conquered, lost and won again.

It had given its name to a great people, a great empire. It had been a city of immense wealth and still housed some of the richest treasures, the most celebrated museums in the world.

They had by no means seen most of the sights but they had seen a lot, bounced along by Alan and his almost encyclopaedic knowledge of the capital. Now, they sat at a table in one of the many trattoria in the ancient Piazza Navona, which was crowded with people taking an evening stroll: large Italian families with many children and dogs running at their heels, tourists clutching their guide books, clergy in long cassocks and hard black hats sweeping past with a purposeful air.

It was very hot and the couple sipped long cold drinks before ordering their evening meal.

It had been a long, exciting day with plenty to see and talk about. Alan had digested an enormous amount of information in the relatively short time he had been in Rome and proved an excellent, if exhausting, guide.

'It *is* a lovely city,' Peg murmured, putting her drink down on the table, 'and you know so much about it. Lucky you.'

'Why lucky me?' Alan looked rueful. 'Don't forget it will soon be a Fascist state. Mussolini is clamping down on all opposition. The Fascists have already killed Matteoti, the head of the Socialist party.' Momentarily Alan, who had covered the trial for the paper, clenched his jaw in anger. 'The prisons will be full of his opponents. There is much more to Italy now than its sights. It will soon be a dangerous place to live. Besides I missed the excitement of the General Strike. I could have been there with you demonstrating. I wish I had been.'

Listening to him, Peg wondered if he had been if she'd have met Hubert again. Almost certainly not. But for that fateful day, their paths would never have crossed.

She avoided Alan's eyes, which looked at her with such love, so full of hope. The term 'dog-like devotion' came to her, as if he was hoping to please in order to get a pat from his mistress.

Almost immediately she dismissed the image, despising herself for entertaining it. Alan did look different. He was tanned, he'd put on weight. He had lost his London pallor and filled out, doubtless on a diet of pasta and red wine.

He had been standing on the platform of Rome station, eagerly scanning the carriages as the early morning train pulled in. Peg made her way towards him unseen and the sight of him momentarily filled her with apprehension because she knew how much he looked forward to seeing her, something she had dreaded.

Should she have written? Been honest? Stayed away? No, it was too cruel.

When at last he spotted her, anticipation turned to radiance and he ran towards her, swept her up in his arms and hugged her. It was then that she realized that Alan was like a brother. Her feelings for him were like those she had for Ed. He was a dear friend and companion. He always had been and she should have kept it like that and not have given in to pity, family pressure and the wishes of her dead mother. She loved him, but not the way she loved Hubert.

Hand in hand they had crossed the station and he had taken her in a cab to his hotel near the Spanish Steps where he'd booked a room for her.

After she'd freshened up they had set out on a hectic programme of sightseeing and now here she was. Tired, but also elated.

'Penny for them?'

Emerging from her reverie, Peg looked at Alan.

'I was thinking.'

'About what?'

'About what you just said. The strike. I was thinking that the climbdown of the TUC was disgraceful and the miners gained nothing from it and still have not as they are still out on strike.'

His hand closed over hers. 'I am so proud of you, Peg, and the way you stood up to Oliver. Your articles since have been so good.'

'I think I'm going to leave the paper.' Peg's eyes rested on his thin brown hand covering hers. 'There's a new paper called *Labour Monthly*. I may go and work for that. I want to see real social justice in our country and I won't see it if I stay on the *South London Gazette*.'

'I think you'll have more influence there,' Alan said thoughtfully. 'I mean where you are. The paper is good, well produced and its reputation is growing. I know Oliver has ambitious plans to extend it to the provinces.' He paused, then: 'On a small circulation paper devoted to the Labour Party you'll be preaching to the converted. Your influence won't be as great.'

'Perhaps.' Peg bowed her head. As usual Alan, with his measured, thoughtful opinion, carefully delivered, was probably right.

'I love you, Peg,' he murmured, stroking her hand. His voice was low, tremulous, even diffident. She stared again at his hand for a moment and then raised her eyes.

'I love you too,' she said, wishing she could tell him how and in what way; but if she did it would hurt him terribly.

'Peg,' he said in the same low voice but now with a note of urgency, 'let's get married. Let's not wait. We can get married here. I'm sure we can get our papers and it can be arranged at the consulate. What say, Peg?'

She raised her eyes and saw how excited he was.

'I can't,' she said.

'But why not . . .'

'Because of the family. They'd be so disappointed.'

Alan's face fell. 'Oh, yes. Yes, I suppose they've gone to a lot of trouble. It was just an idea.'

The meal which Peg had been looking forward to tasted like sawdust in her mouth and Alan seemed also to feel that the spell of the day had broken. They wandered back to the hotel still hand in hand, but somehow there was no sense of togetherness.

'Everything is all right, isn't it, Peg?' he asked as they stopped outside the hotel.

'Of course.' She turned away from him and walked inside to

the reception where she collected her key. She waited for Alan as he collected his and they got into the ancient lift which cranked them up to the second floor where they had adjoining rooms.

He saw her to her room and watched her putting the key in the lock. 'Can we try again?' he asked quietly, putting a hand on her waist. 'I know that last time . . . but it was the first time.'

Peg threw open the door of her room, then she turned and looked at him.

'I'd rather wait until we're married,' she said. 'I think it's better that way.

'Very well.' Alan's hand fell listlessly to his side. He pecked her on the cheek and watched her sadly as she went into her room and closed the door.

Her cheeks were burning as she threw herself into a chair and gazed despairingly at the ceiling. She hated herself.

If only she'd had the courage to tell him. But what could she say?

'How was Rome?' Verity asked, looking at Peg closely. She had already been home a day and seemed quiet and withdrawn, not her usual self at all. Maybe she was tired. It was hot and the train journey had seemed endless. She'd stayed a week, during which the tension between Alan and her had slowly mounted, fed by frustration and denial. Their sightseeing was almost frantic to avoid any discussion of issues, any mention of deeper emotion. It was sightseeing and politics, Fascism and the miners' strike over and over again.

'Oh, wonderful!' Peg tried to sound enthusiastic. 'It is a wonderful place.'

'I wish I'd gone. I only ever managed Florence and Venice. They were wonderful too.'

'Well, you've plenty of time.'

'And how was Alan?' They were sitting in the cool of the garden in late afternoon. Peg had only arrived in the morning and the hushed stillness of the country seemed such a contrast to the heat, bustle and noise of Rome.

'Alan was all right.'

There was a long, rather pregnant silence.

Then: 'You don't sound very enthusiastic,' Verity murmured.

'What do you expect me to say?' Peg said angrily and rose. 'I said Alan was fine and Rome was wonderful. What else is there to say? I'm going for a walk.'

'Right.' Verity looked at her anxiously. She knew her sister well enough to detect that something was amiss, but she knew better than to ask. 'I won't offer to come with you, Peg. I think you want to be by yourself, but if and when you do want to talk I'm here and –' she smiled encouragingly – 'you know *whatever* it is, I'll understand.'

Impulsively Peg leaned down and kissed her.

'Thanks, Ver,' she said and walked hurriedly away before she broke down and confessed to an affair which she knew would upset and scandalize her sister, however broadminded she thought she might be.

Not only was Hubert married – Verity might understand that but he was a Ryland, and she herself was engaged to someone whom Verity liked and welcomed as a brother-in-law.

Peg opened the side gate and walked up the path towards the castle. None of the Ryland family were at home. It was the end of the London season and they would still be at the house in South Audley Street.

She knew that Violet was with them, and Hubert and his wife undoubtedly joined them in whatever it was they did during the season. She imagined they went to balls and parties where, according to Hubert, they were exceedingly bored.

Boredom in fact seemed part of Hubert's life. He had a stale marriage and a job as a stockbroker that he didn't particularly enjoy. No wonder he found her exciting. She desperately wanted to see him, but weekends were always busy, or he was away at some country house party or the other, so she had come home.

Peg wandered along the path, acutely aware of the silence of the country: the sweet smell of new mown grass, the bleating of sheep on the hillside.

This was her life. It had been since she was six years old and her stepfather had joined the staff of the castle as head gardener. She could not remember any other life. She and Hubert had grown up in the same place, and although their status was different their values in many ways were the same.

She stood looking for a long time at the ancient family home of the Rylands with its gables and turrets, its tiny mullioned windows glinting in the sunshine. Then she walked along the brow of the hill and down towards the lake which ran from one end of the park to the other, an entrancing stretch of water which drew the crowds in the summer on the days when Lord Ryland opened the grounds. There were rowboats on the lake and a flock of majestic white swans, and in the middle was an island where they rested and mated which was also used by ducks and mallards, peahens and waterfowl, and small birds of all descriptions.

Hands deep in the pockets of her cotton frock, Peg stood by the water's edge looking into its murky depths, her face reflected in the still surface which seemed to offer a challenge to her.

If this was, say, like an analogy of her life should she jump or stay where she was? Remain with Alan or throw in her lot with Hubert? And if she jumped would she sink or swim? Go forward or back? Would Hubert let her down and if he did would she ever want to go back to Alan again, or would he want her?

That, it seemed to her, was her dilemma at this moment, and so far the answer eluded her.

Six

P ale, tense, tight-lipped, Addie sat bolt upright beside
Frank as he drove towards the town and the hotel where
it had been arranged to meet her estranged husband, Harold.

He had pleaded for the meeting and somehow, to Addie's
kind heart, it had seemed cruel to refuse him.

After all he was her husband though they had not been
married very long and not very happily. The marriage had
been consummated, there was no dispute about that, but
only just. Once he had found out on their honeymoon
about her relationship with Lydney Ryland and the subsequent birth of Jenny there had been no more attempts at
conjugal love, and a sterile and increasingly unhappy
marriage had been the result. Oddly enough Harold had
seemed quite happy with the state of affairs and was very
surprised when his wife left him. Now he wanted her back.
To Harold appearances were of paramount importance
and, as a headmaster of a junior school in an affluent
community, he felt that a wife was an important adjunct
to the life of a successful man.

'Are you sure you want to go through with this?' Frank
asked, looking anxiously at the woman beside him. 'You don't
have to, you know. It can be done through solicitors when you
ask for a divorce.'

'Harold has done nothing wrong,' Addie said quietly. 'He
didn't abuse or injure me in any way. He never threatened
physical violence.'

'He just neglected you,' Frank retorted angrily. He knew

75

nothing, and could never have asked, about their most intimate relationship.

Addie and Frank got on well together. Her mother's third husband was a kind, gentle soul who mourned his wife deeply. Her family had become his family and he was bitterly wounded by Peg's taunts in London, something which had caused a rift between them. He had always been non-political, a loyal servant of the Ryland family since he was a youth, trusted and valued by Lord Ryland, who extended to him certain privileges, like the use of one of his cars for personal business whenever he needed it. This proved invaluable for transporting the family around a countryside where there was little public transport.

Their home was in the gift of Lord Ryland and there were many other benefits, including the fact that Lord Ryland had always promised to take care of him in his retirement, and there would be a home on the estate for life. All this, yet Peg, with her unwholesome left-wing views which he deeply deprecated, expected him to refuse to drive one of his lordship's cars when instructed to in order to break the strike of which he, naturally, deeply disapproved.

Addie knew how he felt – she too felt Peg's views were too extreme – and looked across at him, as bowler-hatted and gloved his eyes fixed on the road, he drove at a measured pace towards the town. He was not a handsome man: his frame thickset and solid, baldheaded, with rather bland undistinguished, unexceptional features, and a prominent nose that had been broken once or twice owing to the excesses of a boisterous youth keen on rugby and boxing. But he was a very gentle man, rather emotional with warm brown eyes that easily filled with tears.

He had been a bachelor until his marriage to Addie's mother and he couldn't believe that such happiness and fulfilment as he found with her and her large family could come to him relatively late in life. He had felt blessed, that her children were his children, and he was devastated by her early death.

However, he promptly and gladly took on the burden of caring for her family. They sustained one another in their grief. Between him and Addie, who kept house, there was a special bond and to Jenny he capably filled the roles both of father and grandfather.

'You will stay won't you, Frank?' Addie asked a little timidly as they drew up in front of the hotel.

'If you'd like me to, Addie.' He looked down at her kindly.

'I *would* be grateful.'

He then drove round to the car park at the back, parked and helped Addie to alight. Then with her arm linked through his, they walked stiffly towards the lounge of the hotel where Harold awaited them.

They saw him as soon as they entered, sitting in a corner with a pint of beer, the glass half full, in front of him.

Harold looked as though he was rather surprised to see Frank and greeted him perfunctorily before turning to Addie and attempting to kiss her on the cheek. But she sidestepped quickly, and his gesture embraced the empty air, to his evident chagrin.

'Do sit down, Addie.' He pointed to a chair. 'What can I get you to drink?'

'A cup of tea would be very nice,' Addie said, aware of the heavy thud of her heart.

'Frank?'

'Beer, please,' Frank said, looking at Harold's glass.

Harold waved to a waiter who was attending to customers on the far side of the room and when he came over, ordered while Frank sat down and took off his hat.

Addie, her face flushed, undid her coat as if she was feeling the heat.

'You don't mind if Frank stays, do you?' Addie asked, taking off her gloves and laying them neatly on her lap.

'Well, is it really necessary?' Harold pursed his lips in a schoolmasterly manner as if deciding whether to forgive or reprimand a child guilty of only a minor misdemeanour.

'I think it is,' Addie said firmly.

'I'll go,' Frank began, half rising.

'No, you *stay*,' Addie said, firmly stabbing at his chair with her finger. She turned to Harold. 'Frank is a member of the family. He knows about and understands everything.'

'Well that's all right by me,' Harold said, running a finger uneasily round his collar. He then went on to address Addie as though Frank wasn't there, turning his chair slightly towards her so that he had his back to Frank.

Addie thought that Harold's hair was thinning and was greying at the sides. He was very tall, much taller than Frank, lean and with a slight stoop as if to try and disguise his height. He was pale with sunken cheeks and wore large horn-rimmed spectacles. Looking at him in a detached way, as she could now, she wondered what she had ever seen in him, or why she had ever married him. They had been teachers together at the same school. Their courtship had been long and passionless. She had never really been in love. Was it that she had felt that, if she didn't accept him, she would end up a spinster like Verity, whose fate seemed to be a warning and a threat to all the female members of the family?

Conversation was perfunctory until the tea and Frank's beer arrived. The men toasted each other.

'Cheers, Frank.'

'Cheers, Harold.'

They drank deeply for a few seconds while Addie poured her tea, wishing, as Frank had suggested, that the whole thing had been dealt with by letter. Finally Harold leaned towards her, hands joined loosely in front of him.

'Have you thought about my suggestion, Addie?'

'That I should return to you?'

He nodded.

'I have thought about it and the answer is the same.'

Frank cleared his throat uneasily. 'Addie wants a divorce,' he said gruffly. 'She wants the chance to start life afresh.'

Harold sank back in his chair, an ugly, petulant expression on his face.

'Oh, no!' he said, shaking his head with a slow emphasis. 'No divorce. There is no question of that, at all.' There was a silence for a few seconds while Addie, feeling very hot and confused, went on sipping her tea.

'I'm surprised that you should even suggest it, Addie. I have done nothing to give you grounds for divorce. It is something I would *never* consent to and I am shocked that you, a church-going woman, should even think of it. The marriage bond is sacred and indissoluble.'

'You *are* a hypocrite, Harold,' Addie burst out.

'I *beg* your pardon?'

'I said you are a hypocrite. You know our marriage was a sham. Why pretend otherwise?'

'It was *not* a sham to me. If it was a sham to you, you know the reason why.'

'And that is?'

'You had a child out of wedlock,' he said accusingly, leaning towards her in case anyone else was in earshot. 'You came into the marriage knowing you had committed that dreadful sin, yet saying nothing about it to me. I had taken you to be a good, pure woman and you deceived me. However, I was willing to behave magnanimously and forget it, to let bygones be bygones; to forgive you, in other words.'

'As long as my child was brought up by someone else!' Addie stared at him, feeling that control of the situation was slipping away from her.

'You were perfectly happy to let your child be brought up by your mother,' Harold said loftily, 'as she had been before you even met me. Indeed I often wondered how much you really cared for Jenny . . .'

The words were scarcely out of his mouth before Addie rose and lunged towards him. Completely taken by surprise, Harold fell back in his chair, a look of exaggerated astonishment on his face. With an exclamation, Frank also rose and grabbed Addie by her waist, drawing her back from Harold. A couple who had been sitting in the far corner of the lounge and were about to leave looked at them in alarm, and Frank hissed: 'Sit down, Addie, and control yourself or we shall be asked to go.' He looked at the departing couple and wondered if they might be about to complain to the manager. Happily, because the tension appeared about to increase, the room was now empty. Addie did as Frank had told her and sat with arms crossed, gazing at her lap. She shook from head to foot, her feelings a compound of fear and despondency as though an awful chasm had appeared beneath her.

Harold, trying to regain his dignity, righted himself, adjusted his spectacles and attempted to compose himself.

'That was a terrible thing to say,' Frank addressed him sternly. 'Addie adores Jenny and always has. As a young woman she was forced to work to support her child. She did everything she could for her, and well you know it.'

'I apologize.' Harold's normally pallid complexion had turned a dull red. 'I'm afraid my emotions unusually got the better of me.' He looked across at Addie, who was sitting in the same position, as if turned to stone. 'I'm sorry, Addie. I sincerely ask your pardon. You see I am in the grip of profound emotion. I do love you and I want you to return to me and live with me as my wife. I want us to forget the past and, as I have told you, I am now perfectly willing to give Jenny a home.'

'And how will you explain Jenny?' Addie's expression was full of scorn. 'What will the parents of your well-behaved, nicely brought-up little schoolchildren have to say about her?'

Harold shook his head. 'I haven't thought about it, to tell you the truth. We could perhaps say . . .' he paused, groping for words, 'that she was a niece? Her mother had died and . . .' He gazed at her hopefully.

'You're a bigger fool than I thought, Harold,' Addie said witheringly. 'Do you think I would allow that? Do you think *you* would be believed and, above all, *I* am her mother. What do you think the effect would be on me to deny my daughter in public?'

Harold shook his head as if suddenly conscious of defeat staring him in the face.

'I want a divorce, Harold,' Addie said stubbornly. Her words delivered with vehemence seemed to inflame Harold.

'I will never give you a divorce. Never. Besides you have no grounds.'

'I will give you grounds.'

'And what are they?' he sneered.

'Adultery.' Addie stabbed her finger in her chest. 'I am in love with someone else and we are living together as man and wife. Now what do you think of that?'

Harold gazed at her, horror-struck. Her words seemed to hang in the air and he looked as though he couldn't believe her. Then he struck the arms of his chair several times.

'No divorce,' he thundered. 'No divorce, now or ever.'

August 1926

Peg stood by the round pond at the top of Heath Street looking into the water which was rippled by little waves, the wash from the many boats pushed out by the children playing at the sides. It was very warm and there was no breeze to help the sails along and many of the boats were becalmed in the middle of the pond.

Once again she stood by the water's edge. To jump? Sink or swim? Her wedding was just a couple of months away, planned now for early October. The invitations were ready and her trousseau was prepared. Addie and Mrs Capstick, the cook at the castle, were deep in plans for the wedding feast.

Yet it all seemed unreal. How could she marry a man she did not love when she was in love with someone else?

It was an intolerable situation.

Peg looked around her at the children playing by the pond, flanked by their parents or nursemaids, trying with their long sticks to retrieve the boats which had stopped in the middle. Everyone looked so happy and carefree. This should be a happy time of her life; she was loved and in love. But it was not. She was dreadfully unhappy because her illicit love was not only a folly. Deep in her heart she knew it was wrong.

Peg turned away from the pond and walked slowly across the Heath, following the path that would ultimately take her to the home Alan expected to share with her. It was now fully furnished and decorated. The deeds of ownership were in the bank. The waxy, purple blossoms of the magnolia tree had blossomed that year well into the summer.

As Peg walked down the road leading to the house, she was surprised to see a man standing outside the garden gate looking towards it. He wore an ill-fitting lounge suit and carried a notebook in his hand. A battered trilby was on his head and a cigarette dangled from his lips. The sight of him somehow filled Peg with apprehension, though she didn't know why. She had nothing to be afraid of. She stopped and looked at him for a while and then walked on.

As she approached him he turned, seeming startled to see her.

'Excuse me,' she said, going past him to the gate and opening it.

'Miss Hallam?' the stranger said.

'Yes, why . . .' Surprised that he knew her name, Peg turned towards him and then with a smile and a slight tip of his hat he walked rapidly away.

Now she did feel afraid. But of what? The house was paid for. He looked like a seedy reporter from a second-rate newspaper.

Rather belatedly Peg decided to go after him, but he turned the street corner and seconds later she heard the sound of a motor starting up.

Thoughtfully Peg opened the gate and walked up the short path to the front door. To her surprise it was open and only one person had the key, apart from Alan, who she knew was in Egypt.

'Hubert,' she called softly as she went into the hall and he came slowly out of the drawing room in his casual, relaxed way, arms open wide.

'Hubert!' she cried as she was enveloped in his embrace. 'Oh darling, I didn't expect you to be here.'

'Didn't you see my car?'

'No, I didn't notice it.' She leaned her head against his chest.

'Peg,' he said, his voice filled with concern as, stroking her cheeks, he found them wet with tears. 'What is it, my darling?'

'I feel so afraid,' Peg said, looking up at him. 'I feel we are like two people standing on shifting sands.'

'But, darling, our love is so secure. There is nothing on earth to be afraid of.'

Hubert led her into the drawing room, sat her down in a chair and lit two cigarettes, one of which he passed to her. Peg sighed deeply. 'It is not secure, Hubert. You know it isn't. How can you say that? You are married and I am about to be. Do you realize my wedding is only a couple of months away?'

Hubert's expression suddenly grew solemn and he sat smoking his cigarette and looking thoughtfully out of the French windows across the back lawn. There was something so elegant about Hubert, with his fine head of fair hair, cropped moustache, blue eyes and square-cut chin. He wore tweeds and one leg was crossed nonchalantly over the other. Socialist she might be, but he seemed quintessentially English, not Tory, not upper class, but certainly not a son of the soil like Gilbert, so that it was difficult somehow to pigeon-hole him. He was unique and she loved him.

'You can't marry Alan,' Hubert said. 'It would be insane.'

'I can't let him down.'

'Peg, it would be madness. You can't marry someone out of pity, which is what you'd be doing. Look, darling, we'll work something out. I can't think what now . . .'

'I think you want to keep me as your mistress,' Peg said bitterly, 'and we will go on and on like that for ages. You know that, Hubert. Anything else is impossible.'

'That's not true.' He paused and looked at her as if suddenly realizing the implications of what she was saying.

'We've never discussed the future, have we?' he said.

'We've avoided it. You know we *have* no future.' Peg's tears had dried but her expression was desolate. 'We can never progress from where we are now. You could never divorce your wife and marry me.'

'Why not?'

'Because you know you can't. What would your parents say? Can you imagine? A Ryland marrying a Hallam, the stepdaughter of Jack Hallam, once head gardener to your father, and Frank Carpenter, his lordship's chauffeur. I don't believe it's something you've ever thought about, is it, Hubert?'

'Is it what you want?' he asked quietly.

'No. Of course not. It's out of the question.'

'But why?'

'Because it is. You know it is. You would be ostracized. We would have to go and live abroad and you'd hate that. So should I, incidentally. Besides, your wife would never divorce you and we should be in a situation like Addie and Harold, who, I'm quite sure, will never ever give her her freedom.'

Hubert reached out and began to stroke her hair, tenderly brushing it away from her face.

'Darling,' he murmured, 'let's go and make love. This will resolve itself one day, I'm sure.'

Peg knew that making love would resolve nothing, but that day she felt a particular need of him, and when it happened, their love-making surpassed anything she had known before.

Early in the afternoon she lay in his arms, drugged with love, conscious of supreme happiness.

'I can never let you go,' Hubert declared. 'We must find a way.' Peg, still feeling lazy said drowsily: 'By the way, when you arrived did you see a man standing outside or near the house?'

'No. What sort of man?'

'Well, suspicious looking, I'd say. Suspicious enough for me to want to go after him, but he was too quick for me. He was standing outside the gate looking at the house. As I was going in, he asked if I was Miss Hallam and I said I was, expecting him to say something, but instead he turned and walked rapidly up the street.'

Hubert's arms tightened anxiously around her. 'Peg, this worries me. You don't think it's anything to do with the articles you've been writing? You've been rather critical of the Government.'

'No, I haven't. They only really offend the mine owners, and I think they consider me a nuisance, rather than a real threat. Anyway this isn't a police state. Yet.'

Hubert continued to feel disturbed. 'Well, I don't like it. Did he say anything at all?'

Peg shook her head. 'Maybe he was some sort of house agent and didn't realize it had been sold. I know that sounds a bit far-fetched. He was rather scruffy looking and could have been a reporter actually, for a second-rate newspaper, the type who sticks his foot in the door, anything to get a story.'

'He wouldn't be someone sent by Alan?'

'*Alan?*' Peg looked at him with astonishment. 'Why should Alan send someone?'

'A private detective, you know.'

Peg was shocked. 'Alan would *never* do a thing like that. He is much too straightforward and above board, much too honest. Besides there is no earthly reason for him to suspect anything.'

'Peg,' Hubert said, settling back in the bed, 'I want you to think seriously about your marriage. Do you promise me that?'

'Yes. Yes, I promise.'

Peg looked at the sheets Verity had embroidered so lovingly for her own wedding and which had lain for years wrapped up in tissue paper in a drawer.

'They are very beautiful,' Peg said admiringly, fingering the fine linen stitched in white with an intricate pattern of flowers – forget-me-nots, rosebuds and vine leaves. She looked up at her sister. 'But, Ver, might you not need them yourself some day? I'm sure you'll find someone.'

'If I do,' Verity said briskly, 'I shall embroider some more. In the meantime these are for you.'

'They're really lovely.' Peg's fingers lingered on the linen as if she was reluctant to take them away.

Verity looked at her younger sister with concern, aware that something wasn't right. She felt it in her bones and had for some time.

'Peg, are you *sure*?'

Peg found it hard to withstand that searching look.

'*Sure* . . .' she began and then faltered as tears filled her eyes.

Verity merely hugged her, saying nothing. Then she tenderly wiped each eye, brushing away the tears that had gathered there and handed Peg a handkerchief.

'Have a good blow,' she said.

Peg did as she was told and after a while she tucked the handkerchief into the pocket of her dress and attempted a brave smile.

'I'm not at all sure,' she said, 'but I don't want to hurt Alan. He has waited such a long time and he'd be absolutely shattered. He is such a nice man – he deserves better, he actually deserves someone better than me.'

'I'm sure he doesn't feel like that, but if you do, if you really don't love him, I think you must cancel it. To continue is a recipe for disaster.'

'He will be so hurt.'

'I don't care. We don't want the same situation that we have with Addie and then, like Harold, Alan might never release you if you met someone you really loved.'

'I would want to make it work,' Peg said firmly. 'I would be determined about it. He loves me and I would try so hard not to let him down. We have a lot in common, and that is a very good basis.'

Peg lay in bed, hands behind her head, looking at the hills in front of her dappled by moonlight. She had more in common with Alan than she had with Hubert, and maybe that would be more lasting than the passion she and Hubert shared now. When the passion had gone what would there be to keep them together? They led such different lifestyles and, of course, Hubert didn't share or understand her political views. There were great areas they agreed not to talk about. There were rather a lot of them, so they spent as much time as they could making love, when one didn't have to discuss anything.

She knew that it was much more a basis for an affair than anything lasting; but how could she marry Alan for his intellect, for shared interests, and continue a physical relationship with Hubert?

Some cynic might say that way she would have the best of both worlds, but such a notion was abhorrent to her. She had been on the verge of telling Verity about Hubert and then at the last minute held back.

However broadminded she might think herself to be, Verity would be appalled. To emulate the example of Addie and have a Ryland for a lover would be an intolerable, impossible situation. She recalled her last meeting with Hubert who now had gone north with his wife to join his parents in Scotland where the shooting season had begun. It was a way of life utterly alien to her. She disapproved of blood sports: she would never fit in.

In fact the pair of them were locked into an impasse, and for her there was only one honourable way out.

Later that morning the family went to church as they always did on Sunday: Frank and Addie, Jenny, Stella, Ed, Verity and Peg, dressed in their best, walking up the aisle, past the empty Ryland pew where the family always sat when they were at home. Gilbert was in his usual place, his large workman's hands linked in front of him, his eyes lingering on Addie as they passed by. She gave him a secret smile and then followed her family into the pew they normally occupied near the front.

The vicar preached a sermon about the meaning of trust, at least that's what Peg thought it was about. Her mind kept on wandering on to other matters.

Or maybe the idea of trust was pertinent to her own thoughts, the resolution she had come to in the small hours of the morning after a sleepless night.

The thing about the water's edge was that it was always possible to go back. You could retreat. It was not necessary to jump in, sink or swim, try and cross to the other side. You could simply step back from the brink, and that was what she intended to do.

After church they gathered as usual outside to chat with friends, mostly estate workers, shake hands with the vicar, swap news and bits of gossip about the estate or the village. It was a fine morning, the sun high in the sky, a few fluffy white clouds appearing on the horizon.

As usual, Gilbert gravitated towards Addie, and they stood talking animatedly to each other as though they were unaware there was anyone else there but themselves. He would walk back with them for Sunday lunch as he always did and then he might take Addie and Jenny for a drive or a walk by the lake, or in the woods above the castle.

Peg knew, everyone knew, that Addie would spend quite a lot of time at Gilbert's cottage, and no one was in any doubt as to what went on there; but there were few who condemned them besides the usual busybodies and gossips who put their noses into everyone else's business.

As long as Addie and Gilbert were discreet and did not flaunt their affair, no one really minded. They were both considered good people who would marry if they could, but who were probably bound to this sort of life for ever.

The chattering over, the family turned towards the road that led to the lodge. Frank, Addie, Gilbert and Jenny in front, Stella with Ed in the middle and Verity and Peg at the rear. Peg began to slow down and finally when she stopped Verity stopped too.

'Is anything wrong?' she asked.

'No.' Peg looked at her. 'I came to a decision last night, Ver, and nothing will make me change my mind. I have decided that

I am going through with my marriage to Alan. It is the right, the only thing to do. Why should I ruin his life when it is in my power to make him happy? He is a good man and I can't let him down. If I did I don't think I could ever forgive myself.'

Seven

A lan settled back in his comfortable first-class compart-
ment as the train drew out of Dover station en route for
London. He'd had a good crossing to Marseilles from Alexandria, travelled by train to Calais via Paris, crossed the English
Channel in a storm and was now on the final step of his journey
home, a journey to which he had looked forward for so long –
and marriage to Peg.

He had loved her since he first saw her. She'd come into the
dingy office of the Fleet Street news agency, where he worked,
for an interview and he remembered she was like a breath of
spring air bringing light and sunshine into that gloomy place.
Their rise in a way had been meteoric, and they had helped each
other, but Peg had helped him more. Solely through Peg he had
been offered a job on the paper which now employed him as its
foreign correspondent, a post he'd filled with distinction for a
year and for which he was increasingly being acclaimed by
politicians, his fellow journalists and the general public alike.

It was good to be home. Alan got out his pipe and lit it, then,
as he sat back while the express rushed through the lush
landscape of Southern England, his mind flew over the past
few years.

There was one blip on an otherwise perfect horizon: their first
and only attempt at lovemaking had been a disaster. It was his
first experience and he'd been inept, clumsy and, ultimately, he
thought, stupid. He had pressured Peg into it and he should

never have done. It had coloured their recent meeting in Rome. They both seemed to be holding back from intimacy, the things they should have been talking about: their future life together, children. They had never discussed children though he felt sure that, coming from a large family, Peg would want them.

Such a thing he had taken for granted and he should not have done. But, since that visit, Alan had increased his experience of love-making, as he thought he should if he was to please his bride, in the brothels of Rome and Cairo. Good-class, expensive places where elegant women understood the art of love and passed on their knowledge to their usually well-off clients. Alan had been a willing student. He had even become quite attached to a woman in Cairo who had extended her favours out of business hours and he had visited her home and taken her out.

Nadia. Half-Egyptian, half-French, the mother of two children, abandoned by her husband and forced to fend for herself in the only way she knew. In another age she would have been called a courtesan and been exulted, but in Cairo in the year 1926 she was merely a prostitute. But he didn't think he would ever forget her, or cease to be grateful to her.

Alan had even felt as though he was abandoning her when he left, but she understood. She had known about Peg all along.

The wedding was in two weeks' time. All the arrangements, he knew, were well in hand, and if their meeting in Rome had been less than satisfactory Peg had made up for it since by writing him long, newsy letters full of plans. In the last one she told him how much she was longing to see him. It seemed to him more intimate than the others as if, like him, she anticipated their nuptials with joy.

Alan had bought a sheaf of English newspapers in Dover, enabling him to catch up with the news after his many days of travel. There was only one other occupant of his carriage, and he was a tired business man who had been on the boat and was fast asleep.

Alan shook out the first of the papers lying on the seat by his side and began to read. In the UK 250,000 striking miners had returned to work. Welsh miners had clashed with police at Port Talbot. Peg would have something to say about that. In Italy Mussolini had assumed total power, all opposition had been banned and the Fascist Party was now the government. Well, he had seen that coming. Nothing new there.

He finished the paper, *The Times*, and took up another. The front pages were pretty similar, so he flicked through it, did the same thing with another and was about to abandon the rest and have a snooze himself when a headline caught his eye and he hurriedly smoothed the page out and read it.

PEER'S DAUGHTER SUES FOR DIVORCE
Prominent journalist named.

Lady Ida Ryland, wife of the Honourable Hubert Ryland, is suing for divorce on the grounds of her husband's adultery. The co-respondent is cited as Miss Margaret Hallam, a popular journalist who writes under the name of Peg Hallam for the *South London Gazette*. Miss Hallam is believed to be engaged to Mr Alan Walker, the paper's foreign correspondent. Their wedding was scheduled for the middle of October at the bride's home in Dorset, which is also the family home of Mr Ryland, who is the heir to Lord Ryland.

Peg stood on the platform at Victoria as the boat train slowly chugged in, anxiously scanning the windows as they passed her. All the passengers were standing up in their seats, searching for their luggage and preparing to alight, but there was no sign of Alan.

The doors opened, porters ran along the platform and cases were hauled out and piled high on the trolleys. Some passengers started to descend and walk slowly along the platform, greeting friends or relations who had come to meet them. Placards were held aloft with the names of passengers who were expected by various businesses or hotels. There was an air of bustle and excitement; but for Peg there was only dread.

No sign of Alan. Peg moved swiftly alongside the train, looking through the windows into the carriages, now almost all empty.

Her heart sank. Perhaps he had missed the train. Perhaps he knew and didn't want to see her. One or two of the papers had had the story.

She turned back and walked slowly along the length of the train, and then she saw him, pipe in mouth, a small suitcase by his side, his expression impossible to fathom.

Did he know? Oh, please, God, don't let him know.

She ran up to him, arms waving, but he stepped back as though he didn't want to kiss her, and she knew then that he did know.

'I thought you weren't on the train,' she said, looking at his case. 'Is this all your luggage?'

'I travel light.' Alan gave a bleak half smile. 'Essential for a good journalist not to carry excess baggage.'

'I've got the car,' Peg said as he picked up his case. 'Oliver sent a driver.'

'Very good of him,' Alan murmured and Peg knew he was different, aloof, holding back.

Oliver's driver was waiting for them at the ticket barrier, removed his cap when he saw Alan and took his case from him.

'Is this all your luggage, sir?'

Alan nodded and popped his cold pipe into a pocket.

They walked out to the car, the chauffeur stowed the small bag in the back and Alan and Peg got inside.

'To Hampstead, Miss Hallam?' The chauffeur turned to Peg who nodded. Alan stared straight in front of him as the car swung out into Victoria Street towards Hyde Park.

Finally Alan turned and looked at her, opening his mouth to break the awful silence between them.

'I know,' he said, 'if that's what you're wondering. I read it in the paper on the train.'

'I hoped I could tell you first,' Peg murmured, glancing at the chauffeur. 'Can it wait until we get home?'

'If you like,' Alan said and continued to stare in front of him as the large car was driven rapidly northwards. The chauffeur carried the case up to the front door of the house, was thanked by Alan, who followed him with Peg. She opened the door while Alan stood for a few minutes, as the car was driven off, looking round the garden. It was a mild autumn day and the trees lining the street had not yet shed all their foliage. The dark green leaves of the magnolia in the garden, which they'd both admired when they first saw the house, already seemed to be preparing for the spring. Alan sighed and followed Peg into the house as if reluctant to join her.

It was not the homecoming he had hoped for or, indeed, expected when he sailed so joyfully from Alexandria.

Peg was waiting for him in the drawing room, hands deep in the pockets of her coat. Although it was quite warm she felt cold, shivery as though she was getting a cold or 'flu.

Alan halted on the threshold, looking at her, and then rummaged for his pipe and drew it from his pocket.

'How long has this been going on?' he enquired in a manner that was almost offhand as he produced a pouch of tobacco from the other pocket and started leisurely to fill his pipe. Peg felt that somehow this was an act to disguise his own unease. A pipe was a good camouflage for a man's emotions.

Her reply was given in a bleak tone. 'Four months. Since the strike. We met on a picket line.'

'How romantic.' Alan made a great play of lighting his pipe, using several matches to do so. 'I didn't realize that Mr Ryland was a Socialist.'

'He's not, of course. He was driving past in a car and saw me on the street. Offered to take me home.'

'And did you intend going ahead with our wedding, that is, if I hadn't found out?' Alan's tone was sarcastic.

'It's over between Hubert and me. We knew it was silly and wrong.'

'And then his wife found out, I suppose?'

'We were finishing in any case. I knew how unhappy you would be and he thought his wife would never divorce him.'

'I see.' Alan slowly blew smoke in the air and watched it spiralling towards the ceiling.

Peg had never seen him like this before and thought how much he had changed, even since Rome. He was more authoritative, detached, even remote. It made him somehow seem less human, maybe because it was all such an act.

'In fact his wife was having him followed by a detective because she *did* want a divorce to cover up her own affair which Hubert knew nothing about.'

'How very sordid,' Alan said with a slight sneer. 'The whole thing is overwhelmingly distasteful – for you to have got into such a situation, and what your family or the Rylands make of it, I do not know.'

'Very upset, naturally,' Peg said in a small voice.

'And if Mr Ryland thought his wife *would* divorce him, would you have told me?'

'I think I would still have gone ahead with our marriage.'

'How very kind of you, Peg.'

'Oh, don't be so sarcastic, Alan. I'd rather you lost your temper than behave like this. It's so terribly unreal and artificial. I know it's been an awful shock and it was unforgivable. I'm not proud of myself causing all this misery. Nor is Hubert. The only one enjoying herself is his wife, who gave the story to the newspapers out of spite.

'I know I behaved badly but I wanted to spare you any hurt because I *do* love you, Alan. I love and respect you and I am unbearably sad you've been so hurt.' She hung her head. 'It was something I never expected with Hubert. A *coup de foudre*. It just happened.'

'You always liked him. I used to notice the way you looked at him. It made me jealous.'

'Did you? Were you? I never knew I liked him that much. It was more hero-worship. We all rather looked up to the Rylands. I tell you, the whole thing happened by chance and was not planned. Not at all. I wouldn't have lied to you, Alan.'

'Well, you made a good show of devotion in your letters. I never suspected for a minute.'

Peg hung her head again. 'It was not a "show". I didn't intend to deceive you.'

'One of those things,' Alan said. 'I suppose as a journalist you're a good liar.'

'You're being horrible to me.'

A little voice at the back of Alan's mind whispered 'Nadia' and he began to feel uncomfortable himself. But it was no time to play *quid pro quo* and he wanted to remain on the moral high ground.

'Of course I free you immediately from our engagement. No doubt you will see to the cancellation of all the wedding plans and naturally I shan't stay here. I'll get a cab and go to a hotel.'

'It's not necessary.'

Alan looked surprised. 'I think it is or I might compromise you even more. Or don't you mind about that now, Peg? Have you got so hard, so bold that you don't mind what people think?'

'I can understand that you're hurt, Alan, and I shall never forgive myself for doing this to you, but please don't be so cruel. I have gone through hell too, you know.'

'I'm sure all your plans have miscarried, but at least you have been spared marriage to a man you don't love; and I wonder, Peg, if you ever did? Naturally I expect you and Mr Ryland wish to marry and I hope you'll both be very happy – and his snobby, stuffy parents will be very happy too.'

Alan then walked out of the room, and a few minutes later Peg heard the front door close and she could see him walking up the garden path with his little case, away from the house they once might have shared, and out of her life.

Peg found herself heaving, so choked with tears that she could hardly get her breath, now that the enormity of what had happened and the implications really struck her.

Would she and Hubert marry? She had no idea. They had no chance to talk. He had warned her by telephone what was happening, that Ida had announced she was seeking a divorce and had already informed the press. As yet they had had no opportunity to meet. Hubert had rushed off to see his parents to warn them and Peg had telephoned Verity. Obviously Oliver Moodie had to be informed too and that wasn't very pleasant.

Other than that she had just sat it out, waiting for Alan to arrive home, feeling in some way as though the end of the world had come.

Lord Ryland was an imposing man, now approaching his sixtieth birthday, who embodied some of the best and also the worst traits of the British ruling class. He was honest and honourable, patriotic, a good family man, a thoughtful, even generous, employer and a loving father. But he was also arrogant, opinionated and above all he felt assured of his place in the world by virtue of centuries of breeding, of Rylands living in a castle built by his ancestors, generations of Rylands going back almost to medieval times, of their rightful place in the scheme of things, the sanctity of master and servant.

Rylands had paid their taxes, served the reigning monarch, and often sacrificed their lives for their country in overseas wars. Above all, Rylands were confident of their role in English society and security in the succession from father to son. Until 1917, that is, when Lydney Ryland had been killed at the battle of Cambrai. Then Edward Ryland's world had fallen apart, but only briefly. There were standards to maintain; but his grief at losing a son was far greater than that of losing an heir, because there was always Hubert, four years younger than his brother and every bit as robust, vigorous and trustworthy. Hubert and Lydney had been close as brothers, and Hubert was as grief-stricken as the rest of the family when he died.

Hubert also knew then that he would succeed his father and

he fulfilled his duties as the heir, taking an interest in the running of the estate but with a token, not very demanding, job with a firm of London stockbrokers.

Father and son now faced each other in the great drawing room of Ryland Castle and the atmosphere between them was electric. Lady Ryland sat apart from the men in a chair, her hands resting on the arms. She was a tall, distinguished-looking woman, two years younger than her husband, and the daughter of an Irish peer. In her youth she had been a beauty, the deb of the year, much sought after by the young men surrounding the court. She had a simple, plaited coiffure coiled on top of her head. Her hair, once fair, gently turning to white, deep blue eyes and a pale, remarkably unwrinkled skin. She could pass for beautiful even now. She wore a tailored dress of pale blue mohair with a pleated skirt, and lapels revealing a single strand of exquisitely matched pearls round her throat. She was a exuberant do-gooder, patron of many local worthy causes and, though devoted to animals and all furry and feathered things, still a keen shot and an enthusiastic follower of the hunt, as was her husband.

Lady Ryland had said nothing while Hubert told his story, her reaction hard to fathom. However, Penelope Ryland was adept at the practice of self-control required by someone of her breeding, of keeping herself to herself. As Hubert finished his story her hands started nervously to clench and unclench, her eyes resting on her surviving son full of anxiety and pain. She was a devoted mother and he was a much-loved son, maybe more loved than most because she had lost her first born. She wanted his happiness, but so many other factors were important, like social attitudes and family pride. *Noblesse oblige*.

'Peg Hallam is a very pretty girl –' she spoke before her husband – 'but how *could* you, Hubert . . .'

'A servant . . .' her husband thundered. 'I can't understand you, Hubert.'

'Peg is *not* a servant, Father,' Hubert said icily. 'She has never been a servant. She is a professional woman, a highly respected journalist.'

'Pah!' Lord Ryland snarled. 'Both her stepfathers have worked for me and both were servants. I value Frank Carpenter very highly, but he is still a servant, paid to do as he is told. Her sisters and brother have done well, but that cannot alter their status. It would certainly not be in order for a Ryland to marry into that family. You would be ostracized by society, and rightly so. Why, Peg used to help out in the kitchen.'

'Only in school holidays, dear,' Lady Ryland chided her husband gently. 'She was never *really* a servant and I have always been fond of Peg, as indeed I have of the whole family.'

'Don't say you're on *his* side, Penelope.' Lord Ryland looked at his wife indignantly.

'I don't think it is a matter of "sides", Edward dear. Of course I am not on her "side", as it were. But then I was never overfond of Ida and, from what Hubert says, she has not behaved very well. If she loved someone else and wanted a divorce she should have asked him in the proper way and not have had him followed by a detective. I find that deceitful and very vulgar. I also find having a lover *very* vulgar,' she said as an aside, 'but, alas, it is not all that uncommon, even in the best families.' Lady Ryland grimaced with well-bred distaste.

'Thank you, Mother.' Hubert crossed the room and kissed her on the cheek, whereupon she took hold of his arm.

'That does not mean I approve, Hubert. I agree with your father that you would find it difficult socially . . . I mean it depends what you and Peg . . .' Her eyes anxiously scanned his face. 'For instance, you wouldn't intend to *marry* her, would you?'

Hubert swallowed. 'That's just what I *do* intend, Mother, if she'll have me . . .'

'If she'll *have* you,' Lord Ryland growled. 'I would think that a forgone conclusion. What a lift up in the world for the daughter of a butcher.'

'That is a very cruel and unjust thing to say, Father, and,

incidentally, unworthy of you,' Hubert said stiffly. 'Your snobbery does you no credit. Things have moved on since the war, you know; attitudes in society have changed. I am not at all sure Peg *will* accept me. She has her own sense of pride. She will not relish being looked down upon by you.'

'Now *that* is not a very nice thing to say,' his mother intervened angrily. 'If she became your wife we would, of course, accept her.'

'*I* would not accept her,' Lord Ryland interjected. 'I would *never* allow her to set foot in this place as long as I lived. I would never believe, Hubert, that after all your breeding and training you would even consider having the daughter of a servant for your wife.' He turned to Lady Ryland, who by now was sitting bolt upright in her chair, watching him. 'Your mother might accept her but I never shall, and that's my final word on the subject.'

Peg knew that Hubert was up at the castle at this moment confronting his parents; but they had travelled down separately and were yet to meet.

Verity, alerted by telephone, had got leave and travelled from Bristol the night before. There was an atmosphere of crisis as Peg walked into the house, but the sisters embraced, clinging to each other rather longer than they normally would have. Stella and Jenny were in school; Frank had decided it would be more politic to be absent, so was busy about the estate. But there would be no respite for him there as most of the workers had already seen the paper.

But there was a sense of awkwardness, of diffidence that wasn't usually present when the sisters met. Maybe at last on Verity's part there was a hint of disapproval too. Alan had always been a favourite of hers. But Hubert Ryland . . .

They were sitting in the kitchen, where family discussions normally took place, crises were dealt with and other decisions of household importance made. It was really the centre of the home, its heart. A kettle usually simmered on the well-blackened stove, and a brown cloth covered the kitchen table. Now there were three cups and saucers on it, as well as a pot of freshly brewed tea and a plate of home-baked biscuits.

'I didn't know you even *knew* him, Peg,' Verity began once the tea was poured and some commonplace remarks exchanged.

'Well, of course I knew him,' Peg said, shakily getting out a cigarette. 'We all did.'

'You know what I mean.' Verity said, colouring.

Peg, speaking quickly, almost breathlessly, then told her sisters about the meeting at the picket line and what had followed. When she stopped, neither Verity nor Addie said anything, expressing neither approval nor disapproval. Both, in the past, had had illicit liaisons, so perhaps their thoughts were inclined to be sympathetic, though complicated by the fact that their sister's lover was the Ryland heir, a person of importance, someone deeply significant yet formerly remote in their lives.

'What will happen now, Peg?' Verity spoke at last. Having, like Peg, had recourse to a cigarette, she sat furiously puffing away.

Peg shrugged. 'I have no idea. Hubert is at the castle this moment talking to his parents. You can't expect them to be anything but shocked. It's in the melting pot.'

'He might throw you over,' Addie said quietly. 'The Ryland men have always been afraid of their father.'

'I don't think you can say that, Addie.' Verity looked at her disapprovingly. 'We will never know what Lydney might have done in your case; but you seemed at the time to think that his love was true and I expect Peg thinks the same about Mr Hubert.' It was difficult, even with her sister's lover, to break the habit of a lifetime and simply refer to him by his Christian name alone.

'Lydney still never told his father or mentioned me to anyone in the family. I think he was too afraid of what they'd say.' Addie looked defiantly at her elder sister.

101

'I don't expect Hubert to throw me over, as you call it,' Peg intervened quickly. 'He might want a break or a pause. I shouldn't blame him. This has all happened so quickly. He may want to collect his thoughts before seeing me. Whatever he wants he can have the time.'

'And what do *you* want, Peg?' Verity asked her earnestly.

Looking momentarily bewildered, slightly bereft, Peg shook her head. 'Quite honestly, right now, I don't know. It was a shock to me and a great shock to Alan.'

'I must confess I *am* so sorry for Alan.' Verity shook her head sadly. 'I was and am fond of him. He adored you and this must have been a terrible blow to him.'

Peg nodded. 'He was very unforgiving.'

'You can hardly blame him.'

'I suppose not. I felt terrible about him too. Yesterday was the most awful day of my life, meeting him at the station and finding out that he already knew.'

'I think I'll get in touch with him,' Verity said, 'that is, if you don't mind. I would like to reassure him that we, as a family . . . regret what has happened.'

'I think that would be nice.'

'All the presents to be returned,' Addie said glumly, 'the invitations cancelled. The ceremony . . . Oh dear, there is so much to do.' She stood up as if she was about to begin putting that task in hand at once. 'I'm *happy* for you, Peg, I really am,' she said impulsively, and she bent down and kissed her sister before rapidly leaving the room, perhaps to conceal the emotions that had been unleashed at the memory of her own lost love.

Gravely they watched their sister's sudden exit, perhaps aware of the cause, and then Verity put her hand over Peg's. 'Despite the worry this has caused and the confusion, we must not lose sight of the fact that you've been spared an unwise marriage, about which I warned you. I always knew that you were ready to fall in love with someone else.'

'Right as usual.' Peg gave a wry smile.

'Only I didn't know who that would be.' Verity's expression was sombre. 'Now I do.'

At that juncture there was a light tap on the kitchen door and Hubert Ryland put his head round.

'Mind if I come in?' he said.

Eight

L ong hair flying in the wind, Stella Hallam sped down the lane on her bicycle, pedalling as hard as she could. She loved going home for the weekend, but she also loved returning to Nettlethorpe, the small West Dorset village where she was schoolmistress at the junior school. She would go home on Friday afternoon after school and come back on Sunday afternoon.

But there was also another reason for her speed: Stella, shy Stella, the one people always seemed to forget about, always so eclipsed by her older half-sisters, was in love.

Stella had nursed an ambition to be a teacher like Addie and went to teacher training school in Bristol, as her sister had. Not only was it what she wanted, but she knew Mum would have wanted it too. She was sixteen when Mum died and although her place had been taken by Verity, and in certain ways by Addie, it was never the same.

Stella, eager to learn, and clever, adaptable, easy to get on with, emerged from teacher training with honours. She took a job at this small village school on the edge of Marshwood Vale about an hour's brisk cycle ride from home.

This was the end of her first year. To begin with she had been lonely, but she soon made friends. Shy she might have been, but this added to her popularity. She wasn't pushy. She took part in all the social occasions in the small village, attended the dances, the outings, helped with the charity events for the elderly and destitute.

Above all she was a keen churchgoer and sang in the choir. It

104

was there she met Ernest Pickering, who not only had a beautiful rich baritone voice but was handsome as well.

He was a bank clerk in Bridport and lived with his parents in the village. The Pickering home soon became a second home for Stella. She would ride straight to his house on her return from her weekend at home. His mother was a second mother and his sister, Mary, an addition to her three elder siblings. The two young women became close.

After tea Stella and Ernest would go off to sing in the choir for the evening service, and the nice part was lingering for a long time on the way home where much intense kissing and groping took place among the hedges, well out of sight.

No one at home knew about Ernest. Stella was too shy to tell them, yet they should not have been surprised that she so quickly attracted the attentions of a young man because she was very pretty: dark and petite with limpid brown eyes, a dimpled chin and, though this side of her was carefully hidden from her family, an inborn tendency to flirt.

Stella was twenty. She would soon be twenty-one. Ernest was twenty-two. He had reddish brown hair and a freckled skin, pale blue eyes and a ruddy healthy complexion. He was of sturdy build and played rugger for the village in winter and cricket for the village and the bank all summer long. He was very much a man's man and liked drinking with the boys. They met soon after Stella started at the school and joined the choir. It had been silly to keep a secret like this for so long from her family, but she didn't quite know what to say. Anyway they were all so preoccupied with their own complicated affairs, she supposed that never for a minute would they think she had anything of interest to tell them, other than her life at school. She supposed Verity would assume she was too young to have a boyfriend, and might disapprove if she knew.

Stella was the youngest of the family and until the advent of Jenny had always felt she was Mum's special favourite. She had felt protected by the warmth of her mother's love. Even though it was obvious that Mum loved Jenny a lot she also always had time for her. She was only sixteen when Mum had died and was devastated by her loss. But she was close to Addie and regarded good-natured Frank as a father figure.

Stella arrived outside the Pickering's little cottage on the outskirts of Nettlethorpe, pushed open the gate and wheeled her bicycle up the path, propping it against the porch covered with climbing roses. It was a pretty cottage with a thatched roof and a large garden with a hen run at the end. Stella pushed open the door and walked in and, as usual, the enticing smell of baking greeted her and motherly Mrs Pickering opened her arms to embrace her.

'Did you have a nice time with your family, dear?'

Stella nodded.

'And how are they? How's the baby? Did he get over his cold?'

'Oh, he's quite better,' Stella assured her. Addie and Gilbert, who now lived with them at the lodge, had a baby called Arthur who was nearly a year old. Mrs Pickering didn't know that Addie and Gilbert weren't married, and Stella wouldn't have dreamt of telling her. There were so many secrets concerning her family that Stella felt diffident about confiding in this kind, but rather conventional, church-going family, who might not quite understand.

Nor could she tell them about the divorce scandal that had made her sister Peg decamp to the Continent with Hubert Ryland until it all blew over. Hubert had offered no defence to his divorce in order to shorten the procedure. And it had, but the details were interesting enough to attract the attention of the more prurient newspapers. Much had been made of the relationship between Peg, whose family were servants to her noble lover's family, and her lover and how Lord Ryland had turned his back on his son, and would have disinherited him if he could. But he couldn't. The Ryland estate and the family fortune had been carefully entailed by an ancestor who might have been able to see into the future.

Happily all this had blown over before Stella arrived in

Nettlethorpe, and now Hubert and Peg were legally married and had two babies born in rapid succession. All Mrs Pickering knew was that Stella had a sister who was married to an Englishman and they grew grapes and olives in Umbria.

The tea was laid in the kitchen, the table groaning as usual with newly baked bread, cakes, scones, homemade jam and freshly churned butter, which Stella sometimes brought back with her from the home farm together with eggs and fresh vegetables, or anything else she could safely put on the back of the bike or in the basket at the front.

Mr Pickering, whose name was Jim, was already sitting at the table reading the Sunday paper when Stella came in. He was a jovial, good-natured man, a joiner by trade, and he put aside his paper to exchange a few words as she sat down.

Mary was making the tea, pouring hot water into a large brown pot which she covered with a cosy and brought over to the table, greeting Stella with a smile.

Mary was also a redhead, as was Mrs Pickering, though her hair had faded and was salt and peppery. Mary's was a vibrant auburn, and she was pale-skinned with green eyes. She was of medium height, full busted and lissom and, accordingly, was a considerable object of fascination to most of the young males of Nettlethorpe and beyond, who swarmed round her like bees around a honey-pot. She worked in an insurance office, also in Bridport, to which she and Ernest cycled daily, or took the bus if the weather was bad.

'Had a nice weekend?' Mary asked.

'Lovely, thanks.' Stella eyed the goodies on the table. Her long ride always made her hungry. Mary also sang in the choir, but she never came back with Stella and Ernest because she always had something going on with one or other of her many admirers.

'Ernest is going to be late,' Mrs Pickering clucked, looking anxiously at the clock. 'He's seeing someone about buying a motor car.' Mrs Pickering's voice carried a whole load of doubt. 'I don't really *know* they're safe.'

'Oh Mother, they're *safe* as houses,' Mary burst out, taking her seat at the table. 'It will be lovely to be able to drive to work.'

'Oh a car!' Stella cried excitedly. 'We'll be able to go for long picnics.'

'I suppose you know all about cars.' Mr Pickering put aside his paper and applied himself to his tea.

'Well, we don't have a car ourselves of course,' Stella said cautiously, 'but Frank, my stepfather, can use one of Lord Ryland's cars whenever he likes. We're very lucky.'

The Pickering family, though saying little, were rather in awe of Stella's relationship with the nobility. Not that Stella mentioned it to them much, if at all. But she knew they were impressed by the tone in which they mentioned Lord Ryland's name.

However, they had never connected, or had cause to connect, Stella's sister Peg with the scandal in the Ryland family, and Stella was happy for it to remain like that.

Mrs Pickering looked at the clock again as she covered one of the warm scones, which Mary had brought out of the oven, with a thick layer of apricot jam. She was a comely lady who had little concern for the proportions of her ample figure, or the prospect of it increasing.

There was a sudden roar from outside and they all jumped up in alarm. Mary ran to the kitchen door.

'It's the *car*,' she said excitedly. 'Ernest has got a *car*.'

They all poured out into the garden just in time to see Ernest emerging from a small green Model-T Ford, with a huge smile on his face.

'Like it?' he asked, but his question was directed mainly at Stella.

Stella ecstatically clasped her hands together. 'Have you really got it? Is it all yours?'

'It's all mine,' Ernest declared proudly. 'A man at the cricket club is going abroad. It's almost new. He was eager to get rid of it and I've got a bargain.'

They all gathered round the car whose gleaming exterior and highly polished interior drew gasps of admiration.

'Anyone like a quick spin?' he called out, opening the door.

'It's time for your tea,' his mother said sharply, 'time for spins later, or you'll be late for church.'

Stella sang particularly well that night. She kept glancing at Ernest and thought how fine he looked, his head thrown back in song, his chest thrust out. He was obviously very pleased with his car. A beam of evening sunlight coming through the west window of the church shone on his head, so that momentarily it seemed to be on fire. Then he caught her eye and smiled.

After the service they stood outside as usual for some time talking to their friends among the congregation or members of the choir who had also gathered to admire his newly acquired automobile. Hardly anyone in Nettlethorpe was the possessor of such an impressive contraption.

Finally the crowd thinned. Ernest opened the door and with a smile at Stella said, 'Hop in.'

He shut her door, then, rounding the car, gave the bonnet a pat of endearment and clambered into his seat. He switched on the engine and set off, a little tentatively at first. Stella settled back, conscious of a feeling of euphoria as if Ernest's pleasure in his new toy gave her pleasure too. Of course it did. This was as it should be. She realized she was really in love with him, and what made him happy made her happy too.

Her only sadness was that those slow walks home on a Sunday had been something she looked forward to; the sensuous pleasure of his body against hers, their caresses which as they became more prolonged had come very near to the real thing. But just in time she always drew back, remembering what had happened to Addie. Ernest, however, was a passionate man and if she hadn't cried, 'No!' quite firmly several times and pushed him away she was sure that by now she would no longer be a virgin.

They drove in silence for a while, Ernest's mind clearly concentrating on the mechanics of his car.

'See, she goes like a bird,' he shouted above the roar of the engine. And now, after a few initial bumps, abrupt stops and erratic starts, she did. The little Model-T flew along.

Stella lightly put a hand on Ernest's arm. 'Where are we going?'

'I thought as it was a nice evening we might have a drink at the Baker's Arms.'

The Baker's Arms was a pub much frequented by the cricket team and was in a rather remote part of the countryside some miles out of the town.

'Nice idea,' Stella said, settling back again. 'Oh, how lovely to have a car. But . . .' She looked at him.

'But what?'

'Well I'll miss our walks.' She glanced at him slyly.

'Oh, we can have *walks*,' Ernest replied meaningfully.

As if he knew exactly what she meant by 'walks' and was excited by the thought, Ernest abruptly turned off the road and drove the car along a rough track leading into a wood, stopping about half way.

'We can still have our *walk*, darling,' he murmured, turning to her and taking her in his arms.

Their kissing was passionate. It was also a lot more comfortable than a grassy bank or the hedgerow where they usually did their love-making. Sometimes it had been wet and they'd got soaked.

In the heat of the moment Ernest slid his hand under her skirt, his fingers creeping towards her knickers, feeling under the elastic.

'Stop!' Stella commanded, turning her mouth away and putting a hand firmly over his.

'Oh, go on.' His breathing was heavy, his face puce.

'No, no. It's wrong. You know it's wrong. Besides . . .'

'Besides what . . .'

'My sister had a baby out of wedlock.'

'Oh!' Ernest withdrew his hand, took a deep breath, and his panting gradually subsided.

'Oh, yes, of course. I see.' He mopped his perspiring brow. 'You can take precautions, you know. I know how.'

'*How?*' Stella asked suspiciously. 'I mean, *how* do you know?'

'A bloke at the office told me.'

'Well, I don't think it's right. Not yet. Not after what happened to my sister.'

'Which sister was that?'

'Addie.'

'But didn't she marry him? I thought she was married.'

'He died in the war. She was only seventeen.'

'Did she tell her husband?'

'No, yes.' Stella paused. 'It was rather complicated.'

'Stella.' An amorous look came into Ernest's eyes and he slid an arm round her waist, putting his lips close to her ear: 'Will you marry me?'

'Marry what?' Stella looked at him startled. '*Marry*, did you say?'

'I mean it. I was going to ask you, honest. It's nothing to do with what we just talked about. I mean, I can wait.'

'You don't *have* to, you know.'

'But I want to. Don't you?'

'Oh yes. Well –' she paused 'I don't know. Maybe it's a bit soon. I'm only twenty. I don't know what my family would say.'

'We don't have to rush it. We can get engaged. You *do* love me, don't you, Stella?' He pressed his cheek against hers, his arms hugging her tight.

'Of course I do.' She felt overwhelmed by his closeness, his physical presence. If he put his hand under her knicker elastic again she didn't think she'd be able to resist.

'Then it's "yes"?' Ernest prompted her.

Stella nodded, too overcome by emotion, by the strength of her desire, to trust herself to speak.

*   *   *

September 27th 1930

NOTES FROM AN UMBRIAN VINEYARD BY PEG HALLAM

This is a golden time of the year. The slopes above our farm are covered with vines of the Trebbiano grape which goes towards the making of the beautiful golden-coloured Orvieto wine. The harvesters have started arriving, most of them locals but some travel around Italy assisting at this time of the year.

Or course we are still inexperienced viniculturists and it is only three years since we bought the farm and took over the vineyard. We do not make wine ourselves but send the grapes to be pressed at our local cooperative, which supplies the winemakers in the region. But my husband is rapidly becoming an expert, and in between my house-keeping duties and looking after the children, I must say I find it a subject of endless fascination.

Ours is only one of the many wine-growing districts of Italy. Most of the vineyards were damaged during the war and their owners reduced to bankruptcy. Our farmhouse was practically a ruin when we bought it and the vineyard in a grave state of disrepair. But we fell in love with the countryside and the nearby city of Perugia, one of the most beautiful and historical in Italy.

Did you know that . . .

Peg stopped typing at the sound of her study door opening and Hubert came in carrying a thick bundle of letters.

'Post,' he said, leafing through them. 'Two for you. Mostly bills for me.' He stopped to kiss her and looked over her shoulder at the piece of paper in the typewriter. 'Writing your article?'

Peg nodded, leaned back in her chair and lit a cigarette.

'I was a bit stuck and then I thought I'd write about the harvest and the various kinds of Italian wines.'

'Good idea.' Hubert sat down beside her and began slitting open the envelopes and briefly perusing the contents. 'Oh, Mother would like to come.' He looked up. 'You don't mind, do you?'

'Of course not.'

Peg turned back to her typewriter and read over what she had just written. She was aware of Hubert standing behind her, scrutinizing her.

'Sure?'

She turned and took his head between her hands.

'*Quite* sure, darling. I like your mother,' and she kissed him firmly on the lips.

'In that case I'll send her a wire.' Hubert began to gather up his correspondence. 'She loves coming here.' He turned to look at her. 'She loves *you*.'

Peg smiled and waved him off as though she was busy, but after Hubert had left she sat back in her chair, smoking and looking through the window at the magnificent countryside that surrounded their farm, deep in the Umbrian hills. As well as wine they had an ancient olive grove producing the famous plump green olives of Umbria, which were pressed by hand to make pure virgin olive oil though, again, they sold their olives to a cooperative which did the pressing and manufactured the oil.

For Peg the last few years had been among the happiest in her life. There was no doubt about that. At first the plan had been to get away and then return to England after a suitable time but, instead, they fell in love with Italy and decided to make their home there. Hubert had always had an interest in wine, and how it was made fascinated him. He also developed a talent for reconstruction and cheerfully gave up his stockbroking business to concentrate on the restoration of the farm and its buildings.

Money was tight, but various legacies from relatives in the past had left him fairly comfortably off. Ida had married her wealthy lover and made no claims on him, and there were no children by her to think of.

His and Peg's eldest child, Jude, had been conceived sometime before they were able to marry, but was born in time to be the legitimate Ryland heir. Their second baby, also a boy, Caspar, was born a year later.

Peg soon came to love life in Italy, and she managed to keep working. She had been commissioned by a women's magazine to write a series of articles on life in Italy, far away from the resurgence of Fascism that had gripped Rome and the industrial towns. Here in their tiny village in the Umbrian foothills it was almost possible to believe that Mussolini didn't exist, but how long that would last one did not know. Fascism loved regulations, and plenty of these were creeping in.

Very few local people knew anything about the new arrivals, and that included the few expatriates who lived in various castles or palazzi dotted throughout the countryside.

The Ryland divorce had been only a brief sensation, thanks to Hubert's decision not to contest it. The fact that he and Peg had lived together before they were married was unknown because as soon as they were legally able to do so the ceremony was performed at the town hall in Perugia. Two weeks later Jude had been born.

Her mother-in-law's first visit had been unexpected. She 'happened' to be touring Italy with a friend and had called. It was very difficult meeting Lady Ryland in her new role as Hubert's wife, but the visit had gone well.

Peg had always liked Lady Ryland and indeed her husband too, but to see her now as mother-in-law, grandmother to her children, was something else.

However, she had been tactful, left mother and son together as often as they wished, even suggested they took the grandchildren out for the day if they wanted. So what reservations Lady Ryland might have had quickly evaporated and a warm and loving relationship began, in which Lady Ryland saw Peg as her son's wife and not a member of the lower orders.

So one day at I Pelicano – their farm took its name from the small hamlet nearby – merged happily into the next. The harvesting of the grapes went on and occasionally Peg would join them, cutting the plump bunches with special scissors and putting them in baskets which would then be carried to the carts awaiting them, from where they went to the local press.

In time Hubert thought that when he knew enough – and people said it sometimes took a lifetime – he might produce his own wine 'Casa I Pelicano' but that time was not yet.

He could imagine spending the rest of his life in Umbria and even when he inherited – and given his father's robust good health, this was likely to be some time away – saw no reason why he should return to live in England, provided Peg and the children agreed.

Peg was quite happy to stay away from home. Apart from the animosity of Lord Ryland, who regarded her as a scarlet woman solely responsible for his son's fall from grace, there was the attitude of Frank, who had never forgiven her for her outspokenness during the picket. Frank was of the old school who believed in the social boundary between master and servant, and he thought Peg had strayed beyond this and had somehow lost her way.

But Verity came to stay. She loved foreign travel and Italy especially, and Addie had once come with Gilbert, but that visit was not so successful because Gilbert felt out of place in the home of his employer's heir and found it impossible to be on an even footing with him.

Peg finished her cigarette and had returned to her typewriter when she remembered the two letters Hubert had brought her, both with an English postmark. One bore Addie's handwriting, so she opened that first. The other was typewritten and had a London postmark.

'Dearest Peg,' Addie wrote in her neat schoolmistressy hand:

> I have some surprising news for you. Stella is engaged to be married! Isn't that a surprise? He is a nice young man called Ernest Pickering and she has known him for over a year, but kept it to herself – dark horse! He works in a

115

bank in Bridport and his prospects are good. He popped the question in the summer, but Stella thought she had to think about it. As you know she has only just turned twenty-one and she felt, quite sensibly in my opinion, that she had to experience a bit more of adult life.

She told us at the weekend and brought Ernest home to meet us. We all liked him. He is very keen on sport and he and Gilbert get on particularly well. He is quite nice looking with red hair and freckles. Not very tall.

Stella had told him all about the situation between me and Gilbert, that is that we are not married, and he was very understanding and broad-minded about it.

They are going to wait a little before getting married however, maybe in two years' time, and very much want you and Mr Hubert to be there.

No more news at the moment. We are all well. How are things with you and the boys?

Love,
Addie.

Peg put down the letter, her heart full of deep emotion. The baby of the family engaged! Little Stella in love. How *pleased* Mum would have been that she had found a man in a good steady profession like banking, solid and safe. Peg's eyes momentarily filled with tears, and then she tore open the envelope of the other letter and after reading its contents, flew out of the room and through the house, calling for Hubert. He was in an outhouse, putting on his boots to go up to the vineyard.

'Darling,' she cried, waving the letter high above her head.

'Whatever is it, Peg?'

'Someone asked me to write a book!'

'What, who?' He looked at her excited face.

'A publisher who likes my letters from Umbria. He wants me to write a book in the form of a diary about living here. Isn't

116

that wonderful?' She handed him the letter which he read keenly.

'And there's money too.' He looked up at her. 'An advance of two hundred pounds! We'll be able to extend the olive grove.' He held out his arms and Peg flew into them.

'Oh Hubert, I'm so happy. And, darling, Stella is engaged. Isn't life *fun*?'

October 1930

They sat on the verandah watching the evening sun sink behind the Umbrian hills, a bottle of chilled Orvieto on the small table in front of them. It was that quiet, happy time of the day when work was finished and in the kitchen the cook was preparing dinner. Unlike most Italians the Rylands did not like midday lunch.

Lady Ryland, who had always had nursemaids to look after her own children, relished her new role and had helped put Jude to bed. Peg had just come in from checking that everything was all right in the kitchen and Hubert handed her a glass of wine and patted the chair beside him.

'Everything all right?'

'Everything's fine,' she reassured him. 'About half an hour.'

They had a cook and a maid who lived in, and the farm workers came from the neighbouring hamlet.

'It *is* a beautiful place,' Lady Ryland exclaimed with a sigh, putting her glass back on the table. 'How *lucky* you were to find such a spot.'

'Weren't they lucky?' Verity smiled at her and then sat baby Caspar up on her lap to wind him before giving him the rest of the bottle.

It was lovely to hold her nephew in her arms. She had given many small babies their bottles, but there was nothing as special as one's own flesh and blood. Peg and Hubert had given her a happiness she hadn't expected because not only were they the happily married parents of two children, but they lived in a

117

country she had always loved and naturally gravitated towards, even resuming her old friendship with Geraldine Beaumaurice to do so.

It had been strange, at first, meeting Lady Ryland as a social equal at the home of her sister. But now they had met several times, although she still called her 'Lady Ryland' and Lady Ryland either called her 'dear' or 'Miss Carter-Barnes'. Old habits died hard. She also instinctively thought of Peg's husband as 'Mr' Hubert, but at least had learned to use his Christian name.

Verity finished winding Caspar and Lady Ryland leaned towards her. 'Shall I take him, dear? You haven't even tasted your wine.'

Verity brought Caspar over, sat him with his bottle on his grandmother's lap, and helped herself to olives from a bowl before drinking her wine.

Caspar settled happily in his grandmother's arms, as contented there as he was with his more experienced aunt. He had an extraordinarily happy temperament.

Lady Ryland was thrilled with her grandchildren. She felt a whole new world had been revealed to her by her son's marriage to Peg. Although she had always liked Peg she had inevitably shared her husband's misgivings about the suitability of it all.

Penelope Ryland had always mixed exclusively with members of the upper classes; people with money, titles, breeding, usually all three.

Of course she knew the middle classes through her charitable work; ladies of leisure who gave freely of their time to help the poor and unfortunate, ran the women's institute, the mother's union and so on. But she never mixed with them socially or entertained them to dinner.

The working classes, as distinct from the deserving poor, were represented by all who served the Rylands on the estate and these were people who, on the whole, knew how to keep their place and were soon got rid of if they didn't.

Knowing Peg's family in a different light had given her an

entirely new perspective on the world. Hubert's first wife had, like her, been the daughter of a peer – a cold and remote woman, which she didn't think she was. She had never particularly liked or understood Ida and couldn't say she was sorry when she and Hubert parted, though like her husband she didn't really approve of divorce and considered it a social disgrace.

However those bad times were past. Edward had never become reconciled, but she was sure that in time he would and he would want to see his grandchildren. She knew he suffered, but he was too proud to compromise and Hubert would never be the one to beg. In time she prayed father and son would come together.

Lady Ryland looked across at her son, who smiled at her as if he knew what she was thinking about. He looked so well, his hair bleached by the Italian sun, his skin brown. Above all he was happy and relaxed, and she put out a hand, which he took. Peg, seeing the gesture, smiled her approval. It was a very happy time.

The telephone rang and Peg got up. 'I'll get it,' she said as Hubert started to rise. 'I must just check on the dinner.'

She stooped to put a kiss on the top of his head as she passed quickly into the hall and lifted the receiver.

'Hello?'

'Hello?' The voice came crackling over the line. 'Is Lady Ryland there?'

'Who is it calling?' Peg began. Then, uncertainly, 'Is it *Frank*?'

'Oh Peg, is that you?' Frank's voice sounded anxious. 'I didn't recognize your voice. Thank goodness it's you. Peg . . .' He stopped and suddenly Peg was filled with a deep sense of foreboding.

'Frank is anything *wrong*?' Her knuckles whitened as she tightly clutched the receiver.

'Peg something terrible has happened. I don't know how to tell you this.'

119

'Oh Frank, what *is* it?'

'Lord Ryland has been killed, Peg. He fell off his horse this afternoon during the hunt and has broken his neck. We just had word from the hospital. Oh Peg, whatever will you say to her ladyship? However will you tell her?'

There was silence as Peg wrestled with her emotions, the feeling that the whole world had suddenly caved in.

'And Peg?' Frank went on slowly. 'Do you realize, Peg, that you'll now be the new Lady Ryland?'

Nine

November 1930

L ady Ryland. Peg couldn't get used to the idea. She stood
in front of the Ryland family vault, her coat collar turned
up against the cold, teeth chattering. It was a bitter day for
Lord Ryland's funeral. The morning had dawned damp and
foggy and a pall of gloom seemed to hang over the place as
they'd followed the coffin from its resting place in the castle to
the church where he had been baptized, married and where his
children had been baptized. All the solemn rituals of his family
had taken place there for centuries.

A stream of mourners had got there before them. The church
was packed and several hundred people stood outside, straining
to hear the service. Lord Ryland had been a proper country
squire who was polite and courteous to all, who treated his staff
well and considerately and so they turned out to honour a man
who, though not greatly loved, had been liked and respected. A
good man, a just man.

His death had been cruel. He had been fit and was a superb
rider but his horse had stumbled at a hedge and, in falling off,
Lord Ryland had hit his head on a stone stile and died some
hours later without regaining consciousness.

The vicar had paid tribute to the man. Hubert had read the
lesson in ringing tones, the rafters of the church had echoed to the
stirring hymns chosen to give a good send-off to one whose early
career had been in the Army and who had fought at Omdurman.

Now just the family had gone into the crypt where Rylands

had been buried for centuries, each lead coffin on a shelf one above the other. There seemed an awful lot of them, Peg thought, looking round fearfully. It was a creepy place. One day it would be Hubert's turn. Maybe hers? But she still felt she had no right to the Ryland title. It was very strange, and she wondered if she would ever get used to it.

She stood between Hubert and Violet. Her mother-in-law was slightly in front with the vicar, who was saying the final prayers.

'Ashes to ashes . . . dust to dust . . . in the hope of a blessed resurrection . . .'

Peg's mother too had had her funeral in the church, but she was buried outside in the churchyard, a solitary but well tended grave on the edge of the cemetery, lovingly cared for by Frank.

The prayers came to an end. Hubert bowed towards the coffin, took his mother gently by the arm and escorted her back into the church, Violet and Peg following behind to where the congregation silently awaited them while the organ played softly.

It was a nerve-racking experience walking down the aisle past the crowd of onlookers, whose eyes, were on her, an object of curiosity because, although they all knew her and who she was, her new role was as strange to them as it was to her.

Lady Ryland. There were odd glances as she passed, faces not unfriendly but puzzled as if they, like her, didn't quite know what she was doing leaving the church with the Rylands as part of that family.

The chief mourners walked slowly up the hill towards the castle. The front rows of pews had been reserved for family guests, who had come not only from London but from all over England and Scotland. There were lords, knights and their ladies, members of parliament, retired army generals, an admiral, members of the diplomatic corps and a number of relations and family friends, some of whom were staying at the castle.

The previous evening Peg had uneasily presided at a dinner party to welcome them. None of them had at first known who she was but made polite, if rather embarrassed, noises when introduced, usually by her mother-in-law, as Hubert's new wife. Now these special guests were ushered through the main door of the castle while locals and estate workers were shown the side entrance to the ballroom where the staff parties were held. This made Peg feel even more uncomfortable as she stood on the steps leading to the castle, undecided what to do until Hubert put his arm lightly round her waist and pushed her forward.

'Go on, dear, you're holding up the traffic.'

'I feel I should go to the ballroom, Hubert.'

'Don't be silly, darling.'

'But those are my people.'

'*These* are your people now, Peg,' he said quietly and kissed her swiftly on the cheek.

It was confusing. In a way it was humiliating to separate, as it were, the sheep from the goats. Alan, she knew, would have thought it very wrong. But she did as she was told and was swept up on the tide of distinguished guests who were ushered into the drawing room where there was a cold buffet and whisky and champagne to drink.

She slipped up to her room to remove her coat and hat, smooth down her black dress and, as she powdered her face and applied fresh lipstick, she took a long hard look at herself. She thought that in a very short time she seemed to have lost the bloom of Italy and grown pale, tense and, she thought, old.

Lord Ryland's death had been a terrible shock. They had led an idyllic life in Italy and she had never given any thought to the day when Hubert would inherit. Though she knew it had to happen one day she had thought that day was many years off. The Rylands had always enjoyed robust good health and why should Hubert's father be any different? He could have lived to his eighties or nineties, by which time Peg felt she would have been well able to cope with the duties of life at Ryland Castle. Maybe one of their sons would have taken over the estate while they remained happy and content in their Umbrian farm.

What a foolish dream it had been.

Peg gave her nose a final pat of the powder puff, did her hair and with a last glance in the mirror left the room. She walked quickly down the grand staircase and entered the drawing room where the crowd seemed, if anything, to have grown.

Hubert, who had been watching the doorway, came to her with a smile, hand extended. 'Peg, let me introduce you to people.' He swept her into the middle of the room, singling out a tall, military-looking man with white hair and twirling moustache.

'Peg, this is General Alder. He was in Dad's regiment in the Sudan.'

'How do you do?'

'How do you do?' the general said stiffly and then, turning to the woman beside him who was staring at Peg, 'May I introduce my wife, Priscilla? My dear, er . . . Lady Ryland.' He pronounced the name as though he had a piece of hot coal in his mouth.

'How do you do?' Priscilla's expression was frigid and she turned away without making any further attempt at conversation.

Apparently unaware of this snub, Hubert and General Alder fell into some sort of conversation without taking any more notice of Peg.

Of course they had all known Ida. But she was an adulteress too. Maybe an upper-class adulteress didn't matter, whereas a lower-class one did? Maybe they thought she had ensnared Hubert.

'Peg, do let me introduce Lady Frobisher.' Violet came up with her arm in that of a woman of about her own age.

'Janet, my sister-in-law, Peg Ryland.'

'How do you do?' Janet said but her eyes were flinty too, her smile false and superficial.

'My dear, and so I said . . .' Lady Frobisher turned pointedly to Violet to recommence a conversation that had obviously been interrupted by Violet, who, Peg knew, was only trying to be helpful. She liked Violet. She always had, but even she

124

seemed to have some reservation about Hubert's marriage into a family they had always seen as servants, and had hardly ever visited them in Italy.

Hubert was back again, this time with a man with a glass of whisky in his hand. 'Darling, this is Admiral Mountjoy, a very old friend of the family. He fought in the Battle of Jutland.'

'How do you do?'

'How do you do, my dear?' The old man had a kindly twinkle in his eyes as he clasped her hand.

'Do you mind if I leave you two alone together? I've just seen . . .' and Hubert sped off.

'Gladly,' the Admiral said, still holding on to Peg's hand, and Peg was conscious of his keen scrutiny. 'Do you know many of these people here?'

'Not a soul,' she replied.

The Admiral nodded as if he understood.

'Hubert of course has kept you tucked away in Italy.' He nodded sagely at her as he patted her hand. 'You shouldn't worry. You'll be all right.'

Peg felt a sudden urge to confide in this stranger.

'But you see it is *very* difficult. My family . . .'

'I know.' The Admiral nodded again. 'I live not very far away in Somerset and was close to Edward Ryland. I saw him quite often, especially lately. I also rode with the hunt, but unfortunately not on the day he died.'

'I see –' Peg lowered her eyes – 'then you do know everything.'

'Much as I loved him as an old and valued friend I thought he was a very silly man, very pig-headed, and told him so to his face. I think he would have got round to it if . . . well, these things happen.' He gently clasped Peg's arm. 'But do take courage, my dear. No one really liked Ida and I am sure that knowing how happy you are making Hubert, everyone will soon love you too.'

'How kind,' Peg said and then looking around, she realized

125

two people were missing. 'Do you mind, Admiral? I must go and find my sisters. I thought they had followed us in.'

But of course they hadn't and she should not have expected them to. She squeezed past the chattering groups and crossed the hall running down the stairs to the ballroom, whose doors were half open.

As she entered, those nearest the door all stopped talking and pressed round her. The atmosphere here was so different. She was among friends, people she had known all her life. They too would consider the situation strange, and one or two didn't quite know how to handle it and stood shyly back. But others pressed forward to greet her and some she kissed warmly on the cheeks, others she shook by the hand.

She had not seen any of them for many years and there were some faces she didn't recognize. She at once spotted Addie and Verity in the centre of the room chatting to a group of local farmers, most of whom she did know.

Then Mrs Capstick, who had been supervising the catering arrangements, appeared with a full plate in her hand, which she held out to Peg. 'Would your ladyship like a sandwich?'

'Mrs Capstick,' Peg said, outraged. 'You *know* I am not to be called that. You *know* how cross it makes me. In fact I think you do it just to annoy me.'

'Oh no, Peg,' Mrs Capstick said contritely. 'I don't do it to annoy you. But you know things have changed. You are now married to his lordship. I don't think he would like to hear us call you Peg.'

'Of course he would,' Peg protested stoutly.

But Mrs Capstick shook her head. 'You'll see how different things will be, and there is nothing you can do about it.'

Shaking her head a little sadly, she moved off with her plate of sandwiches, offering them around.

Peg felt close to tears. This was a woman she had known ever since the family came here when she was a little girl. She used to help her in the kitchen where she was often scolded for doing the wrong thing. She had been one of her mother's best friends.

'It is something you must get used to,' Verity murmured quietly. 'Because now you *are* Lady Ryland.'

'I hoped you'd be upstairs,' Peg addressed her sisters. 'I badly needed some support.'

'We don't feel comfortable there,' Addie said firmly and looked over to where Frank was dispensing drinks. 'None of us do.'

'Do you think I do? I'd much rather be here with you, with all my friends.'

Peg's tone bordered on the hysterical and Verity took her gently by the hand.

'I'll come upstairs with you if you want me to. If it will help.'

As she looked at her the end door opened and Hubert appeared, looking anxiously round. A hush fell on the room again as he saw Peg and crossed over to her.

'I wondered where you'd got to. There are a lot of people I want you to meet. It is a unique opportunity to get to know our friends. They are all anxious to meet you.'

'These are my friends too,' Peg muttered under her breath. 'Don't you think you should say "hello" to them, Hubert?'

'Of course I shall.' Hubert flushed. 'But they will be here for some time, I hope. Many I greeted outside the church already, and some guests upstairs will soon be leaving to catch trains.'

Verity's expression became even more concerned.

'I think Peg has had a very tiring day . . .' she began, but Hubert turned to her sharply.

'The day has hardly started, Verity. As my wife, Peg has a lot of entertaining to do. I see this as a great opportunity . . .'

'Then why don't I come up too?' Verity said tactfully, taking Peg by the elbow, 'and perhaps I could meet some of your friends as well? After all, we're all family now.'

Finally the last of the guests had left, the last car drove away. The family went back to the lodge, the locals drifted off, some the worse for wear, and Peg and Hubert were left alone on the steps waving goodbye.

The morning mist and drizzle had turned into a surprisingly mellow autumn day and Hubert tucked his arm through Peg's.

'Let's have a stroll?' he suggested. 'I could do with some fresh air.'

Peg nodded, although she was desperately tired and would prefer to have lain down.

'Are you warm enough?' he enquired solicitously. 'Or shall I run up and fetch a wrap?'

'I'm quite all right, darling, thanks.' Peg took his arm and they strolled down the steps and towards the lake. She felt she owed Hubert some sort of an apology, but didn't quite know where to begin. The atmosphere between them was strained and she knew he was tired too.

It had been a desperately busy few days, and a couple of weeks ago they had still been in Italy, completely unaware of any impending catastrophe.

Although they were arm in arm, somehow Peg felt there was a strangeness, a distance between them, one she badly wanted to bridge.

'I feel I failed,' Peg said at last. 'Thank heaven Verity came to the rescue. Of course she's used to meeting people.' Verity had in fact appeared quite at home in a room full of strangers and was soon chatting to people as though they were old friends. But on the other hand the guests knew she wasn't Hubert's wife and they could be more relaxed with her.

'But so are you, darling.' Hubert looked at her curiously. 'Dozens, I would have thought, in your job as a reporter.'

'It's not quite the same,' Peg said defensively. 'I think their attitude to me is different. They regard me as some sort of interloper.'

'Oh nonsense, you're imagining it.'

'I am not imagining it, Hubert.' Peg disengaged her arm from her husband's and for a while they walked along together in silence until they came to the water's edge and stood looking into the murky depths of the lake.

'When we go back to Italy it won't be so much of a problem.'

Peg tried to tuck her arm through Hubert's again but he seemed to resist her.

'What do you mean?' he asked.

'Well, we're not staying here for ever are we? Our home is in Italy.'

'Darling ' Hubert turned and looked solemnly at her 'I don't think you realize what has happened.'

'Of course I realize what has happened, and it's awful but it doesn't mean we have to live here for ever. You always said that we loved Italy and that would be our home.'

'But I never expected my father would die so soon. I imagined he would live, if not for ever, at least for a very long time. He was so active, in perfect health . . .'

'What difference does that make?' Peg asked sullenly.

'I have a duty now towards the estate, one I can't fulfil in Italy. Don't you understand that?'

'I thought your mother was going to be around to look after the estate?'

'Of course she can't. Be reasonable, Peg. She knows nothing about it.'

'And Violet?' Peg persisted stubbornly. 'Are you suggesting two women are incapable of looking after the estate?'

'No, I'm not but they don't want to. I discussed it with them both last night after you had gone to bed.'

'I see.' Once again Peg felt excluded from those important family councils.

'Violet has her life in London and Mother . . . well Mother would quite like to go back to Italy too.'

'Your mother knows absolutely nothing about growing grapes, Hubert.'

'And almost as little about the estate. Mother is over sixty and although she is by no means "old", as you know, she shows no interest in it at all. It has to pay and can't be left to the bailiff, good as he is. In Italy it will be easier to get someone to look after the vineyard and the olives, and of course we can spend long holidays there.

129

'But, Peg, Ryland is my heritage. It is my life and this is where we must both stay and rear our children. You do see that don't you, Peg? Darling?' His tone became wheedling. 'Everything has changed.'

Peg moved nearer to the water's edge. 'I never thought it would be like this. I never wanted to be Lady Ryland or I suppose if I thought about it at all it was that, as you said, one day, very far distant, when your father was an old man it might happen. I imagined us living out our lives in Italy, which we love and where we were so happy. I'm only twenty-seven. It's like being sentenced for life to something I didn't really want.'

'But you wanted me. You don't regret that, do you?' Hubert tenderly put his arm round her waist and hugged her gently to him.

'I did want you and I love you, and I don't regret it. But I feel so strange in the company of your friends. They seem to look at me as if I am some kind of freak. The scarlet woman: the cause of the scandal, their eyes seem to suggest.'

'They don't look at you in that way at all. They just don't know you. Most of them know you were not the cause of the scandal. Some people are shy as well, you know.'

'They didn't seem very shy to me. They didn't seem to want to get to know me. The Admiral, though, was very nice,' she added as an afterthought. 'He was an old friend of your father's and seemed to understand.'

'They will get used to you and you will get used to them. We can lead a life here very similar to what it was in Italy.' He took a deep breath and gazed around him. 'It is so beautiful here. It is our native land, the county where we were both born. We don't have to go to London unless we want to. We can just stay here with the children, happy as bugs in a rug. Nothing will change. I promise.'

Peg leaned against him, but her heart felt very heavy.

If only it could be like that.

*   *   *

The Water's Edge

Stella lobbed the ball over the net and Ernest had to run from one end of the court to the other to try and return it, but he missed.

'Game!' Stella shouted triumphantly. 'Five-two.'

She seldom got the better of Ernest but today was one of those days. Five-two up. However she was beginning to feel tired and her limbs had begun to ache. 'One more game and call it quits?' she suggested, but Ernest won the next game to bring it up to five-three.

He appeared to want to go on but Stella resisted.

'Go on,' he nagged, sensing that he was in the ascendant. 'Let's go on to the first one who gets six.' Ernest never liked to lose.

'Oh, all right.' Stella returned to the base line and served, but her strength was flagging. Ernest was a good player and always gave her a hard game. But she was good too. However, she lost the game and the next two as well, so that Ernest won the set and seemed well pleased with himself.

They walked together off the court and into the club house, where Ernest bought them each a lemonade at the bar. These they took outside, slumping on to the grass to watch the other players on the courts.

'Feeling better now?' Ernest enquired solicitously. He had noticed her tiredness, which was a little unusual for her.

'I'm fine,' Stella insisted robustly. 'You're too good for me.'

Ernest rolled over and put his arm round her waist, nuzzling her cheek.

'Be careful,' Stella warned, looking anxiously towards the pavilion. 'Someone might see.'

'No one's looking.'

'Still, you never know. You can't be too careful.'

No, you couldn't be too careful. Ernest, devout churchgoer that he was, was very physical. The sexual attraction seemed to dominate their lives, maybe because it remained unfulfilled. At times it was very difficult for Stella as Ernest was so persistent and she felt a spoilsport. But at the moment of surrender the vision of Addie and what had happened to her came to mind and she drew back.

She knew it was very frustrating for him, and also for her because she was a sensual person too; but she was sure that it was the right thing to do. The thought of facing her sisters, especially Verity, if she got in the family way was too awful to contemplate.

In the months since they'd been engaged she and Ernest had discovered how much they had in common, apart from enjoying a frolic in the back of the car, or sometimes at his house when his parents were out. It was then that it got very dangerous, and they were occasions that common sense had taught her to try and avoid.

But it was so difficult to be sensible all the time. They were youthful and hot-blooded, but the best thing was to keep mind and body active and there was nothing like a vigorous game of tennis to sap all that energy and blunt the emotions.

Ernest was lying on his stomach, his head propped on his arms, face turned sideways, looking at her.

'Time we went back and changed,' he said, glancing at his watch, and he rose and took their empty glasses back to the bar. There was to be a dance that evening at the tennis club. They liked dancing and were good at it. They were an active couple and enjoyed doing things together like playing tennis, dancing and walking. They belonged to a ramblers' club and most weekends they went on some outing or other, covering miles. Stella was a keen supporter when Ernest played football, and was a regular on the sideline, cheering him on no matter what the weather. She took turns making teas for the players at the cricket club, or acted as a scorer home or away.

She knew she would be a dutiful and supportive wife because instinct as well as common sense told her that that was the best way to a happy marriage. She didn't share Peg's political, feminist views and never had; and look what rebellion had done for Addie, living in sin with not one illegitimate child but two. Stella was a conventional person who valued and wanted a conventional, regular life.

She went after Ernest into the clubhouse and collected her cardigan and handbag from a locker. They stopped to talk to another couple with whom they often played a foursome and then they both went out to the car, stowed their gear and rackets in the back, climbed in and Ernest drove off.

After a few miles he turned off the main road, drove up a narrow lane and stopped.

Then, as usual, they both climbed into the back of the car, came together like magnets, and started kissing until they were both hot, sticky and breathless, and clawing at each other's clothes.

Ernest put his hand up her tennis dress and attempted to pull down her knickers and, as usual, she clamped a hand firmly on his wrist and said no.

This was the ritual part, and usually Ernest did as he was told. But this time he didn't stop and rather roughly tried to get her knickers right down and insert his hand between her legs.

Angrily, face flaming, Stella wriggled away and fell into the space between the back seat and the seats in front of the car.

Ernest tumbled on top of her, and she was shocked to see that the flies of his tennis shorts were already undone, the veins bulging in his neck and his face scarlet.

'Ernest, stop at once,' she commanded and she began to beat his chest with her fist. Suddenly Ernest closed his eyes and his head lolled on to her chest. She could feel his heart thudding away and desperately tried to push him off.

Finally, with much squirming and shoving, at last she wriggled free and climbed out of the car, pulling up her knickers and trying to straighten her crumpled dress as best she could.

She felt indignant and undignified and sat on the grass by the side of the lane, trying to pull herself together. Men really were beasts, she thought, smoothing her crumpled pleats and noticing a small tear.

A few moments later Ernest shuffled out of the car, fastening his flies. His shirt hung over his shorts and his tousled red hair and dishevelled appearance made him look as though he'd been pulled through a hedge.

He went round to the front seat and rummaged in his blazer pocket, producing a pack of cigarettes. He took one out and lit it, then he sank down beside her.

'Sorry,' he said gruffly.

Stella felt guilty and angry at the same time, shoddy and dirty, and also a little afraid of the forces they'd unleashed.

'We can't go on like this,' Ernest said, speaking through clenched teeth.

'Well, what do other couples do?' Stella gazed at him nervously.

'They just "do it". Lots do. I don't know what you're so afraid of. After all, we *are* engaged. Just because your sister—'

'I want to,' Stella said tremulously, 'but . . . I think we should wait until we're married. I do think that's the right thing to do.' She looked at him appealingly, placatingly, but his face still smouldered, adding further to her feelings of guilt and anxiety. She didn't want to lose him. 'After all, we both belong to the church. We don't *want* to do anything underhand and wrong –' she reached nervously for his hand – 'do we dear?'

'No, I suppose not.' Ernest limply took hold of her hand and lay back in the grass, gazing at the sky. 'You know what? I think we should bring our wedding forward. I can't wait until this time next year. What's to stop us getting married, say, in a few months' time?' He squinted up at her. 'I mean, you're sure, aren't you?'

'Oh, I'm sure. Perfectly sure. No doubts at all.'

'And you want to?'

'Yes, I do. Of course I do. Like you I find it hard . . . to . . . well, hold back. It isn't that I don't love you. I do, but somehow I feel . . .'

'I know, I know.' Looking relieved, Ernest jumped up and began tucking his shirt into his shorts. 'Don't say it again. I don't want you to do anything you don't want to do. But let's bring the date forward. Say September. Is there any reason why it shouldn't be then instead of this time next year?'

'None at all,' Stella said and suddenly she was filled with eager anticipation. 'Oh Ernest, I think September would be *lovely*,' and she leapt to her feet and hugged him.

Peg sat on the lawn in front of the castle reading a letter, the children on a rug at her feet. Caspar had just started to crawl and Jude was running about, watched over carefully by his nursemaid who was a local girl from the village called Nelly, a marvel with small children.

Peg put the letter down on her lap and leaned back in her chair, gazing at the sky. She was aware of a deep sense of peace and fulfilment at last. The past six months had been difficult, but a lot had been achieved. She had found that it was possible to equate being Hubert's wife and Lady Ryland with being herself, Peg. She had not needed to be a rebel to bring this about, but had slowly and quietly transformed the rather paternalistic and autocratic regime of Hubert's parents into a more informal and democratic structure.

The old order had changed, yielding place to the new.

The senior Lady Ryland had gone to live in Italy, thinking that was the best way to give her son and daughter-in-law the chance to settle. Peg took over many of her charities, but she knew the people concerned and the workers on the estate in a very different way from the older Lady Ryland. She worked with them, as one of them, a person who understood their needs in a way Penelope Ryland never did or could.

Meanwhile Hubert had continued as a hard-working farmer, managing the estate and extending its range, introducing new methods. Yet he still belonged to some of the same London clubs as his father had done; he also became a magistrate and the patron of any mumber of causes, mostly connected with the land or the Army.

So although much had changed, much too remained the same.

Peg looked up as Hubert came out of the side door and strolled over to her. Jude saw him immediately and ran towards him, and his father lifted him in his arms and carried him across to his mother, about to plop him down on her lap.

'Careful,' Peg said, shifting her position. She was six months pregnant and he was a heavy toddler. This time they hoped for a daughter.

Hubert took Jude on his knee instead and sat down in a chair next to Peg.

'Great news,' Peg said, waving the letter she'd been reading at her husband. 'Stella and Ernest want to bring forward the wedding.'

'Oh? What brought that on?'

Peg referred to the letter again.

'They decided there was no point in waiting until next year. Their minds are made up. They've begun to look for a house.'

Hubert nodded. 'Very sensible. Why wait?'

'That's what I think. Oh, I do like him,' Peg said with a sigh of satisfaction, 'he is such a nice young man. Perfect for my sister. Mum would be so pleased.' She looked at her husband, who was now nursing a rather sleepy baby. 'They suggest September twenty-first. We'd have to be sure that everything is all right here and . . . I mean you wouldn't mind having the reception here, would you?'

'Of course not,' Hubert said. 'It's a tradition.' He paused for a moment, looking at her carefully. 'You know, Peg, you don't have to ask me every time you want to do anything. It's your home now as well as mine.'

'I know, darling, I just thought it was polite to ask, to be quite sure it was OK by you.'

'It's absolutely OK,' Hubert said, smiling. 'Is there time to do everything? The baby is due in September too, don't forget.'

Peg frowned. 'That's a point. It is due the first week of September, so I think I'll suggest October. How about early October?'

'That's also fine by me.'

At that point Jude struggled to get off his father's knee and went over to Nelly, who looked up from her game with Caspar.

'The baby's getting tired, my lady,' she said, addressing Peg. 'Shall I take him inside?'

As Peg nodded Hubert said: 'Take Jude too, Nelly, he looks as though he could do with a nap.'

Hubert then helped the nursemaid gather up the rug and playthings, which he took over to the castle as Jude trotted by his side and Nelly carried Caspar.

Peg sat back watching them, feeling very lazy, very relaxed, very happy, and as Hubert returned she held out a hand to him. 'We are so fortunate, aren't we, darling? Very blessed.'

'Very,' Hubert replied, sitting down beside her again. 'What makes you say that at this particular moment?'

'Because I was thinking as you walked across with the children how perfect it is here. How lucky we are.'

He studied her face for a moment, wondering if she realized how perfectly she fitted into this setting, how right she was for it, in a way Ida, had that happened, would never have been with her love of London life and parties.

'Do you miss Italy, darling?' he asked her.

Peg shook her head. 'Not any more. But we'll go there next year, won't we, for part of the summer?'

'Part of the summer, I promise.'

Hubert's attention was suddenly distracted by a figure running up the path from the lodge to the castle.

'Someone in a big hurry,' he observed to Peg, 'I think it's your sister.'

Peg sat up, arms round her knees, and looked in the same direction. 'It *is* Addie,' she said. 'I wonder what she wants?'

It seemed then that Addie saw them too and, changing direction, ran across the lawn, halting breathlessly by the side of Peg's chair. Peg, by now seriously concerned, sat bolt upright.

'What is it, Addie? Did something happen? Is Jenny all right?'

'It's Stella,' Addie gasped and threw herself on the grass to try and catch her breath. 'She's been rushed to hospital in Dorchester. They think she's got polio.' She gazed distractedly at Peg. 'They want her close relations to go and see her at once. Oh Peg, I think she's dying!'

And she broke down in tears.

Ten

October 1931

S tella, her leg propped up on a stool in front of her chair, gazed sadly out of the window.

'This is the day we should have been married,' she said wistfully. 'I wonder if Ernest remembers?'

Verity put down her knitting and anxiously studied her sister's woebegone face. Since her illness Stella looked older, sadder and still far from well.

'Oh, I'm sure he does. Perhaps he'll come later.'

She accidentally dropped a few stitches and bent her head to recover them and then began counting them again. She was knitting a matinée jacket for Peg and Hubert's new baby, who was just four weeks old.

But to her dismay Stella gave a loud sob and then burst into tears.

Verity quickly put aside her knitting and went over to her, perching on the arm of her chair.

'Darling,' she said, putting her arm around her. 'What is the matter?'

'You *know* he won't come,' Stella said in a burst of sudden anger, 'so why pretend? We haven't seen him for weeks.'

'Only two,' Verity said doubtfully, 'or is it three?'

'It's a lot more,' Stella banged the arm of her chair as if to emphasize her point. 'You know that, so why pretend? You know he hardly ever comes and when he does he doesn't stay long.'

'Well . . .' Unusually Verity felt lost for words. Ernest's

139

behaviour, his neglect of his fiancée, was of concern to all who had helped her through her serious illness.

'He doesn't love me any more,' Stella went on, stormily staring at her paralysed leg. 'In this state I'm no good to him.'

'But Stella –' Verity reached for a handkerchief to wipe her eyes – 'you know you are so much better. Why, at first no one expected you to live. You've made a wonderful recovery.' She paused and then continued dutifully, 'And Ernest was good at the beginning. He came to the hospital every day even though he wasn't allowed to see you. He was really terribly worried and concerned. We all were . . .' She tailed off, looking at the sister who had so nearly died, remembering what an awful time it had been for them all.

Stella's eyes turned again towards the window as though she was trying to recapture not recent events but those happy memories of the past.

At the onset of her illness Stella had been isolated for two weeks with a high fever and severe paralysis. For a short time she was even placed in an iron lung to assist her breathing. Her condition had been aggravated by the fact that she had played a vigorous game of tennis when she had not been feeling well, unaware that her tiredness and vague sense of malaise were signs that she was sickening for the illness.

However, slowly she recovered, the paralysis began to disappear and all the affected limbs responded to treatment except for her right leg. Even this slightly improved with massage and electrical treatment, but the doctors' consensus was that it was likely that she would walk with the help of a caliper for the rest of her life.

Her recovery, which was deemed even by doctors to be almost miraculous, was attributed to her strong desire to live, and the fact she was to be married and had named the day. But slowly all wedding plans fell by the wayside and were not referred to again.

Eventually she was moved to Ryland Castle, where Peg had engaged a full-time nurse.

It was then that Ernest's visits gradually tailed off, becoming so rare as almost to cease altogether.

Stella gave a deep sigh and turned towards Verity, holding out her hand.

'You have been so good, Ver. You have *all* been good. I don't know what I'd have done without you. You all helped to make me well.'

'That's what sisters are for,' Verity replied. 'We can all help one another.'

And they had. It was a sad and ironic fact that while Stella was recuperating from her near fatal illness Peg had given birth to the longed-for daughter who was called Catherine after their mother. It was so strange, Verity thought, how sometimes grief and happiness seemed to go together. It had been so often in her and her family's life in the past and it was so now: joy and sadness, sadness and joy.

But Stella, whose moods were mercurial and unpredictable, had gone moody again and was gazing at her stricken leg.

'I shall never walk properly again, shall I?'

'It's hard to tell,' Verity said truthfully, but she knew quite well that if a limb failed to recover completely within the first six months then it was unlikely it ever would. They were only three months on from the onset of the illness, but Stella's right leg had only marginally improved. She couldn't even wriggle her toes and it seemed hard to imagine that it would ever be completely normal.

'You know I won't, Ver,' Stella burst out. 'Why pretend?'

'I don't know for sure. I really don't.' Verity tried hard to sound reassuring.

'You do and you're pretending you don't.' Stella seemed to be deliberately trying to whip up a storm within herself. 'You know that I'm never going to be able to walk without that awful iron contraption. That Ernest doesn't want me, won't want me and neither will any man and I'll end up an old spinster like *you*!'

Verity felt stung by Stella's words, rather as though she had been physically abused, and for a moment she remained sitting rigidly in her chair as if she'd suddenly been turned to stone, stifling a strong impulse to leave the room.

But Stella's contrition was instantaneous and she clasped a hand across her mouth, her eyes wide with horror. 'I'm sorry, Ver,' she said, noting the shocked expression on her sister's face. '*Please* forgive me. It was a horrible thing to say.'

'But you meant it,' Verity said quietly. 'I know you did. It doesn't matter. It's best to get it all out.' She leaned towards Stella and spoke softly but quickly. 'I can honestly say that I don't know whether your leg will ever completely heal. I don't think anyone does. But I can assure you there are far worse things that can happen to a person in this world than remaining unmarried. At one time I felt as you do now, but I have become accustomed to my single state. I even enjoy it. I am free to do as I please, within the constraints of family responsibility, of course. I have a job that I love and do well and have my own money. I don't know if I will ever have a husband. It is, I suppose, within the bounds of possibility that I might meet someone. But even if I don't I think I am able to see that a good and satisfying life lies ahead of me even without a husband and the blessing of children.' She paused and looked at her sister and when she spoke again her voice was stronger. 'It may not seem like that to you now, Stella, but if that is to be your fate – and I am by no means sure it will be – I am certain you will adapt to it as I have been able to and, despite it, enjoy your life and all that it has to offer you. Humankind, you know, is infinitely adaptable.'

Stella had been listening intently to her sister, but when she had finished, Verity's words seem to have offered no cheer and she put her head in her hands.

'But I love him, Ver. I adore him and it is almost impossible for me to accept, when there was so much between us, that he no longer cares for me.' She looked woefully at Verity. 'I like to pretend to myself it's because he's so busy. Sometimes, I even manage to convince myself that *is* the case. That Ernest does love me and one day I'll be his bride.'

Ernest looked up, startled, as the woman, her face partly concealed by the brim of a brown felt hat, leaned towards

142

him over the counter and hissed sharply: 'I would like to see you, Ernest, in private if I may.'

Ernest looked anxiously first to one side then another, but his fellow clerks were busy either serving customers or counting money.

'Could it wait until lunchtime, Verity?' he whispered back after looking at the clock. 'Only another twenty minutes.'

'Of course,' Verity said, straightening up 'I'll wait outside.'

Verity had told no one about her decision to confront Ernest and ask him exactly what his intentions were towards her sister. She knew that if he had been free Frank would willingly have driven her but, wanting to keep her mission secret, she had gone by bus to Sherborne and then caught another bus to Bridport. The whole journey had taken several hours while she changed buses and endured the slow ride across the hilly countryside.

She walked out of the bank and waited in the high street. It happened to be market day and both sides were thronged with a cheerful mêleé of people inspecting stalls which offered goods of all descriptions: meat, fish, a variety of cheeses, fresh vegetables, local honey, homemade jams and cakes. Then there were stalls selling clothes, new and secondhand, small items of furniture, junk, books, bric-a-brac and every kind of material you could imagine – woollens, muslins, cottons, silks, alpaca, bombazine and heavy duty worsteds – by the yard.

It was a bustling, happy scene but Verity dreaded her interview with Ernest, and as she stood there waiting she began to regret that she had ever decided to come.

The clock in the market place struck the hour and soon afterwards Ernest appeared from around the side of the bank, buttoning his coat.

'I hope I didn't keep you waiting, Verity?' he said, politely doffing his hat to her; but she thought he looked anxious, an emotion that mirrored her own unease.

'Is there somewhere we can speak in private?' she said.

'There's a café round the corner.'

'That's not very private.'

'We can sit in my car,' he looked at her doubtfully. 'It's in the car park just behind the bank.'

'That's a good idea,' Verity said. 'What I have to say won't take very long.' There was, however, a slight menace in her tone.

Ernest set off ahead of her and she followed. It was a very short distance to the bank's car park, in which there were few cars.

'Not many people have cars,' Ernest explained. 'Most of them live locally. We'll be quite private here.' He opened the passenger seat door for her and she climbed in. A moment later he got in beside her and they sat for a moment or two looking rather awkwardly at each other. Ernest was the first to break the silence.

'Well, Verity, what brings you here?' His manner was shifty, his expression worried. Verity began to wonder how she had ever liked or, in particular, trusted him. 'There's nothing wrong with Stella, is there?'

'A lot you seem to care,' Verity said sharply. 'Maybe you don't. I don't know with you, Ernest . . .' She paused.

'I don't understand . . .' he began, but Verity went on: 'Stella has been very, very ill and continues to be weak.'

'I know, Verity,' Ernest spoke quickly, avoiding contact with those accusing eyes, 'and I have been greatly concerned, but I thought she was much better last time I saw her . . .'

'And when was that, Ernest?'

'Well . . .' Ernest pursed his lips and looked thoughtfully at the car roof. 'Two weeks ago? Maybe three?'

'I think it's more like three. Whatever, it is a long period not to see someone to whom you are, after all, engaged to be married.'

Ernest cast his eyes downwards and made no attempt to reply.

'I have to ask you this,' Verity looked at him intently. 'Do you still consider yourself engaged? Do you still love Stella? Do you still intend to marry her?'

Ernest shook his head, his eyes still lowered.

'I asked you a question, Ernest,' Verity said impatiently after almost a minute had passed. 'Please answer it.'

'I don't know,' Ernest replied haltingly, blinking up at her. 'The truth is, I really don't know, Verity.'

She looked, or pretended to look, amazed. 'You don't *know* whether you love her or whether you want to marry her, or both?' Verity's voice rose to a sharp pitch.

'Both,' he answered and his expression was haunted.

'Then it sounds to me your mind is made up.' Verity's tone was scornful. 'What kind of love was there, Ernest, if it couldn't survive serious illness . . . a time when a person has most need of the beloved? Or is the truth that you can't face the fact that she may be crippled for life? Able no longer to run about, dance or play tennis? Have you fallen out of love with her on account of that? If so what kind of love was it?'

Ernest shook his head and played with his fingers, interlacing those of one hand with another. 'I *thought* I did love her,' he mumbled, 'but now I'm not sure. I'm not very proud of myself. In fact I feel ashamed; but I can't force myself to love someone, can I? I can't marry someone I don't think I love. I feel very bad about it, Verity, very ashamed.' He looked at her humbly. 'I wonder if you could tell her for me, as nicely as you can, you know.'

'*Nicely!*' Verity squawked. '*Nicely*, did you say? How do you tell someone "nicely" that the man she loved – she told me recently she adored you and still does – and thought she was going to marry no longer feels the same way about her?' She leaned towards Ernest, her expression ferocious. 'Do you expect her *not* to suffer pain? To take it, as it were, on the chin? How do you say it "nicely", Ernest, can you tell me that?'

Ernest shook his head. 'No, I can't,' he said abjectly. 'Believe me, I really am sorry.'

'She knows of course,' Verity went on bitterly. 'It will hurt but it can come as no real surprise. You gradually stopped coming to see her. At first it was every day, or nearly every day.

Then when it dawned on you she wasn't going to be the woman you knew, the one full of fun, loving sports and vigorous pastimes, as much as you, you slowed down until you almost stopped. You may even have thought you would have to look after her, a semi-invalid, and that didn't suit your book at all. Did it? Not a selfish, self-centred man like you?' Verity thrust her face aggressively up against his. 'One excuse after another came tripping off your lying tongue. How do you think Stella felt about that? It was hardly likely to help her recovery, was it? After all, *you* were the one who was so keen you wanted to bring forward the wedding. Do you deny that?'

Again Ernest, looking wretched by now, shook his head.

'You were all eagerness to marry as soon as possible. In fact the date was last week. Did you remember it, Ernest? Stella thought you might have visited her that day, but in fact I don't suppose you even remembered, did you? *Did* you?'

Ernest, face ashen, seemed speechless in the face of the elder sister's onslaught.

'You know we all liked you, Ernest, once,' Verity went on giving him no respite. 'The whole family liked and respected you. Now we despise you, or they will when they hear what I have to tell them. *Totally.*' She made an abrupt cutting gesture with her right hand.

'But the woman you have spurned, my sister Stella, is made of much sterner stuff than you. Despite the trauma of her illness and the additional suffering inflicted on her by you, you miserable little coward, she has come through. She is a woman of character and strength, far, far too good for the likes of you, incidentally.'

Verity's spate of words, as if borne along by a strong gust of wind, suddenly ceased. She looked at him contemptuously for what seemed a very long time. Then: 'Do you know what, Ernest?'

'What?' Ernest stammered timorously, by this time thoroughly cowed.

'You are a horrible, base, contemptible little worm, not

146

nearly good enough for my sister. I'm *glad* you revealed your true colours before Stella made the awful mistake of marrying you.' She gave him a smile of cloying, almost evil, sweetness and raised her right hand. 'And now let me give you a little present to remember me by,' and before he could duck or swerve she hit him twice quite sharply across the mouth, a blow which immediately drew blood from his lip.

As he folded up, hand to his mouth, crouching as if fearing another attack, she tumbled out of the car and beat a hasty path towards the exit.

Verity couldn't believe she had actually hit him. She had never performed an act of violence towards anyone in her life. She felt that for a brief moment she had been completely out of control.

She was glad of the long bus journey home because it helped her to get some perspective on what had just happened: her utter inability to control those feelings of hatred and even resentment against a man who, for the moment anyway, had ruined the life of her sister. How wonderful it would have been if Ernest had been one of those rare human beings who was able to put others above self. But how many were there? How many young men, faced with a lifetime of marriage to a cripple, would willingly accept such a fate? It was hard, it was cruel, but it was true. If they had been married, the situation might have been different, but with someone as weak as Ernest had proved himself to be, Verity didn't think that would have been the case. He might have neglected her, eventually left her and caused more misery than ever.

At least now Stella was surrounded by her family, fortified by the strength of their love.

It was after dark when she got back to the lodge. There were no lights on to welcome her and no fire in the grate to warm her. Then she remembered that Addie had told her she was taking Jenny to a friend for tea and would be late back. Frank would probably be about his duties somewhere on the estate.

Verity removed her hat and coat and then, changing her

mind, put them on again and went out of the house and up the road to the castle, where welcoming lights gleamed in the myriad of tiny windows.

It still felt funny to be able to approach the castle as though one were coming home, to know that one had the right of access to it at any time and not just to the kitchens or the ballroom, where the servants' parties were held, but upstairs, right to the heart of power: Lord and Lady Ryland themselves. Verity had not yet become accustomed to the idea of Peg being in such an exalted position. It seemed flukish, bizarre. Yet it was true. Not only was she Lady Ryland but she was the mother of the next Lord Ryland, her position secure, her destiny safe.

Verity had liked Alan, a working-class boy made good, but she liked Hubert too in a way she had never anticipated. To have got beyond that apparently hard, protective carapace that people like the Rylands had surrounded themselves with for centuries had been no mean achievement.

Hubert had emerged a modern man, a good husband and father, a democratic hard-working employer, generous to his staff, someone to whom others turned in time of trouble. He was very different from his father. The old order had indeed changed.

Verity entered the castle by one of the many side doors and went along the hall to the drawing room. There was a light under the door and she tapped on it before pushing it open. Hubert and Peg were sitting in companionable silence on either side of the fireplace, in which a huge log fire burned. Hubert had the paper on his knees and his head jerked up as she entered as though he'd been dozing. Peg was reading a letter, which she put aside as Verity came in.

'Hullo,' she said, and then, noticing her apparel: 'Have you been out?'

'I have.' Verity looked about to sink into an armchair.

'Let me take your coat and hat,' Hubert said, getting up. 'You look all in, Verity. Can I get you a drink?'

'If it's time for a whisky I wouldn't say no.' Verity smiled up at him. 'And a ciggy perhaps?'

'You shall have both.' Hubert passed her a silver cigarette box and when she had selected one, took one himself and then lit both their cigarettes. 'Darling?' He turned to Peg, who shook her head.

'No, thanks.'

'Drink for you too, Peg?'

Peg glanced at the clock. 'I must go up to the nursery and help bath the children. I'll wait until I come down.' She passed the letter she'd been reading to her sister.

'Ed is coming down next week. He's got a girl. She seems rather nice. Her name is Maisie.'

'I said she sounds like a barmaid.' Hubert chuckled and then pretended to duck as Peg glanced angrily at him.

'I told him not to be such a snob,' she said to Verity. 'Ed doesn't say anything more, but if he likes her she must be all right.'

'How long is his leave?' Verity took the glass Hubert had placed in her hand and glanced at the letter.

'He doesn't say. But he's to be stationed in Plymouth for the time being. Hopefully we'll see more of him.'

Ed had, after all, made the Royal Navy his career and was a gunnery officer on one of His Majesty's ships. He had been abroad for over a year and this was the first time they were to see him since Peg had been back.

Peg was looking curiously at Verity. 'You do look tired,' she said sympathetically. 'Had a hard day?'

'Very hard.' Verity took another sip of her drink and gave Ed's letter back to Peg. 'I went to see Ernest.'

'Oh dear!' Mouth turned down, Hubert looked at his wife and then stooped to place another log on the fire.

Verity brushed back a piece of hair from her face. 'I know it was a bit silly, a bit foolish perhaps, but I wanted to know why he had neglected Stella and what his intentions were. I suppose I knew, but I wanted to be sure.'

149

'And they are?' Peg prompted.

'As we thought.' Verity flicked ash into the tray beside her. 'He didn't think he loved her and now doesn't want to marry her.' Verity began to choke as the memory of that awful encounter almost overwhelmed her again with rage. 'He asked me if I would tell her "nicely". I ask you – "nicely"! In fact I hit him.'

'You *what?*' Hubert looked at her in amazement.

'Hit him,' Verity repeated, now almost with a sense of pride in her achievement.

'You actually *hit* him?' Peg gasped in admiration.

'Right across the mouth,' Verity finished triumphantly with an accompanying gesture. 'Made it bleed, in fact.'

'He will probably sue you for assault,' Hubert said.

'I don't think so.' Verity's tone was malicious. 'I think he will want to forget I exist as soon as he possibly can.'

'Oh dear,' Peg sighed, tucking Ed's letter back in its envelope. 'And I *did* so like him. He seemed so suitable. They had such a lot in common.'

'Not any longer.' Verity spoke grimly. 'Stella can't dance and play tennis any more. He doesn't want a wife with a caliper, dependent on a stick, and that's the grim truth. I think he is utterly rotten and unworthy of Stella, and good riddance to him, I say.'

'But who is going to tell Stella?' Peg asked in a whisper. 'Is anyone?' And then, after a long pause during which no one spoke. 'It had better be you, Ver.'

Stella sat for a long time staring in front of her, face impassive, but her eyes smouldered. Verity, sitting close to her, pressed her hand.

'I'm awfully sorry, darling . . .'

Stella said nothing and her silence was more alarming than any kind of outburst which Verity had been expecting.

'You're really well rid of him . . .' Verity began and then Stella suddenly wrenched her hand away and looked at her sister with an expression of cold fury.

'Why did you have to interfere? What business of yours was it to go and see Ernest without telling me?'

Knowing the interview would be difficult, but completely dumbfounded by this unexpected attack, Verity was momentarily lost for words.

'I . . .' she began.

'Don't you think that is something Ernest and I can work out for ourselves? Why should my big sister stick her nose in? Ernest didn't like my family much anyway. That's why he hasn't been to visit me so much here.'

Verity looked at her aghast. 'Did he say that to you?'

'No, not exactly but I could tell, and then *you* have the cheek to interfere. Why, Ver, I can't get over it. Ernest must have been furious, and it must certainly damage our chances of marriage.'

'You don't think they were damaged already?' Verity said in a small, tense voice.

'I certainly don't. Ernest loves me and I love him. He had a shock. We both did. Our lives had changed dramatically. He'd have come round. Anyway I'm going to get better. At one stage I couldn't move a muscle in my body, now it's only my leg. I can feel some movement already. I'll show you how I can wriggle my toes.' Stella looked down at the foot propped on a stool. Verity followed her gaze, but no ripple was discernible beneath her stocking. They both averted their eyes, and from anger Stella's expression turned to one of despair.

Verity suddenly felt extraordinarily tired. She had done the wrong thing and it had alienated her from her sister. She should at least have discussed it with Peg and Addie. It had been a silly, impulsive thing to do. She felt thoroughly dejected and deflated.

'I'm sorry,' she said, stooping to try and kiss Stella's cheek, but she averted her face. 'I really am sorry. I didn't mean to do any harm.'

'Well, you did,' Stella said. 'You have to understand, Ver, that you can't control my life as you have controlled and manipulated everyone else's.' Then, seeing her sister's expression, 'Don't look so indignant, so innocent. You have. The eldest sister, we always had to defer to you, and yet you hardly knew any of us, not really well. For years you lived away from home and when you did come back we couldn't understand you. You even started speaking in a posh tone of voice as though to distance yourself from us.'

'Oh, that is not true!' Verity felt her cheeks flame with indignation.

'Well, that's certainly what it seemed like, and now you have the nerve . . . the nerve . . .' Stella seemed to make an effort to control herself but failed, overwhelmed by weeks, months of suppressed frustration and rage, 'the bloody nerve,' she shouted, 'to come between me and my fiancé. Now kindly get out of this room and don't you dare attempt to come and see me again or interfere in my life any more.'

It was very late at night but still Stella couldn't sleep and tossed and turned in her bed, words, thoughts, actions spinning around in her mind. She knew she had been unfair to Verity, but her own emotions and feelings about Ernest were hopelessly confused: anger alternating with regret, helplessness, longing, forgiveness. If only she could get through to him, to convince him that one day she would be completely well. Now more than ever she was determined to succeed.

It was certainly true, she thought, again resentfully, that Verity's visit would not have helped, would be sure to have angered Ernest, who would resent her interference.

Then at last she rose, with difficulty as always because so much inactivity had made all her limbs stiff, and hopped across the room to a table on which were books, pen and ink and, in the drawer, writing paper.

She thought for a long time, made several false starts which she committed to the waste-paper basket and then began again:

Dearest, darling Ernest,

I know you must feel very angry with me, probably on account of Verity's visit. I swear to you I knew nothing about it and didn't ask her to try and see you.

I'm very cross with her and have told her not to come and see me. I wish she'd stay in Bristol permanently and not keep on hopping back here and sticking her nose into our business. Maybe she will, now that I've given her such a telling off.

I know, dear Ernest, how very difficult it is for you, as it is for me, and you hate to see me suffering.

But I am ever so much better, believe me. I'm improving every day and can now wiggle my toes. I know that I will fully recover the use of my leg and one day will be able to dance and play tennis just like always.

I only ask you to be patient, dearest, and perhaps come and see me from time to time though I know how busy you are. At least write and say I am forgiven.

When all this is over I'll be able to walk up the aisle with you – next summer perhaps? – and we can be married and live the life we planned in our own little house . . . and, you know what? No more back of the car . . . need I say more???

We had such fun together, darling Ernest. I'm sure we will again. In the meantime forgive me and forgive Ver and don't let your justifiable anger keep you away from me.

Your ever loving
Stella.

Feeling exhausted from her labour, the many versions she'd tried of the letter, Stella sat back and screwed the cap on the pen.

She read the letter through again and before putting it in the envelope kissed it, letting her lips linger lightly on the page as though she held his face between her hands.

She would give it to one of the maids to post tomorrow and wait for his reply.

Then she crept back to bed and lay for a long time wondering, as Verity had, if she was doing the right thing.

Verity had said, as gently as she could but quite firmly, that Ernest had changed his mind and she should forget about him. But surely it wasn't true? How could he, and how could she, after all that had passed between them?

Eleven

'Isn't she lovely?'

Two pairs of eyes turned to look at the woman standing by the window engaged in animated conversation with Hubert. She certainly was: tall, lissom and very beautiful with high cheekbones, a sculpted, sensuous mouth, deep blue eyes framed by very long, dark lashes and blonde, shoulder-length, silky, wavy hair. She was heavily but skilfully made up, her mouth a slash of scarlet highlighting her fine even white teeth.

'She certainly is.' Peg looked at her brother. 'What does she do?'

'She's a dancer.' Ed took out his cigarette case and offered it to Peg, who shook her head. Then he stuck one into his mouth and lit it. 'I met her a few days after I came on leave. A crowd of us went to a club in Soho and I fell for her at once.'

'You mean this time round?' Peg opened her eyes wide.

'Oh, yes. This leave.'

'Then you've only known her a few days.'

'Have a heart,' Ed laughed. 'Two weeks is a long time for a man in love. She knew one of the men in the party I was with and joined us after the show. I asked her for a date that night. I'm going to marry her.'

Peg gasped. 'Have you asked her?'

'Not yet, but I will soon. Maybe while I'm here?' He studied her face. 'It's so romantic. Fancy *you* living in the castle, Peg. Lady Ryland. I still can't quite take it in.'

'You'll get used to it.' Peg tucked her arm through his. They had seen very little of him in the past four years. His naval career had taken him all over the world and he only visited them in Italy when his ship berthed in Genoa for a few days.

'It's so lovely to have you back,' she said. 'Will Maisie mind being a sailor's wife?'

'I don't know. I haven't asked her, but I think she feels the same about me as I do about her.'

'But, Ed, it's *very* short notice, isn't it? I mean, how can you be sure?'

'I'm sure. It's long enough when you're in love. I know and you should know that, Peg. Your romance was very quick too.'

'I knew Hubert a *very* long time before.'

'Yes, but not in the way . . .' Ed stopped and drew on his cigarette. 'You know what I mean. Not as lovers.'

Lovers already. Peg gulped. It was hard to equate this handsome, self-assured, debonair man of the world with the pious, shy, self-effacing Ed, who, gifted academically, had wanted to be a priest.

Life and the Navy had completely transformed him.

He and Maisie had arrived in the late morning racing up the drive in a jaunty sports car. Gaiety and laughter had seemed to blow in with them, just as now Maisie had brought warmth and sunshine into the great drawing room, which she appeared to dominate by force of personality. She wore a red silk dress which matched her lipstick, its pleated skirt swirling mid-calf, and very high-heeled white shoes. For the journey in the unheated car she'd worn a white fur coat and this was casually slung over the back of one of the chairs. Although she was not a barmaid her voice, with its pronounced London accent, her carefree, extrovert manner would immediately have branded her in the eyes of Hubert's family as 'common'.

Or they would have in the past, but Hubert was chatting away to her quite amiably as they sipped their drinks, as bewitched by her as the rest of the family. Verity had remained in Bristol since the scene with Stella, judging it best to keep out of the way, but Addie, Jenny and Frank had been introduced and were suitably awestruck. No one quite like Maisie Reed had been seen at Ryland Castle for as long as anyone could remember, possibly never. Gilbert was the one person to remain out of sight. He always felt awkward in company at the castle and invariably kept away. Despite their best efforts, he could never forget that he was an employee, and a lowly one at that.

Ed looked more contented than Peg had ever seen him. Love for Maisie had completed the task started by the Navy of turning him into a fulfilled, happy human being.

Having welcomed Ed and his girlfriend, Jenny and Addie had gone off to complete some household tasks. The children had been brought in and paraded before their admiring uncle. There was to be a family dinner. Peg thought that possibly after that, or even before, Ed might pop the question and make his announcement. Or would he wait for a more romantic moment, maybe tomorrow by the lake, where Harold had proposed to Addie (not such a good omen!) – Goodness knew how many other troths before, or since, had been plighted in that propitious spot. She still thought it was a bit soon, but she could tell Ed's mind was made up.

'Addie looks well.'

'Doesn't she?'

'Jenny's so tall. How old is she now?'

'Nearly fourteen.'

'She gets more and more like –' Ed stopped and glanced across the room at Hubert. 'Well, she does have a look of the Rylands. No doubt about that. I wonder nobody has noticed.'

'So do I frankly.' Peg wore a troubled frown.

'Does Hubert never say anything?'

'Not a word.'

'One day he'll have to be told. She'll have to be told.'

'Do you think so?'

'Oh yes, Peg. Of course. You can't hide something like that forever.'

'It's going to change everything.'

'I don't see why. You have changed everything by marrying a Ryland.'

'Perhaps you're right.'

'How is Stella?' Ed lowered his voice as though she was in the room. 'Is she able to walk yet?'

'She can hobble around all right but she didn't want you to see her like that, so she's stayed in her room.'

'And the boyfriend? The engagement?'

'Well, it's off but she doesn't want to accept it. It's now got to the stage that we don't talk about it. She and Ver have already completely fallen out about it.'

'I'll go and see her,' Ed said quickly. He took Peg's arm and they began to stroll over to the couple by the window. 'You get to know Maisie. You'll love her, Peg, I know you will.'

Ed popped his head round the bedroom door.

'Hello, funny one.'

'Ed!' Stella shrieked from her chair, holding out her arms. He walked rapidly across the room and hugged her. It was a very long time since he'd seen her and her thinness, the frailty of her body, shocked him.

'Oh Stella, it is so *good* to see you!'

'And you,' Stella replied, brushing away the tears of happiness from her eyes.

Ed sat down beside her and took her hand.

'You were very ill, but you're very much better, I hear.'

'It's only my leg,' Stella looked down at her foot, 'and I can wiggle a toe. See.'

They both gazed fixedly at her foot and, indeed, there did seem to be a very slight movement at the extremity of her stocking.

'It may not seem much,' Stella said, looking anxiously at her brother, 'but believe me it is. That's how gradually I got the use back of my other limbs. To start with I was completely paralysed and in an iron lung.'

'I know.' He put his arm round her. 'You've made wonderful progress, but you mustn't stay here all day like an invalid, Stella, stuck in your room. You must get about.'

'Oh, I do,' she assured him. 'But I didn't want you to see me like this, especially your girl.' She looked at him shyly. 'What's she like?'

'She's lovely. The most wonderful woman in the world, apart from my sisters.'

'Do the family like her?'

'Very much. I could tell.'

'You must bring her to see me.'

'Stella,' Ed said sternly, 'you must come and meet her.'

'I don't want her to see me walking with a crutch. And I'm so thin.' Stella turned her eyes deprecatingly upon herself. 'Is she very beautiful?'

'Very, but you're beautiful too. And . . .' He paused as if not quite knowing how to proceed.

As brother and sister with a different father from the others they had been so close they could practically read each other's thoughts.

'You're going to ask me about Ernest?'

Ed nodded. He had met Ernest on a brief leave just before he and Stella got engaged.

'He wanted us to be married in the autumn. It was *his* idea to bring it forward. It has been a difficult time for him.'

'And you.'

Stella nodded. 'Me too, of course; but at first I was allowed no visitors for fear of contagion. He came every day and left flowers. Then I was in an iron lung and I didn't want him to see me like that. We were all very frightened, thinking it might be permanent. But I got better, though I was still paralysed, and I think that was what frightened Ernest. His visits got fewer. Of course he had a long way to come and a lot of things to do. He is a very busy person. Then –' a gleam came into Stella's eyes and her voice hardened – 'then Ver went to see him. I don't know what she said or did but she frightened him away and he hasn't been to see me since. I blame Ver for that, not Ernest.'

Ed lowered his head. 'Oh dear. That is too bad. But surely Ver wouldn't do anything—'

'She did something, or said something,' Stella insisted. 'She interfered and she shouldn't have done. It was simply no business of hers. Well –' Stella looking and feeling very emotional swallowed hard – 'I wrote to him and told him I had nothing to do with Ver's visit and I was sorry about it, but he never replied. Not yet,' she added quickly. 'When he gets over his anger I'm sure he will.'

'Would you like me to go and see him?' Ed asked gently.

Stella's pale face registered shock. 'No, no! Enough harm has been done by my family. Frankly I think they put him off, not me.'

'I assure you I won't . . .'

'No, I say.' Stella squeezed his arm. 'I know that in time he'll come back to me. I expect one day I'll get a letter.' But when she looked at her brother her eyes were full of pain. 'It's just a question of waiting.'

'Come and meet Maisie.' Ed reluctantly rose and held out his hand.

'Oh no, I couldn't.'

'Yes, you could. You must. Look I'll carry you as far as the drawing room and then you can lean on me.'

'I can't,' Stella cried tearfully. 'Don't you see I'm a cripple? How can I meet a beautiful woman looking like this?'

It was a lovely morning. There had been a slight frost in the night but it had quickly cleared once the sun was up, although traces lingered in the hills surrounding them and on the branches of the skeletal trees.

Arm in arm Ed and Maisie emerged from the castle and stood blinking in the sunlight. Maisie shaded her eyes and looked around, then back to the castle standing tall and splendid at the top of the hill. For a moment she seemed to fasten on a particular window as if she had seen movement.

'It's a fantastic place, Ed. I never dreamt you came from somewhere like this.'

'I don't.' Ed took out his silver case and selected a cigarette.

'My family are not noble. Not in the least. They were servants of the Rylands. They still are. My stepfather is the chauffeur to my brother-in-law. He does all sorts of jobs on the estate. The fact that my sister married the Ryland heir was a fluke. As a boy growing up in the lodge it was the last thing I ever expected.'

Maisie frowned. 'But she seems so, well, like a proper lady. You know, a titled one.'

'Peg was always a bit different. She was ambitious, oh not to marry a lord but to be unlike the others. She was one of the first women journalists and quickly made a name for herself. We thought she was going to marry someone called Alan, a journalist too but a working-class man like us, to whom she was engaged. But one day she and Hubert Ryland bumped into each other in London. She told us she had always liked him and he said the same about the few times they'd met at the castle, usually at servants' balls and so on. The Ryland family always used to attend these as part of their job – *noblesse oblige*. But I had no idea there was an attraction between Peg and Hubert, and nor had anyone else.'

'It's very romantic.' Maisie moved closer to Ed. 'I like her.'

'She likes you.' Ed's hand closed over hers and they began slowly to walk down the hill towards the lake, the sides of which had partly frozen, imprisoning the small boats moored close to the bank.

'Tell me about your boyhood,' Maisie said as they began to walk slowly round the lake.

'Not much to tell. I was, it may surprise you to learn, very shy and –' he laughed – 'even more surprising, very pious. Oh, I'm not now.' He gave a wry smile as Maisie flashed him a knowing look. 'That has all changed. But I did want to enter the Church. My mother particularly wanted it, and she was a very powerful influence in our family. I was quite studious, very shy about girls and not really interested, but I did like games. I went to university to study theology but I became very ill with meningitis. Like Stella I nearly died and the experience seemed to do something to me. I decided I didn't really believe in God. He hadn't been much help to me, giving me this awful illness, and that I didn't want to be a priest after all.

'But my sister Verity persuaded me to return to university which I did and then I joined the Navy. And then I met you.' He paused and looked at her shining eyes, studying him, enraptured as though she was drinking in every word, couldn't hear enough about him.

'Will you marry me, Maisie? Do you think you could bear it – being a sailor's wife? You know . . .' His voice trailed off as he tried to fathom the message in those expressive eyes.

'Oh Ed!' Maisie cried, throwing her arms around his neck, and for a long long time they embraced.

As they drew apart he said hopefully, 'I suppose that means "yes"?'

'Yes,' Maisie cried. 'Yes, yes, yes.'

Stella sat by the window looking at the birds hopping about on the lawn, feeding from the crumbs that Mrs Capstick had been out to throw to them just as Mum used to do at the lodge. Mrs Capstick made a point of doing it every morning on the front lawn below Stella's window so that she could sit there watching the blackbirds and robins, the chaffinches, thrushes and sparrows, and the tits that swung from the pieces of fat hanging from the tree, the nets full of nuts and sunflower seeds.

She loved the life of the birds, and she couldn't quite have explained why but their enormous energy gave her hope that one day she would be able to walk again. She would try wiggling her toes and it was true that the day before with Ed she had seen and felt a very slight response to her efforts in her big toe. Looking at it, she tried again and, yes, she was sure there was movement, very slight but movement nevertheless.

Just after ten she saw Ed and a very tall, beautiful woman come out and stand in front of the castle looking around. The woman had shaded her eyes and for a moment Stella felt she had looked straight at her. She was wearing a white fur coat, white suede boots and a red woolly scarf wrapped round her neck. After a while they disappeared out of sight and she guessed they were walking towards the lake.

Stella loved her brother best of all her family. They were more of an age, they had the same father and they had both been of a rather shy disposition as though they lived in the shadow of their ebullient older half-sisters. Peg was the nearest to them in age. Addie had gone to live with their aunt and then went to college, after which she got married, so from the age of sixteen or so she had never lived at home. Verity left home before they were born and never seemed like part of the family however hard she tried, though she visited in the holidays.

So brother and sister were thrown together. They grew up feeling somehow as though they were apart with different friends and doing different things. Later on they had both suffered severe illnesses which had profoundly influenced their lives.

She and Ed had sung in the church choir, diligently attended Sunday school and she had always thought that Ed would be a vicar as Mum had wanted and she would teach, also according to the wishes of Mum. Mum had been such an important part of their lives. When she died it was as though a bough had broken from the family tree.

But Ed had joined the Navy and she, well. . . . she would be married now if everything had gone according to plan, if only a cruel fate hadn't intervened.

Stella knew there was that slight movement in her toe but it was very slight and in the rest of her leg there was no feeling at all. Maybe she should have let Ed go and see Ernest and at least find out what Ver had said or done to him. Daily she waited for a letter, but so far there was no reply.

There was a tap on the door and as Stella looked towards it, it opened and Ed put his head round.

'I brought you a visitor,' he said. 'Is it all right if we come in?'

Stella went red, her hand flew to her mouth and she pulled the rug quickly over her leg to cover it. Then Ed came in with his hand in that of the most beautiful woman she had ever seen:

163

tall, willowy, blonde with wonderful bright deep blue eyes. She looked even more stunning close up than she had from a distance and she came straight towards Stella with a long effortless stride and stopped in front of her, those wonderful eyes brimming with interest, sympathy, love?

'I'm awfully pleased to meet you,' Maisie said, stooping to take Stella's outstretched hand and holding it in hers. 'Ed has told me so much about you.'

'You're very beautiful,' Stella said in wonder. 'Much more beautiful than you were when I looked out of the window.'

'Oh, you saw . . .' Maisie laughed nervously and looked across at Ed who was watching the scene.

'I saw you come out of the castle and look around,' Stella continued.

'You didn't see anything else?' Ed wondered, gazing out of the window. 'No, of course you can't see the lake from here.'

'What was there to see?' Stella enquired archly.

'We were kissing. I asked Maisie to marry me and she said yes.' Maisie held out a hand to him, which he clasped and brought to his lips. 'You're the first one we've told. I wanted you to be first.'

'Because you're so special to Ed,' Maisie said. 'And I *do* want you to be special to me.'

'Oh, I *will* be,' Stella said devoutly, clasping her hands. 'Oh, that is the most wonderful news in the world. When will the wedding be?'

'Before my next posting. Maybe the spring. I shall be in Plymouth for some time as the ship is in for overhaul. Maisie is going to come down and live in Plymouth.'

'You're both so lucky. I know you'll be happy. You're so well suited.'

Stella felt close to tears, but she realized they were tears of joy and not envy. She was thrilled that this stunning woman was to marry her brother and thus to be part of their intimate family.

'Now, tonight you're going to come to dinner,' Maisie said, sitting down next to Stella. 'Ed is quite right, you mustn't stay here all the time cooped up. There is nothing to be ashamed of, you know. Nothing at all. You had a very serious illness, life dealt you a hard blow but it is not shameful.'

Stella reached for her hand. 'You're quite right,' she said. 'You're so sensible. How lucky Ed is. Oh, I know we're going to be friends.'

Addie finished fussing with Jenny's hair. She wanted to look at her best for this grown-up party for her uncle and his new fiancée. Jenny was thirteen but she could pass for someone a lot older. She had a mop of golden curls, a complexion well described as peaches and cream, a dimpled chin, a pert, retroussé nose and eyes the colour of light blue cornflowers. She was also tall, bright, intelligent and good, a credit to any mother. In addition she was blessed with a sunny disposition and she wriggled about anxious to be in her best dress and off to the party, while Addie kept on telling her to be still.

'*Now* you can dress yourself,' Addie said when at long last she had the recalcitrant curls in place and a pretty blue ribbon securing them, 'and I'll go and see to Gilbert.'

'Yes, Mummy,' Jenny said obediently, dashing to the wardrobe to take out her frock.

Smiling to herself, Addie went to the door and down the stairs, hoping to find that Gilbert was all dressed and ready for the walk up the hill. But she knew it would be difficult. He liked to keep away as much as he could from being a guest at the castle where he felt uncomfortable and ill at ease.

Gilbert was a rough, uneducated man, but a tender lover, a good father and in the four years they had been together, Addie had been very happy with him. To her he was solid gold and although he never said much they were at ease in each other's company. They had a son of two called Arthur and they all lived together in perfect harmony except that Addie had this nagging wish that they should be married. She knew that Mother, with all the emphasis she had put on respectability, would not have liked her living in sin with a man to whom she was not married and by whom she had an illegitimate baby.

But it was strange how this state of affairs had been absorbed by everybody, or almost everybody. There were few people who ignored them or went to the other side of the street if they saw them coming. They were never ostracized at church. It was known that it was a situation that Addie had not wished for. Her husband would not divorce her and if she could marry Gilbert she would. In fact by now most people thought of them as man and wife.

Addie had hoped that this time he would be ready but instead when she opened the kitchen door her hopes were dashed. As she had feared he was slumped in front of the fire in his working clothes, staring into the flames.

'Gilbert,' Addie said sharply, 'won't you go and get ready? We'll be late.'

'What for?' Gilbert asked morosely without looking up.

'The dinner in honour of my brother and his fiancée. You *know* it's a special occasion.'

'I really don't want to go,' Gilbert said, his eyes returning to the flickering flames. 'You know I don't like it there. I'll stay and look after Arthur.'

'Oh *Gilbert*!' Addie said crossly. 'You know that one of the girls is coming down. It's all arranged.'

She went over to him and put a hand on his shoulder. 'Go on, Gilbert, please. For me.'

He reached up and in an awkward gesture, for he was not a demonstrative man, took her hand. 'I'd rather *not*, Addie. I feel so uncomfortable there. I don't know what to say. I don't belong.'

As he let go of her hand Addie sat down by the kitchen table and looked across at him. She too had on her best dress, green velvet with a neat white lace collar and a large amber brooch that had belonged to her mother pinned at her throat.

'Gilbert, we've got to talk this out. It's silly. Your attitude is silly. What happens up at the castle with Peg and that doesn't make any difference to us.'

'It doesn't make no difference to *us*, Addie, but it doesn't

166

mean I have to go and sit with folks I'm not comfortable with. I don't know what to say to them.'

'But Frank will be there,' Addie pleaded. 'He doesn't say much either.'

'That's not the point, Addie. Frank is comfortable with them. I'm not. Your brother is an officer in the Royal Navy. Your sister is married to a lord who be my employer.'

'But *Frank* is happy with them.'

'Well, I'm not. Frank is more used to it than I am. Just let me stay here. I'm an ordinary working-class man and that's what I want to remain.'

'But Gilbert –' Addie went across to him and put her cheek against his – '*I'm* just an ordinary working-class woman, aren't I? We love each other and that's what's important.'

'Important to us, but I don't think your sister likes the fact we aren't married, whatever she may say to you, and nor does his lordship. He is always awkward with me when we meet on the estate as though he's ashamed of his connection with me.'

'Oh, I'm *sure* he isn't.'

'It's not natural,' Gilbert said, edging away from her. 'It's not natural and I don't like it.'

'Maybe we should move away?' Addie said in a worried tone. 'Right away? Would you like that, dear?'

'But you can't leave Frank or Jenny . . .'

'Oh, I wouldn't leave *Jenny*. She would come with us and Arthur. Frank well . . . he does have Peg. He is not as bothered by the situation as you are.'

'How would we live? And where?'

'I could work. I'm a teacher after all. We could find a nice little house to rent . . .'

She paused and looked at him, but she knew her heart wasn't in the idea, and so did he.

'Please, Gilbert,' she pleaded. 'Just for tonight. To please me? And then, I promise you, we'll think about moving away, starting a new life and where to go.'

*　　*　　*

The dining room looked splendid. It was entirely lit by candles, and the best plate and highly polished silver sparkled on the shiny mahogany table. Despite the occasion the men wore lounge suits not dinner jackets – perhaps out of consideration for Gilbert, after all – and the women pretty dresses. Gilbert in his best suit and only tie, his usually unruly hair combed, the stubble on his cheeks freshly shaved, felt like an overstuffed turkey. He was seated next to Addie and as soon as his wine was poured he put the glass to his mouth and, drained the lot, to Addie's concern as he had already had a quantity of whisky in the drawing room before dinner. She pinched him beneath the table. But when the butler, seeing his empty glass, refilled it, he did the same thing again.

Jenny on the other hand was so excited she could hardly sit still, and Frank kept on putting a restraining hand on her arm accompanied by a kindly smile. She had on the dress she had worn for her confirmation in Sherborne Abbey the previous summer; white organdie with a pleated bodice, a round collar and long sleeves edged with lace. Her fair curls had been brushed until they glowed. She sat between her mother and Frank and, unlike Gilbert, she adored the glamour of this grown-up occasion. Stella too, under the spell of Maisie, had agreed to come. She wore a long dress and had entered in on Ed's arm, and now sat beside him determined to enjoy herself.

Peg wore black velvet, Maisie blue organdie over a tight-fitting taffeta blue sheath exposing her arms, neck and the top of her bosom. She had put her hair up and long pearl earrings dangled from her ears. On her finger was a sapphire and diamond engagement ring that Ed had bought in the almost certain expectation that she would agree to be his wife. She sat at Hubert's right as the honoured guest.

Peg sat at the head of the table, opposite Hubert, with Gilbert on one side of her and Frank on the other. It was a mistake. Instead of appreciating the honour Gilbert felt confused and out of his depth and kept looking at Cyril the butler, whom he knew well, to keep his glass topped up.

Mrs Capstick had at short notice excelled herself and produced Stilton soup, goujons of sole and roast lamb from the home farm. There was Montrachet followed by a fine claret to drink, and a sweet Sauternes with the crème brulée, which was one of Mrs Capstick's specialities.

Peg attempted to converse with Gilbert, but it was hard work. She noticed that he ate very little but every time Cyril came round his glass was refilled. She and Addie kept exchanging anxious glances. Gilbert was not known as a drinker, was not used to drink and Addie kept on nudging him and trying to flash him a warning signal, but he took no notice of her and went on drinking.

Peg tried to catch the butler's eye, but he proved elusive, perhaps because he thought, out of a sense of mischief, that it would be fun to make his old friend drunk.

Towards the end of the meal Hubert gently tapped his glass for silence and rose to speak.

'This is a very happy occasion,' he began, clearing his throat. 'All the family are gathered together to greet Ed home on leave and meet the lovely woman he is to marry. This is the happiest of occasions for us all. Now would you raise your glasses and join me in a toast to the happiness of Ed and Maisie.'

After the toast Hubert sat down to approving glances from Peg. Then Ed rose and all eyes turned expectantly to him.

'I would like to thank my brother-in-law and sister for their amazing hospitality. For welcoming Maisie and loving her as I knew you would. This has been the happiest day for us, made happier by the fact that we are with the family, all except Ver. But we know Ver is busy and so I raise my glass to the family present and absent.

'Thank you all for taking Maisie to your hearts. I know she will be a great enhancement to our lives, an adornment to the family.'

Everyone rose except Gilbert who sat where he was, looking stupefyingly at his glass. Then, aware that all eyes were on him, he started to lurch to his feet. Peg put out a hand to steady him

169

but too late. He slipped from her grasp and fell sideways on to the floor where he was violently sick.

Addie woke and lay for a moment gazing into the dark. Then the awful horror of the previous evening hit her. Gilbert. He had been so drunk, so disgustingly drunk that after being sick, he had passed out. She and Frank and Ed had between them managed to get him home and put him to bed in the spare room where he could sleep it off. She had not dared to go back to the house because she felt so ashamed, and wished she'd left Gilbert at home where he wanted to be.

Eventually Frank had arrived back with Jenny, both rather subdued. No one had mentioned the matter, Frank told her, after a rapid exit from the dining room because of the appalling smell; but he said Hubert had given the butler, who should have known better, a good talking to on the side. Everyone at the table had noticed how much Gilbert was drinking, but it was so hard to do anything without appearing rude, which would have diminished Gilbert's notorious lack of confidence even more. It seemed an awful way to end what had been such a happy evening.

Addie guessed it was about seven, and reluctantly she pushed back the bedclothes and got out of bed, jumping eagerly into her dressing gown because it was so cold.

She opened the door of the bedroom she normally shared with Gilbert, crossed the hall and gently pushed open the door of the room where he'd spent the night. She didn't want to put on the light, so she crept across the floor to make sure he was all right, that he hadn't been sick again in the night and choked.

She leaned over the bed and tentatively put her hand to touch him. The bedclothes were thrown back, the bed was empty. Puzzled, but not too concerned, she returned to the door and clicked on the light switch. No Gilbert lying on the floor as she'd feared.

She rushed downstairs but all was quiet. Not even Frank, usually an early riser, was up and the fire was unlit. She opened the back door and looked out on to the landscape covered by a thick frost. There were one or two lights on at the castle where the servants there would be boiling water and lighting fires.

She had thought that perhaps Gilbert had gone out to see to the animals, but she had a cold, bleak feeling in her heart. She went back into the house, climbed the stairs and looked in the drawers where Gilbert kept his few items of clothing. They were empty. He must have crept in during the night and removed everything.

She stole downstairs again and looked for his boots, his best pair of shoes, his coat, his copy of the Bible which had belonged to his mother and which was one of his very few treasured possessions. They were nowhere to be found. Nothing was left. He would have put everything into the rucksack which was all he had when he moved in with her. A man who had been used constantly to being on the move travelled very light. She realized now that in fact, in his heart, Gilbert had never really settled.

She could imagine him leaving the house and making for God knows where, but somewhere where he would no longer be an embarrassment to her or her family; to fade away as quietly as he had come.

She knew, then, that Gilbert had gone.

Twelve

P eg said in her letter that Maisie was like no one they'd ever
known. She was tall, beautiful with shoulder-length wavy
hair. She had been a dancer at a number of London nightclubs
but had now gone to Plymouth to be with Ed. The wedding was
to be in the spring and as Maisie had only a widowed mother it
would be at Ryland.

Verity thought about Ed as she walked along the street
towards the house she hoped to buy in the smart Clifton district
of Bristol. It would be her first real home, a home of her own at
last.

It was, she thought, so amazing that Ed, who had always
been rather shy and had never shown much interest in girls
should have found such a glamorous and unconventional bride.
A nightclub dancer! Verity wondered what Mother, always so
much yearning for respectability for her children, would have
made of that.

Verity was thirty-five but she looked and felt older. Her
brown hair, which she wore in an old-fashioned bun at the nape
of her neck, had a few grey streaks in it and, although by no
means fat, she was well rounded. Her height helped to set off
any hint of corpulence.

She had a strong face full of character that could terrify
members of the nursing staff who had failed to give of their
best. She was the bane of junior doctors, but she sometimes
fawned on consultants because that was the way she had been
trained. She was an excellent nurse, a disciplinarian of the old
school, now superintendent of midwives at a large hospital.

She never wore make-up and when out of uniform her dress tended to be conventional rather than smart; low-heeled, sensible shoes, good for walking, and serviceable dresses, twin sets and costumes that were destined to last. She always wore a hat, usually felt with a brim.

Verity had by now firmly eschewed any thoughts of marriage. The war had taken too many eligible men and she kept very clear of those who were married and who stopped to linger in the wards or in her office. She had been caught once and would not be so foolish again.

There was an air of suppressed, perhaps unfulfilled, sexuality about Verity which attracted men, but of which she remained deeply unaware. For, despite her formidable appearance, she was a good-looking woman with her thick brown hair, soft skin and hazel eyes that contained the merest hint of passion.

Verity stopped outside the house to look at it before going in. It was of red brick and gabled, quite a substantial house because she wanted plenty of room for her family to stay, her nieces and nephews now growing in number. She had seen it once and now it was time to make up her mind.

She finally knocked on the door and was admitted by the vendor, a smiling elderly woman called Mrs Binns who now found the house too big for her and had been offered a home by her daughter.

'Have you family?' she asked Verity, admitting her to the drawing room.

'A *large* family,' Verity smiled at her. 'A brother and three sisters, lots of nephews and nieces.'

'But none of your own?' The woman looked at her with an unnecessarily exaggerated air of sympathy.

'No.' Verity turned to the window and gazed out on to the pretty garden. She didn't care about the woman's patronizing attitude. It was her house she was interested in and her thoughts were still on her sister's letter.

Peg said that Stella really seemed to be getting some of the feeling back in the toes of her right leg, and it was thought

173

possible that one day she might actually be able to walk without a caliper. Ed's visit had done her so much good and now she was talking about getting a job and returning to teaching.

'Might I see upstairs again?' Verity asked.

Mrs Binns smiled and motioned towards the stairs. 'You know the way,' she said. 'My arthritis is bad today, and I try and avoid stairs. Did you say you were a nurse?'

'A midwife,' Verity replied. 'I don't know much about arthritis, I'm afraid.'

'Such a *pity* that you never had any of your own,' Mrs Binns said, standing back for Verity to pass up the stairs. Verity ignored her.

There were four bedrooms which, despite the fact that they were badly in need of redecoration, had tall windows and were bright and welcoming. There was also a large attic which would make a nice nursery. There was a rather cold linoleum on the floor, but the old lady had lived there a long time and Verity intended to put down warm carpets and modernize the plumbing. The house would be repapered throughout and that with new curtains would transform it.

She stood in the back bedroom, looking out on to the garden, which was a good size with apple trees, and she could imagine the children playing there while the adults took tea on the lawn. Catherine was to be christened after Christmas and Verity had been asked to be a godmother. She could imagine little Catherine with all her young cousins playing on a swing that could be hung between the apple trees, and her heart filled with joy and love.

There was something special to her about Catherine, named after Mum, and Verity knew she would be close to her and do all she could to make her life happy and fulfilled. She had a warm glow about Catherine as though she was in fact her child, the child she had so badly wanted, the child she had never had. But one could live through the children of others. It was a rich and satisfying thing to do. Maybe Maisie and Ed would also have children, and it was not impossible that Stella would eventually marry. After all, she was only twenty-one. Far too early to be resigned to spinsterhood, despite a paralysed leg.

Yes, she, Verity, would be surrounded by the children of her brother and sisters and would never really miss not having any of her own.

She wandered through the other rooms, a rather old-fashioned bathroom with a cast-iron tub in the middle of the floor, maybe one of the first to be installed in that area when the house was built in the 1880s.

Peg said in the long letter she'd had that morning that Addie had taken the disappearance of Gilbert very badly. She had become morose and withdrawn and Peg feared she might be having a nervous breakdown. She blamed herself for not understanding Gilbert and especially for insisting he come to dinner at the castle when he had pleaded to be left alone. Gilbert, catapulted from his role as a herdsman to a guest at the table of his noble employer, had been deeply uncomfortable and unhappy. Addie felt she hadn't realized just how unhappy and lost he was and had thus failed him.

They were all upset. They had liked Gilbert, so different from Harold, a solid son of the soil who had given Addie not only love and affection but much needed stability. She was now on her own again, mother to two illegitimate children, one of them only two years old. Hubert was trying to find out what had happened to Gilbert and, if successful, attempt to persuade him to return to Addie and his son. But tracing an itinerant farm worker was a bit like looking for the proverbial needle in a haystack. Gilbert had covered his tracks well and would be hard to find.

Verity walked slowly down the stairs back to the small hall where the anxious vendor was looking expectantly up at her.

'Well?' she asked.

'I'd like to buy it,' Verity said. 'It is a pretty house and will admirably suit my purposes. I'll speak to my lawyer and ask him to proceed with the formalities.'

*   *   *

December 1931

Walking in the early evening through the Piazza Navona on his way to a reception, Alan passed the restaurant where he and Peg and sat during that last visit to Rome, and once again he felt a pang of nostalgia and longing for her, so acute it was like a physical pain. It was a longing which had never really left him despite the passage of years, and often when it did return, it was worse than before.

If only he hadn't been stupid enough to try and sleep with her before she was ready, possibly they would be together even now, and married.

Oh, what joy to have been Peg's husband. Tears almost filled his eyes as he looked at the table where they'd sat in the restaurant, where nothing was different. The tables with encrusted candles in Chianti bottles were in the same place. Even the red check tablecloths seemed unchanged.

Some little thing, a gesture, a memory would bring her back, reminding him of her vibrant presence and how much he longed for her. Yet he knew it was foolish. Peg was gone, married to another. She would never ever, in any circumstances, return to him again.

It was not only her character and physical beauty that Alan missed but her vitality, the sharpness of her mind, her grasp and understanding of political and international issues. He did not deny her right to opt for marriage and motherhood, but he thought she was a loss to journalism and female emancipation, of which she had been such a shining example.

For Alan such a companion would have been a boon. He had lived in Rome now for four years. He loved and was at home in the city. He spoke fluent Italian, had a number of Italian friends, all left wing and anti-Mussolini, as well as acquaintances in almost every profession from all over the world. There were also certain members of society who found him interesting and amusing and who were useful to him mostly because they had access to Il Duce, who had by now crushed almost all opposition to him. Recently several prominent Italians had been seized, accused of plotting to overthrow him.

Alan had come a long way from the young, gauche journalist of extremely left-wing views and with little regard for his appearance, who had first fallen in love with Peg in the seedy Fleet Street news agency where they had both worked. He still had his ideals, but they had been refined by his increasingly sophisticated lifestyle and the milieu in which he lived, his comfortable flat within sight of the Pantheon, his entrée into every strata of society. He was now the chief European correspondent of the *South London Gazette*, which had expanded and was achieving national status, thanks largely to its team of skilled reporters like Alan.

But though he kept his nose to the ground and knew everything that was going on, Alan kept clear of conspiracies. He neither wanted to be thrown into prison nor deported from the country.

As he made his way through the narrow streets on this particular cold evening Alan was able to reflect on the growing transformation of Europe in the face of the Fascist threat, not only from Italy but also from Germany, where Hitler's National Socialist Party seemed unstoppable.

England now had a National Government under Ramsay Macdonald, but the whole of Europe – indeed half the world including America – was still in the grip of a savage recession, and in England alone over two million people were out of work.

Yet now Peg, ardent Socialist that she was, or had been, was married to a lord and Alan, in contrast to the principles he supported, lived in great comfort, wanting for nothing, and on his way now to a soirée given by the Principessa Paola de Filippi-Montebianco, a member, through her late husband, of one of Rome's most prominent and aristocratic families.

The Montebianco villa was set in acres of land on the edge of the Borghese Gardens. As Alan passed through the enormous wrought-iron gates a procession of chauffeur-driven cars, some with diplomatic flags flying on the bonnets, proceeded in stately

177

fashion along the drive. Approaching the magnificent double stairway leading to the Doric stone portico, he saw a stream of people, either alighting from cars or arriving on foot. He joined the queue up the staircase and produced his embossed invitation, awaiting his turn to enter.

Inside the massive marble hall a team of flunkies took the cloaks, hats and overcoats of the guests, who then formed themselves into an orderly procession wending their way up the massive marble staircase, at the top of which stood the Principessa together with her son and daughter, welcoming the guests.

The Principessa, who was about fifty, was a handsome woman magnificently gowned in a long evening dress of stiff gold brocade, the bodice encrusted with semi-precious stones and tiny pearls. Around her neck were the famous Montebianco pearls which were believed to be priceless. She was heavily made up and wore a tall feathered headdress which enhanced her already considerable height. She inspected each guest through a pearl and onyx lorgnette, sometimes saying a few words, sometimes merely smiling before passing them on to her son and daughter who were a charming, good-looking couple in their early twenties. From the reception rooms came a babble of voices and the dulcet tones of a string orchestra playing melodies from operas by Verdi.

As he reached the Princess Alan took her hand and bent low over it.

'I expect you know everyone here, Signor Walker,' she said in Italian in her low, rather seductive voice and then, in scarcely more than a whisper, 'We are expecting Il Duce.' She gave a little shiver of excitement before handing him to her son, Prince Giuseppe, who bowed, and her daughter, Princess Filomena, who gave him a glowing smile. Then he was free to wander into the salon, where instead of knowing everyone he found that in fact he seemed to know no one.

He took out a cigarette and lit it, nonchalantly blowing away the smoke. Then he accepted a glass of champagne from a waiter carrying a laden tray. Once he would have been cowed by this experience, but no more.

He had come a long way, enough to give him more self-confidence than he had in those far off days.

Alternately sipping champagne and smoking his cigarette, Alan moved at ease through the crowd in the great green and gold drawing room, hung with priceless paintings and tapestries, and with a magnificent chandelier of a thousand pieces of glass glittering in the centre of the ceiling which was decorated with frescoes by Pietro da Cortona. At the far end of the room windows from floor to ceiling would, in daylight, have afforded a spectacular view of the Borghese Gardens, which was now concealed by green velvet curtains.

At last Alan recognized a few faces and acknowledged their smiles, sometimes with a nod sometimes a wave of his hand, but there was no one he particularly wanted to talk to and he thought he would make this a brief visit and then spend an hour or two in the offices of his newspaper before going home. He had made an appearance and that was enough: to see and be seen.

For once he would welcome an early night in a life plagued with receptions and dinners, hardly any time to call one's own.

His attention was suddenly diverted by the figure of a woman, her back to him, a cigarette in a long holder in her right hand with which she was gesticulating as if describing something to her companion who was a short, distinguished-looking but elderly man who Alan didn't know.

But not so the woman. She wore a white evening gown and her fair hair, styled in a shoulder-length bob, was covered by a very fine net which sparkled with hundreds of tiny sequins.

He continued walking until he stood just behind her companion so that he could be sure, and as he did she looked up and seemed to recognize him, which surprised him because she had not seen him for a very long time.

But bored, it seemed, by her elderly companion, she flourished her long cigarette holder in Alan's direction calling out: 'Why, *hello!*'

'Good evening, Miss Ryland.' Alan inclined his head and Violet's companion, surprised, stood to one side, looking indignantly at the interloper.

'This is an old, old friend from home . . .' Violet began and then stopped as if she couldn't remember his name.

'Alan Walker. We met at Ryland Castle a few years ago. You were kind enough to look after me when I had an accident with your horse.'

'How nice to see you again.' Violet nodded dismissively to her companion who moved away without waiting to be introduced.

'Thank you for rescuing me,' she breathed *sotto voce*. 'What a bore that man was.' She peered more closely at Alan. 'But tell me, how are you?'

'You didn't really remember me, did you, Miss Ryland? I was once engaged to Peg.'

'I remember you very well. I thought I'd killed you, silly man. Of course I remember you. But you've changed.' Violet described another, even wider arc in the air with her cigarette holder, which Alan could see had the potential of being or becoming a dangerous instrument. 'We all have, I suppose. It's a sad fact of life, isn't it? And what are you doing here in Rome?'

'I am European correspondent for the *South London Gazette*.'

'Yes, of course. You were a journalist, like Peg.'

'How is Peg?' Alan said, desperately trying to sound offhand.

'Very well.' Violet paused. 'You knew she married my brother?'

'Of course.'

'Of course you did. I wonder if you also know she had a little girl a few months ago?'

'No, I didn't know that. That makes three?'

'Yes, two boys – delightful boys, really lovely children – and the dearest little girl. I am to be godmother sometime in the New Year.'

'Do you live in Rome, Miss Ryland?'

'Oh, no. I am only just visiting. But I have known Paola Montebianco ever since I was small. Her mother, who was English, was a friend of my mother, with whom I am staying at her home in Umbria.' Violet put a hand to her mouth pretending to yawn. 'But, oh dear, I am so *bored* with the country and came to Rome to do a few days' shopping—'

Suddenly all the noise in the room ceased abruptly. There was a commotion at the far end as a posse of uniformed functionaries swarmed in, and in the middle it was just possible to see the shining pate of a fat little man who walked self-importantly towards the Princess, whose receiving line had by now broken up and who was now talking to the German Ambassador.

'Mussolini,' Alan murmured, adding beneath his breath, 'pompous little twit.'

'I think that's enough to get you thrown into the Castel Sant Angelo,' Violet said, giggling, referring to Rome's notorious prison. 'At least he gets the trains to run on time. Look,' she added impulsively, 'it's terribly hot in here and *very* boring. Shall we go outside or do you want to speak to Mussolini?'

'I certainly don't,' Alan protested. 'Even if I got the chance, which I doubt I would in this company. How about a stroll in the gardens, if it's not too cold?'

'If it is, come back to my hotel and have a drink,' Violet said invitingly and, to his astonishment and slight discomfiture, tucked her arm through his. 'When it seems polite to go,' she whispered in his ear, 'lead on Macduff.'

'What bliss it was to find you!' Violet said, pouring whisky into a glass. 'What a spot of luck. Ice?'

'No, thank you. Yes, wasn't it lucky?' Alan crossed one leg over the other and took the glass she offered him, smiling up at her. 'An extraordinary coincidence.'

'But don't you think life is full of coincidences?' she challenged, standing before him, her long cigarette holder at an angle in her hand, as if she was striking a pose.

He thought she really was very attractive. He was not quite sure how old she was but certainly a bit older than him. But with her attraction, indeed adding to it, went the used look of an older woman, bowed by experience, a kind of world weariness emphasized by the lines on her face and the dark shadows under her eyes, which even her clever use of make-up had been unable to conceal. She had a rather narrow determined mouth, a thin aristocratic nose and, definitely her best feature, deeply recessed eyes, which were violet like her name.

Maybe her world weariness was sadness, Alan thought, because for some reason she had been unable to find her niche in life. He remembered that long ago while she had looked after him at the castle they had become almost intimate. They really got to know each other very well. Yet she had almost forgotten him, perhaps because he was at that time considered so unimportant. However, he recalled quite clearly now that he had once found Violet intriguing. But then he had been madly in love with someone else. Someone who had since jilted him quite ruthlessly. Suddenly Alan found himself again deeply interested in Violet Ryland and even, perhaps, a little attracted by her.

'Would you like to have dinner?' he said, glancing at his watch. 'I think I could get a table at the Excelsior.'

The Excelsior was one of Rome's grand hotels dating back to the middle of the previous century. Its dining room, rich and ornate, was half full, mostly with people in evening dress like themselves, but there was also a heavy, and to Alan unwelcome, sprinkling of military and naval uniforms adorned with plenty of gold braid and rows of medal ribbons. A string orchestra played softly in the background.

'Do you eat here often?' Violet looked teasingly at Alan. They had eaten well and he felt replete and happy in this elegant ambience in the company of an attractive woman. 'If memory serves me right you were something of an extreme Socialist, weren't you?'

'Something of.' Alan leaned back in his chair, his hand round the stem of his glass. 'I have grown a *little* wisdom I think, but not completely lost my principles.'

'Oh no, I didn't want to suggest that. I mean I admire you, and all that sort of thing.' She lowered her head. 'I've never really had any principles. I've just been swept along by a tide.'

'Oh, I'm sure you haven't.' Alan leaned forward, gazing intently at her.

'No it's true. I don't really believe in anything very much. I don't have any faith,' she faltered, 'or hope . . .' She looked up at Alan with pain-filled eyes. 'You know my fiancé was killed in the war?'

'Yes, you told me at the castle.' Alan produced his cigarette case and held it towards her. As Violet selected one, an observant waiter sprang forward to light it, then waited to do the same for Alan. Violet blew a thin stream of smoke into the air.

'It was a terrible blow. I've never really got over it, though it was such a long time ago.' She pointed to her finger. 'You see I still wear his ring.'

'It's very pretty.' Alan wanted to put a hand over hers because she suddenly seemed so vulnerable, but he didn't dare.

'I've just been so lost.' Violet's eyes were suddenly suspiciously bright and she flicked a finger across them as if to brush away tears. 'It sounds pathetic, I know, but no one really seems to want me. I wander about with nothing to do, no real friends. No purpose in life. My mother, who is busy all day long doing don't ask me *what*, thinks I'm useless and an utter failure – of course, because I'm not married.' She paused dramatically and dashed her hand across her eyes again. 'Oh dear, I don't know why I'm telling you all this. You must think I'm a fool.'

'Not at all.' Alan at last did reach across and lightly place his hand over hers. Her response was immediate. Instead of withdrawing her hand as he'd feared she might, she compulsively clasped his, as if clinging to an anchor.

'I know how you feel,' Alan said. 'You know Peg and I were engaged . . .'

'Of course.' Violet bit her lip. 'How very selfish of me. And then she met Hubert.'

'She never loved me,' Alan said bleakly. 'I know that now. I knew it then. She was sorry for me and, really, it was just as well we didn't marry because you can't force someone to love you, can you?'

'No, you can't, I suppose. But I do think Ted did love me very much, and I loved him. Has there –' she paused – 'has there been anyone since, I mean like Peg?'

'Oh no.'

'Nor me. Funny how alike we are, isn't it? We've both lost something, haven't we? Something we treasured?'

Christmas in Rome was very quiet, very peaceful. The city seemed almost empty. Many of the restaurants were closed but there was life at the big hotels and they danced every night at the Excelsior or the Grand or the Quirinale, eating well and drinking expensive champagne.

Alan had intended to go to Egypt for Christmas and Violet was supposed to go back to her mother, but instead they stayed in Rome and they met each other every day, rather excitedly, like two people who might be on the verge of falling in love.

On Christmas Eve they went to midnight Mass at St Peter's and afterwards strolled through the great square, arm in arm. Just by one of the tall colonnades they stopped and embraced.

'I don't know what I'd have done without you,' Violet said.

'Or I you.' Alan looked at her tenderly.

'Two orphans in the storm?'

'Not quite.' He laughed rather shakily as they resumed their walk, arms again entwined. 'We are free people, you know. The past is the past and we must not let ourselves be dragged down by it. I think we both have. I know that now.'

They reached the door of her small hotel and stood looking uncertainly at each other.

'Well . . . see you tomorrow,' Alan began, but Violet put a hand lightly against his chest.

'Why don't we walk back to your place,' she said quietly, 'just for a nightcap?'

When Alan woke, the light was streaming through the window and bells were pealing out from, it seemed, all the churches in Rome. At first he didn't realize that his lonely bed was lonely no longer. Beside him Violet was curled up, fast asleep like a baby. She was nude and he could just see the top of her small but beautiful breasts above the sheet.

It had been very late when they finally fell asleep or very early, depending how you looked at it. He thought dawn was breaking, but right now he felt as fresh and reinvigorated as if he'd slept for eight solid hours.

He felt like a new man – powerful, vigorous. How very different this experience with Violet was from the one he'd had with Peg.

He was about to creep out of bed when he felt a hand round his waist and he turned to where Violet lay smiling up at him, lazily and looking very seductive.

'Happy Christmas, darling,' she said, pulling him down towards her.

Thirteen

January 1932

Darling Hubert,

A happy new year to you all. I'm so looking forward to seeing you again and being one of Catherine's god-mothers. Darling, do you remember Alan, who for a ghastly moment I thought I'd killed when Champion reared up in front of him? Of course you do. He was engaged to Peg, though I must say it was so long ago that I had difficulty remembering who he was when I met him again here in Rome a few weeks ago.

Well he's actually rather nice and a big shot in news-papers, and we're having a bit of a fling! I don't suppose it will last, but I'd love to bring him to the christening. He *is* rather a darling and so different from most of the blokes I've met these last few years.

Longing to see you, darling Hubert, and all the family.

Violet

Peg handed back the letter to Hubert. 'Well, I am surprised. Astonished would be a better word. Alan and Violet. I can scarcely begin to imagine it.'

'But you don't know Violet very well, darling,' Hubert said defensively.

'No, but I know Alan. I would never have thought even in the briefest acquaintance that she was his type.'

Hubert put the letter back on the pile on his desk and looked

across at his wife, who was standing by the window of his study.
'Are you a bit jealous, Peg?'

'Of course I'm *not*,' Peg said angrily. 'Not a bit.'

'Then would you mind if he came?'

'Why should I mind? It would look extremely odd if I said no.
This is Violet's home and, of course, she is entitled to bring
whom she likes here. It is true Violet and I don't know each
other very well. I sometimes think she keeps away because of
me.'

'Now, that's *not* true.' Hubert leaned back and lit his pipe.

Peg, who could feel the temperature rising, went over to his
desk and placed a kiss on the top of his head. 'Darling, don't
let's have an argument. By all means tell Violet she is most
welcome here, and to bring whomever she likes. I shall be
pleased to see her . . . and, of course, Alan.'

Hubert reached up for her hand, kissed it, let it go and started
to sort through the rest of his post as Peg left the room.

But she did feel rattled. It was strange to hear Alan's name after
all those years, and to think of him staying here. She would have
to alert the housekeeper that they would have a very full house.
Every room would be occupied and the lodge too.

And then, what sleeping arrangements were expected concerning Alan and Violet? Well, there was no doubt in her mind
about that. She would do what her mother-in-law would
certainly have done. Separate bedrooms. Let them come and
go as they pleased, but the formalities must be strictly adhered
to.

There was a lot to do before the christening, which was in
three weeks' time. They would have had it in the spring but Ed
and Maisie had planned their wedding for May and that would
cause enough upheaval, with numbers, catering and so on.

Peg found managing a large household, even with plenty of
help, quite onerous after what she had been used to. Why, she
scarcely had time to read the newspapers or keep abreast of
events. Alan would find her woefully lacking in knowledge of
the international situation.

Peg never asked herself if she missed her old lifestyle, what she might have been as the wife of a journalist based in central Europe. She loved Hubert so much, and they were so happy, that she had settled down quite contentedly, first in their home in Italy and now back at the castle. She supposed some people would say there was more to life than this domesticity, but it seemed to suit her and she never had a bored or idle moment.

They, Hubert and she, were also in a way pathfinders, creating a different way of life to the one that had predominated before. They were banishing a form of enlightened mediaevalism in which patronage and condescension were paramount, and bringing life in the castle and on the estate into the twentieth century.

She remembered, sometimes with amazement, how she and her family had venerated the Rylands, the gratitude they had felt for their brief visits to the servants' parties, or the various receptions that had taken place there when a member of staff married or was buried. The parties were still held, and so were the receptions, but she and Hubert would stay all the time and participate. And yet sometimes she couldn't help thinking the staff rather despised them for it. Some of them, not all, undoubtedly longed for the deference and forelock touching of the old days.

Peg had her own sitting room and to this she summoned the housekeeper, Amy, and spent some time with her going over the arrangements for the christening and making lists.

Then she ran downstairs to see Mrs Capstick in the kitchen to discuss not only the christening but the menus for the house for the following week.

She had a naturally easy relationship with Mrs Capstick, who by now was used to Peg as lady of the house and treated her with respect but not deference. She still called her by her Christian name while Peg would never have dreamt of referring to her by any other name than that by which she had known her all her life: Mrs Capstick.

It had been difficult for Mrs Capstick, as it had been for all the staff, to get used to the new regimen with the added complication of one of their number now being their mistress. Not that Peg had ever been a servant, but part of a family who had served the Rylands.

After speaking to Mrs Capstick, Peg made her way to the nursery where Nelly had, since the advent of Catherine, been assisted by another nursemaid, Clara, whose sole charge was the baby. Like Nelly, Clara was a local girl whose family had been known to the Rylands for generations.

Nelly was preparing Jude and Caspar for a walk, wrapping them up well against the cold, and Clara was giving Catherine her bottle.

For a while Peg fussed over the little boys and saw them off with Nelly, warning her not to stay outside for too long, and then returned to the nursery. Taking Catherine on her knee, she gave her the rest of her bottle while Clara popped her dirty nappies into a pail to soak and began to sort through her baby clothes, chatting to Peg about nothing in particular.

Peg stayed for a while playing with Catherine until she got tired and then she tucked her up in her cot and told Clara that if the weather held she would take her for a walk in her pram that afternoon. Peg did not leave all the children's upbringing to the nurses, but made sure she was an active mother herself and that they saw plenty of their father.

With a little time left on her hands before lunch Peg went down to the cloakroom, changed her shoes and put on a warm coat and scarf and, leaving the castle, went down the hill to the lodge. There she found Addie and Stella sitting at the kitchen table, having a cup of tea. Arthur was in his pen in front of the fire, playing with his toys.

Pink-cheeked with cold, rubbing her hands, Peg warmed them in front of the fire after greeting her sisters, and leaning over the pen to kiss Arthur. Then, as Addie poured her a cup, she unfastened her coat and sat down at the table.

'Guess who's coming to the christening?' she said with a mysterious smile.

'Give up,' Addie said immediately, knowing it was almost an impossible question to answer.

'Alan Walker.'

'Alan Walker,' Stella repeated. 'You mean your one-time fiancé?'

'The same.' Peg nodded.

'Did you invite him?' Addie asked, returning to her chair.

'I certainly didn't. He has been living in Rome, I understand, and guess who he should bump into, but Violet Ryland, who was visiting. I don't know how or why, so don't ask me,' Peg concluded firmly, finishing her tea and putting her cup back on the table. 'According to Violet, they are as she puts it . . . having a bit of a fling.'

'*Alan*!' Addie cried in astonishment. 'With *Miss Violet*!'

'I must say,' Peg said, 'I find it rather difficult to believe, but then I haven't seen Alan for years. I can't judge what he's like now. It's possible there have been big changes. There must be because Violet hasn't the slightest interest in politics.'

'It must be sex!' Stella spluttered.

'It could be, but Alan was always a very nice man,' Peg murmured. 'He may not have set the world on fire but he was nice and he was good. I was the one who behaved badly, not him.'

'You didn't behave badly,' Addie protested.

'I did and I hurt him. It will be very difficult for me to see him again, but he must want to come or else Violet would not have invited him.'

Addie got to her feet to check something on the stove. Peg watched her with an expression of concern on her face. Concern that, these days, was always present about Addie.

'Addie, I don't think you're eating enough . . . you're getting very thin.

'I never seem hungry,' Addie said, turning slightly. Then, in a broken voice, 'Oh, I *do* miss Gilbert. Has Hubert . . .' She looked anxiously over at Peg, who shook her head.

'No news. I do think that one day he will come back.'

'How can you say that?' Stella burst out angrily. 'I think it is irresponsible of you, Peg, to raise Addie's hopes. I personally don't think he will come back. He's gone and that's that.'

'And so has *Ernest* gone,' Addie spat at her. 'Only you will never accept it.'

'That's very different.'

'In what way is it different?' Addie wanted to know, her expression one of outrage.

'Ernest and I were properly engaged.' Stella twisted the ring she still wore on her finger. 'For him it's just a matter of time until my leg . . .' She looked down wanly at her stricken limb. 'I know he will come back, I just know it.'

'Well, I think you're deceiving yourself. You had nothing but a promise, while Gilbert and I . . .' tears sprang to Addie's eyes as she looked in the direction of the playpen, 'had a baby, a real human being, part of us, part of our bodies. Why you and Ernest . . . well . . .'

'Well, *what*?' Stella asked, outraged.

'You never even went to bed together!'

'Oh, *please*,' Peg begged, intervening as she so often had to do between the unhappy sisters. 'Stop this nonsense.'

'Well, I don't want to go on living here,' Stella said, stamping her good foot. 'I'm going to move back to the castle. I came here to try and be of help whereas all I get from Addie is abuse and ingratitude.'

'That's all you deserve,' Addie shouted and rushed out of the room, undoubtedly to fling herself on her bed in a storm of tears.'

'*Now* what have you done?' Peg said almost in despair.

'I have done *nothing*. I find Addie intolerable these days, and as for that poor baby –' She looked over at Arthur, who, however, seemed quite unconcerned about all the fuss and was playing contentedly with his brightly coloured wooden bricks.

Peg sat down beside Stella and put an arm round her shoulder.

191

'You know Addie is unwell,' she said. 'You must be gentle with her. These depressions are quite serious.'

'She should pull herself together. I have.'

'Yes, and you have done wonderfully well; but you are sustained, rightly or wrongly, by the feeling that one day you and Ernest . . .' Peg trailed off, feeling the hopelessness of the situation.

'But don't *you* believe that Ernest . . .' Stella faltered. 'I mean that he will come back when I am completely well?'

Peg passed a hand wearily over her brow.

'I don't know,' she said. 'I really don't know.'

Going up the hill a little later, Peg felt depressed on account of her two sisters, one struggling with a paralysed leg and a hope that was undoubtedly a delusion, and the other with dark depressions that came on suddenly and seemed to alter her whole mood. She would stay in her room, neglect her household tasks and Arthur would be taken up to the castle until his mother was well enough to look after him again. Stella, who had moved back to the lodge to try and help Addie, now wanted to return to the castle.

Peg had spent some time trying to pacify once again her two sisters and get them to forget their grievances and make up. But she knew it was becoming more and more difficult and she worried about both their futures. They did, indeed, love each other but they grated too and these spats were all too frequent.

One day, possibly quite soon in Peg's opinion, Stella probably would return to the castle and Jenny would have to take on more of the work of helping her mother care for her baby half-brother and, of course, Frank, who was actually very good for Addie and able to cope with her moods.

For Peg her singular good fortune seemed all the more incredible, indeed almost unreal. Of the four sisters she was the only one who had a really happy and fulfilled life. Verity could almost come into that category, now. She was contented, she was stable and had just bought a house. She loved her work.

But Peg also knew that Verity would dearly like to have been married and had children of her own, and to the extent that she had not yet achieved this one could perhaps say that she was not really happy.

Peg stopped for a moment and looked up at the castle which was her home. How fortunate she was. Inside was a loving husband, three beautiful children and everything she could possibly want. She was, indeed, blessed. But as she walked on in the bright winter sunshine she felt a little flicker of apprehension at the prospect of seeing Alan again. A man she thought she had left behind forever was to re-enter her life, possibly to disturb her equilibrium, like a ghost from the past.

And there it was at last – the letter! Just as she had known one day it would be, lying on the kitchen table where Frank had left it for her when he went out to work. She had always known he would write, Stella thought, with a glow of contentment, as she picked the letter up and held it in her hand.

It had just been a matter of time.

She slowly sat down at the kitchen table and stared at the envelope, not daring to open it, the sense of anticipation was too intense.

> Miss Stella Hallam
> The Lodge
> Ryland Castle
> Norton Parva
> Dorset

The address was in his rather faint, spidery writing, not the sort of firm, bold, decisive hand you'd expect from someone as strong as Ernest.

It was also rather thin. She shook the envelope between her fingers. Was this a good sign or a bad one? She would have preferred – after all this time, expected – an outpouring of his love which would go on for pages, telling her how much he regretted what had happened and so on. But maybe its brevity was to explain how much he missed her and longed to see her? Or, Stella tore frantically at the envelope, perhaps it was to announce a visit.

It was a single sheet and at the bottom was his signature, a full signature that looked rather formal. The words suddenly blurred on the page.

Stella felt a little faint and steadied herself with her hand against the kitchen table. Then she began to read.

Ed walked down the hill from the castle, hands in his pockets. As he approached the lodge he stood for some time looking at it, its air of quiet tranquillity, smoke rising from the chimney, one of the cats sitting on the lawn washing itself.

It was difficult to contrast this peace with the turmoil he knew was going on in the hearts and minds of those living inside. Yet once that had been so peaceful too, or so it had seemed to the young boy, though there were undercurrents of discord between his mother and father which he only began to understand when he was much older.

He had not been born there, as Stella had, but he'd been very small when his father came to work for Lord Ryland as head gardener.

It seemed odd to think now that he was staying as a welcome guest in the castle instead of sleeping in the lodge which had been his home for most of his life.

As Ed was approaching the cottage, the kitchen door opened and Addie appeared on the threshold with Arthur holding her hand, both dressed as if for an outing. Ed hurried towards her and threw his arms around her and for a long time they hugged each other. Then he stopped to give his attention to Arthur, who regarded him gravely, even backing away a little.

'This is your Uncle Ed,' Addie said gently, pushing him slightly forward, 'give him a kiss, Arthur.' But Arthur stubbornly shook his head and hung back. 'He's shy really,' Addie said apologetically, as Arthur tried to hide his face in her coat.

'I heard you came late last night.' She looked back at her brother. 'Where's Maisie?'

'Still in bed,' Ed confessed. 'She's never liked getting up very early in the morning. It's a habit because of the hours she used to work in the clubs. She never went to bed until dawn. Now she can't sleep unless it's well after midnight.'

'You won't like that' Addie said, smiling. 'You were always an early riser.'

'Still am. I try when I can to get the early watch at sea. Are you off somewhere?'

'Just going to see my friend in the village. We won't be long but she has a little boy too and he and Arthur like to play together. Her husband ran off with another woman, so we're company for each other.' Addie grimaced. 'I suppose you came to see Stella?'

'And you,' Ed insisted. 'How *is* Stella?'

Addie impulsively put a hand on his arm. 'She's had some rather bad news. I'll let her tell you herself. I'm sure you'll be able to cheer her up. Now we really must go or my friend will wonder where I am. I'll see you when I get back.'

'Perhaps,' Ed said with a farewell wave and watched her as she clasped Arthur firmly by the hand and set off down the path towards the main gates. Addie obviously valued the friendship of a woman whose situation was similiar to hers although, as far as was known, Gilbert had not left her for another woman. He had simply disappeared and there was still no news as to his whereabouts.

With a sigh, and wondering what the bad news that Stella had had was about, Ed gingerly pushed open the back door and peered in. Stella was sitting by the fire and at first didn't seem to hear him until he gently shut the door and coughed discreetly.

'Oh *Ed*!' she cried, raising her head sharply, 'you startled me.'

She got awkwardly to her feet and held up her face to be kissed. Ed thought she looked very pale, not well at all.

'How's the leg?' he asked sympathetically, taking a seat

beside her as she sat down, noticing the stick by the side of her chair.

'I can hop about indoors. I always need the stick when I go out.' Stella firmly pursed her lips. 'One day I'm going to manage without it, only . . .' she paused and gave a great gulp, 'only it doesn't matter much now.'

'What do you mean, it doesn't matter?' Ed glanced curiously across at the letter which lay on the table in front of her.

'Ernest is going to marry someone else.' Stella's hand fluttered towards the letter and then fell limply to her side. 'He doesn't love me and never has.' And she lowered her head while her body shook with silent sobs.

'May I look?' Ed said and when she nodded he pulled the letter towards him and read it.

> Dear Stella,
>
> This is a very difficult letter for me to write because I know you still feel a great deal of affection for me, as I do for you. Believe me, please.
>
> However, I have also come to the conclusion that our engagement was a mistake. I have fallen in love with another woman and asked her to marry me, which she has agreed to do.
>
> This has nothing to do with your illness, but I think reflects misgivings I had before.
>
> I know this will probably upset you, Stella, but I hope we can remain friends because I truly do have a high regard for you and wish you well.
>
> Yours sincerely
> Ernest Pilkington.

Reading it, Ed's heart filled with rage and he felt like screwing it into a ball and hurling it into the fire. Instead he put it back on the table and when he looked up Stella was regarding him with a tear-stained face.

'It's all over,' she whispered, 'isn't it?'

'It seems like it.' Ed still felt angry. 'Just as well, perhaps, that you found out now what sort of person he really is.'

'Signing himself as if I didn't know his name. Did he think I was going to ask: "Ernest? Ernest who?"' Her tone was scathing.

'Well ' Ed reached for her hand and rubbed it because it was so cold – 'he's not worth another thought.'

'But I loved him.'

'I know you did.'

Ed wanted to hold his sister in his arms and comfort her, but her still, quiet form was also somehow forbidding as if surrounded by an invisible fence.

'I thought he loved me.'

'I'm sure he did. He is just a rather fickle person and you must try and forget him.' Ed stopped suddenly as though an idea had occurred to him, and he leaned forward earnestly, studying her face. 'Stella, you know that as Ernest formally engaged himself to marry you, and as you have not released him from that engagement, you could sue him for breach of promise?'

Stella still staring ahead as if in a state of shock, refocussed her eyes on on her brother.

'What does that mean?'

'Well you can take him to court.'

'*Me* take Ernest to court? Never. Besides if he really does love someone else what good would it do? The court couldn't make him love me, could it?' She seemed at that moment almost childlike in her simplicity.

'It might help to relieve your feelings. It's just a suggestion. It would show everyone what a cad he was.'

'But would it make him *love* me, Ed? That's the point, isn't it?'

Ed hung his head. 'I don't know. I am truly sorry, Stella. I truly, truly am. I would do anything I could, anything in my power to help you forget him.'

*   *   *

Stella didn't know how long she'd sat there staring into the dying embers of the fire when the door opened once again and this time it was Addie and Arthur, both with faces pinched with cold.

'Whatever are you doing sitting there?' Addie cried, looking at the kitchen range. 'The fire's nearly out. You must be frozen.' She went over to her sister and gazed at her with concern. 'Stella, are you all right?'

Stella shook herself. 'Yes, I'm all right,' she assured her. 'I was just thinking.'

Addie sat Arthur on a chair and began to remove his top clothes. Then she gave him a biscuit and a cup of milk and put him in his pen before moving her own things and placing some logs on the fire.

'It's freezing in here,' she murmured, rubbing her hands together. 'Shall I make us a nice cup of tea?'

'If you like.'

Addie brewed the tea and made two strong cups, one of which she passed to Stella.

'When did Ed go?'

Stella shook herself. 'I don't know. Hours ago, I think. I told him about Ernest.'

'Of course.' Addie looked up and paused when she saw Stella's expression. It seemed to her curiously vacant, as though somehow a light had gone out somewhere inside her sister. 'What did he say?'

'He said that I should sue Ernest because he has broken his promise to marry me.'

'Oh!' Addie said, not knowing what else to say.

'I asked him if it would make Ernest love me.' Head on one side, Stella looked questioningly at Addie. 'Well, would it?'

Addie shook her head. 'I wouldn't have thought so.'

'Well, I don't think so either. So I shan't. I told Ed I wouldn't.'

'Did he agree?'

'He said it's up to me but I think he's very angry with Ernest.'

'And you . . .'

'*I'm* not angry,' Stella said after seeming to consider the question for ages. 'Frankly I don't know how I feel. I've been writing to Ernest without telling any of you. I thought you'd think I was silly and I was. Very silly. He never replied. Well, that was an answer in itself, wasn't it?'

Addie got up and went round to the back of Stella's chair, putting her hands on both her shoulders and gently massaging them.

'Would you sue Gilbert if you could? Get money from him for Arthur's upkeep, that sort of thing?'

'No,' Addie said firmly

'Then neither will I sue Ernest.'

'These men make silly fools of us, don't they?' Addie said, renewing the comforting firm pressure of her hands. 'You know it's funny that of us all Peg was the only real feminist in the family, whereas all we wanted was a stable marriage and to be happy. Now Peg has the husband and happy home, and we . . .'

'We've got each other,' Stella said, her voice suddenly stronger, clasping her sister firmly by the hand. 'We've got Jenny and we've got Arthur. Why, we've even got dear old Frank – a man all to ourselves who we can share.'

And for some reason they both dissolved into helpless laughter.

Fourteen

P eg almost didn't recognize Alan as he came up the steps
after Violet. He had filled out, he even looked suave with
his hair sleeked back instead of hanging limply over his forehead. He had heavy black-framed spectacles, instead of the
thin, wiry tortoiseshell ones he used to wear, which made him
look important. He wore a dark grey overcoat over a double-
breasted grey striped suit and carried a dark grey felt trilby.
Yes, he'd changed.

Yet after she'd kissed Violet on the cheek, when Peg turned to
him she thought he looked apprehensive. 'How nice to see you,'
she said in what she felt was a high, rather artificial tone of voice.

'And you.' His was rather quiet, normal.

They didn't kiss but shook hands.

'You remember Hubert, don't you?' Peg said, turning to her
husband.

'Yes, we did meet.'

'A long time ago.' Hubert and Alan shook hands without
much warmth.

Silence fell, then everyone spoke at once.

'Did you have a good journey?'

'It's nice to be home.'

'Yes, thank you.'

'Isn't the weather foul?'

'How was it in Rome?'

'Has Mother arrived?'

'We've given you your old room, Violet,' Peg said when
silence abruptly fell again. 'We thought you'd like that.'

'And Alan?' Violet raised her eyebrow.

'Next door. Amy will show you both up.'

Peg turned to Amy, who had been standing deferentially in the background.

'This is Amy, our new housekeeper.'

'D'yer do, ma'am, sir.' Amy managed to include them both in her awkward bob.

Alan made as if to shake her hand but stopped when he saw Violet's frown.

'We've lots of luggage in the car,' Violet said imperiously.

'I'll get one of the men to see to that.' Hubert smiled at her reassuringly.

'Well then, we'll see you later in the drawing room –' Peg stood back – 'for drinks before dinner. At about seven thirty. Is that all right, Violet?'

'Sounds perfect to me,' Violet said. 'To you too, darling?' She turned to Alan, who was looking extremely uncomfortable.

'I'll go with anything anyone says,' he mumbled and Peg thought he avoided her eyes as he trooped after Amy and Violet up the stairs.

Dear Alan, she thought, just as diffident, just as shy, just the same after all.

Dinner that night was a glittering occasion, the men in black ties, the ladies in long dresses, all except Addie and Stella who didn't have long dresses and made do with their Sunday best. The family plate and silver was on show, gleaming amidst the glittering tall wax candles. Mrs Capstick, despite all the other preparations she had to make for the christening, had excelled herself and the wines were of the finest vintages, laid down for many years by Hubert's father.

Looking at Peg across the table, Alan thought she was even more beautiful than he had remembered. She had blossomed, matured, put on a little weight but not too much. Above all, she seemed to possess a certain serenity she certainly had not had before.

It was quite an extraordinary transformation.

She was no longer his Peg, no longer feisty and impulsive. He remembered what good times they had had in those early years in London: political meetings, concerts at the Queen's Hall, visiting art galleries, seeing the latest film, discovering new restaurants, walking in Regent's Park or listening to the band there. Sometimes even walking all the way back to Hampstead.

Success had come to her quite early but she was, he was sure, unaffected by it, and remained so now despite being the chatelaine of the castle, a peeress of the realm.

Peg had been careful not to put Alan next to her. Instead there was Uncle Charles, her late father-in-law's brother, who had come over from Wiltshire with his wife, Clarissa, who now sat next to Alan. Uncle Charles said very little but Aunt Clarissa never stopped talking and Alan was giving her all his attention, though from time to time she saw him looking at her.

On her other side was the vicar who would christen Catherine and who was new since she had lived at the lodge. So he had no hang-ups or prejudices about the change in the circumstances of her or members of her family.

All in all there were fifteen people round the table including Lady Ryland, home from Italy. She sat on the other side of Alan and would occasionally converse across him in a loud voice with Aunt Clarissa, who was a little hard of hearing. Hubert had the vicar's wife on one side and Verity on the other. Verity and the vicar's wife knew each other well and from time to time exchanged remarks across the table.

Ed sat next to Verity, and Violet on the other side of the vicar almost opposite Alan, so she was able to keep her eye on him. From time to time they exchanged smiles though she did notice the surreptitious glances he kept on giving to Peg, who did, in fact, look rather fabulous in black velvet which set off her golden hair. It made her feel a little jealous.

Violet Ryland was a bored and rather lonely woman who had tried to fill her empty life with travel. It was true she had never really recovered from the death of her fiancé. Or was that because she had clung to his memory because there had been so little else in her life?

She had been very attached to her home and missed her father. She knew she was snobbish, and much as she liked Peg didn't really think she was a suitable wife for her brother, so she had kept away deliberately, as Peg had suspected.

By choice neither would she have selected Peg's ex-fiancé for a lover, but she didn't have much option. She was thirty-six and there were so few eligible men around. She liked clever, intelligent men and Alan was both. Furthermore he was a loose cannon like herself.

Alan might not have been ideal, but he was better than nothing. She decided, however, that bringing him to Ryland had been a bad idea and she would not do it again.

Violet, also in black but in grosgrain from a French couture house, knew she looked good too, but Peg was nearly ten years younger.

Maisie wore clinging green lamé, which accentuated her almost perfect figure; but she was no rival.

Verity also wore a long dress, but a sensible number in blue taffeta which she kept for hospital gala occasions. She was greatly enjoying herself, delighted to be home and to see Ed and meet Maisie at last. Her arrival at the lodge had been so late that there was no chance for a talk with her sisters as they hurried to get themselves ready for dinner and squeeze Frank into his dinner-jacket.

Stella, however, to her surprise seemed happy and relaxed. She was chatty and gay and not the brooding, unhappy woman Verity had feared and expected to find.

Addie too looked cheerful. She had an excited Jenny next to her once more wearing her treasured Confirmation dress. If Addie had a bad memory of the last dinner here with Gilbert she didn't show it.

Verity thought about her house, the new bathroom installed, the decorations now well under way – the prospect of all her family with their children soon to be gathering there as she had planned was a source of much pleasure. So Verity too sparkled on that happy evening when, for once, all her family were together under the same roof.

Verity had always liked Alan and had talked with him over drinks before dinner. She was still not quite convinced that, excellent husband though Hubert was and happy though she seemed to be, Peg might not have been better off, and ultimately more settled, with Alan, with whom she had so much in common. How much really would a clever, accomplished woman such as her sister settle for evermore to domesticity and a dull, conventional rural life? Even though she had been brought up in the country, London had been where she'd found her métier, her spiritual home with all its excitements and attractions, its risks and the opportunities it offered for adventure.

Verity's attention then turned to Maisie, who seemed to be thrilling, and perhaps shocking a little, the vicar with her account of night life in London. Verity felt she had to admire honest and outspoken Maisie, who never pretended to be anything she wasn't. She had taken her to her heart, and knew that Mum would have too.

An old established ritual dictated the ladies withdrew before the men, who joined them later in the drawing room, where coffee was served and where the carpet had been rolled back in case anyone wanted to dance. They did. The gramophone in the corner was vigorously being wound up by Ed, who then seized Maisie, already impatiently tapping her heels on the floor.

Peg, pouring coffee, turned to find Alan at her elbow and handed him a cup.

'Thank you,' he said. 'I was just thinking at dinner how well you looked.'

Peg took her own cup and they moved to a sofa which was a safe distance from the dancing. After all, they were old friends and had scarcely had the chance to talk. Violet seemed quite happy dancing with Uncle Charles, scarcely with a glance in their direction. The tiny bit of floor was quite full. Lady Ryland was dancing with her son, and Frank and Jenny stumbled about on each other's feet.

'You look well too. And different.'

'How different?'

Peg laughed. 'Oh Alan. Of *course* you look different. Your hair used to be all over the place. Your glasses . . . I can't begin to tell you how different. You must know.'

Alan reached in his breast pocket for a narrow leather case that contained two cigars and selected one.

'You don't mind, do you?'

'Of course not. You didn't used to smoke cigars either.'

'Oh, that's an acquired taste.' He took out a lighter and began to put a flame to his cigar. 'I was just,' he said between puffs, 'I was just thinking of the dinners we used to attend at Oliver's. Somehow tonight reminds me of them. It was very splendid.' His cigar drawing, he put his lighter away and looked closely at her.

'I can't quite get used to you in this situation.'

'Have *I* changed?'

'A bit. Well, a lot really.' He gazed at her defiantly. 'If you really want the truth I thought you looked more beautiful than ever.'

She saw that he spoke emotionally and felt confused. She tapped his arm lightly.

'How is Oliver?'

'Oh, he's very well. He's offered me the job of Assistant Editor.'

'Congratulations. Will you take it?'

'I don't know. It's a big honour, a big promotion but I don't know that I want to live in England again. I like the Continent, and a lot is happening over there. You'd be so interested, Peg.'

'And what about Violet?' she enquired, ignoring the rest of his remark.

'I haven't asked her. I'm not really in her league, am I, Peg?'

'Any more than I was, you mean?'

'I didn't say that. I think you've fitted in extremely well. Watching you tonight, I would have thought you were born to the role. I'm the one who doesn't fit in. Incidentally Oliver misses you too. He says any time you want a job you have only to ask.'

Peg looked surprised. 'Really? Has he forgiven me?'

'Oh, he forgave you, of course he did. We all forgive you, Peg. Even I forgive you.'

Alan lay in bed looking at the tops of the trees in the park outlined against the sky by the full moon.

He felt very emotional, melancholy, and knew he shouldn't have come. He knew now that he didn't want to live in England, anywhere near where he might risk seeing Peg, and that he would not accept the assistant editorship.

At that moment there was a click as the door opened. A beam of light shone in and disappeared again as the door was gently closed. Violet glided towards his bed and, dropping her nightie on the floor, climbed in.

'All right, darling?'

'Fine,' Alan answered, aware of her naked flesh beside him, but somehow repulsed by it.

'What a boring evening, didn't you think?'

'I rather enjoyed it.'

'You mean enjoyed seeing *Peg* again,' she said accusingly.

'No, not at all. All that was over between us years ago.'

'I'm glad.' Violet cuddled up to him and slid her hand under his pyjama top. 'My God, what a common woman Maisie is! All that fake jewellery. A night-club dancer at Ryland. I ask you. I wonder what my mother thought. Father would have *died*.'

'I rather liked her,' Alan said stiffly. 'Maybe because I'm common like her.'

'Nonsense, darling, you're not common.' Violet ran her fingers lightly across his chest. 'Certainly not. You're an intellectual. I could never love anyone who was common.'

Love. Alan looked fearfully into the dark. How could anyone possibly love Violet, or even consider making love to her with Peg sleeping under the same roof?

'I baptize thee Catherine Margaret in the name of the Father and of the Son and of the Holy Ghost.'

Verity gently lowered the baby in her arms towards the font as the vicar poured the baptismal water over her head. Violet leaned forward, dabbing her with a beautiful lace handkerchief to prevent it running into her eyes. Catherine seemed delighted with the proceedings, wetness and all, smiling round cherubically as her name was given, just as a beam of sunlight burst through the window on to her shining head.

The vicar prayed over the baby and then over the congregation, who had come from all parts of the estate.

The organ crashed out as the ceremony ended and everyone poured out into the sunshine, pausing at the door of the church for photographs taken by Mr Flood of Sherborne, who, with his old-fashioned camera, had recorded the major happenings in the Ryland family for more years than most people could remember.

It was a tremendously happy day for Hubert because the past year had been a mixture of sadness and joy; sadness at the death of his father, even though they had become estranged, happiness because so far his return home had been a success and he was now the father of a beautiful daughter.

It had not been easy for Hubert modernizing the estate, adapting to new circumstances, getting rid of old-fashioned habits and antiquated procedures. However, he never for a moment regretted his marriage to Peg, who had brought him more joy, stability and fulfilment than he could ever have imagined, certainly during all those sterile years with Ida.

Hugging his newly christened daughter, Peg beside him carrying Caspar, and Nelly bringing up the rear with Jude, he led the way back to the castle for the feast that had been prepared, the celebrations that had only just begun.

Addie and Jenny went ahead with Verity, Alan with Violet, who tucked a proprietorial arm through his. Frank escorted Maisie, while towards the end Ed, with Stella on his arm, walked slowly, carefully because she had left her stick behind.

'What a lovely day,' she said to Ed. 'How happy everyone was. I thought Maisie looked *so* beautiful. The next ceremony at the church will be your wedding.'

'I hope so,' Ed said guardedly.

'What do you mean you "hope". It's all fixed, isn't it? I mean there is no doubt, is there?'

Ed hurried to allay her anxiety. 'Oh no. I mean I hope I don't get sent to sea and we have to do it quickly in a register office.'

'Oh, that would be awful – Maisie will make such a lovely bride.'

It was so generous of her, someone who had hoped to be a bride herself. Ed looked at his sister gratefully. 'And what about you? Did you enjoy the ceremony?'

'I thought it was *lovely*. Everything has just been so good. You know –' she tucked her arm more tightly through his – 'I'm glad you told me what you did. You know what I mean, about Ernest. It helped clear up a lot of things for me. Thank you for it, Ed.'

He stooped and kissed her forehead.

'I'm glad it's all right and that you're happy. You know one of these days I'll be here giving you away to the right man too. I'm convinced of it.'

Stella looked less convinced, but she had shaken her arm away from Ed and stood tugging at her finger. 'There's something I want to do,' she told him. 'Can we just go down to the water's edge for a few minutes?'

'If you like.' Looking surprised, Ed turned towards the lake and slowly they walked down while the last people from the church, the stragglers and those who had paused to light cigarettes, went on ahead.

A gentle breeze ruffled the smooth surface of the lake and a couple of mallards swam towards them, perhaps in the optimistic expectation that it was supper time.

Letting go of Ed's arm, Stella gave a final tug and, wrenching the ring off her finger, held it high above the water so that, momentarily, it gleamed golden in the sunlight and they both seemed mesmerized by it. It had, after all, a diamond in the middle and had cost Ernest quite a wad of his bank clerk's salary. Then Stella threw it as far out as she could and watched the splash it made on the water as it sank beneath its depths.

'Well, that's gone,' she said cheerfully, turning to Ed. 'And good riddance.'

'Well done,' he said, gently tucking her hand in his. 'Well done indeed.'

And then they turned their backs on the lake, with its new found treasure, and joined the tail of the procession wending its way slowly up the hill.

The christening had been at three and the party went on until nearly midnight. However, it was very different from the celebrations following such important family occasions in the past. The estate workers, of course, had always been welcome, part of the festivities. But they had been housed in a separate part of the building and given different food from the family guests upstairs in the great white and gold drawing room. It had been like that for generations, possibly hundreds of years. Now to celebrate the christening of Catherine Margaret there was no separation by social class as there had been after the funeral of her grandfather. Everyone mingled; there was no more upstairs downstairs, or at least not officially. It was nevertheless true that people still did tend to forgather in groups who were familiar with one another.

A new spirit had permeated the castle since the arrival of Hubert and Peg. The change, it must be said, was probably due more to Peg than her husband, who would undoubtedly have continued in the old tradition just because it was the old tradition, and certainly his mother and sister would have preferred it that way.

That the era of lord and lady, master and servant was over was typified by the way Peg kept on disappearing from entertaining her guests to assist the staff, even to the extent of helping to carry plates containing mountains of food from the kitchen to the long tables set out in the hall.

There were, however, those among the estate workers of the older generation who deplored this state of affairs, this abandonment of an old way of life based on those who ordered and those who served. Habitual cap-doffers and curtsiers, they found it hard to abandon the manner in which they had been brought up, and therefore impossible to mingle freely with people with clipped vowels, whose usual habitats were the salons or drawing rooms of Mayfair and Belgravia or large country houses like Ryland Castle set in vast estates.

But it would change, it had changed and, Peg knew, for the better.

She was hurrying across the room, preoccupied with a hold-up in the supplies from the kitchen, when her way was blocked by a man with a kindly twinkle in his eye.

'Admiral Mountjoy!' she exclaimed, clasping his extended hand.

'Do you remember me?' he enquired, looking gratified.

'Of course I remember you.' Peg lowered her voice.' At the time you seemed my only friend.'

'You have introduced so many changes so quickly, I see,' he said, looking around.

'Does it upset you, Admiral?'

'Not at all. I think it's an excellent idea to mix people up. It is done on the hunting field. People don't realize how democratic the hunting fraternity is. This is the future, you know.'

'Thank you, Admiral.' Peg leaned forward, lightly kissed his cheek and as she sped off, he watched her with an admiring but slightly regretful look in his eyes, as if wishing that he too were her age and could somehow turn back the clock.

In the kitchen Verity and Addie were also helping to take
sausage rolls from the oven and put them on silver trays held by
perspiring waiters. Frank was in a corner uncorking bottles, a
full glass by his side as such activity was thirsty work. Jenny ran
back and forth, clearly excited, torn between the desire to help
or chat to her young friends, who had come with their parents,
many on their first visit to the castle. The little Ryland boys
played with other children in the upstairs nursery, supervised by
their nursemaid, and baby Catherine lay in her crib, surrounded
by admirers until she, who had been so good all day, began to
cry and it was time to put her to bed.

'Going well.' Verity, red faced from the heat of the oven,
looked at Peg.

'Admiral Mountjoy said he liked to see people mixing. I
think he meant it.'

'Everyone seems very happy. Oh,' Verity gasped, dropping a
hot sausage roll and shaking her fingers. 'Hot.'

'That's what they're meant to be,' Mrs Capstick said briskly.
'Now, Peg, you should not be here but looking after your
guests.' She made a shooing gesture with her arms. 'Off you go.
Else your mother-in-law won't be too pleased.'

It was true that the elder Lady Ryland had rather kept her
distance. She would not have dreamt of going to the ballroom,
let alone the kitchen, but remained upstairs with a coterie of her
London and county friends. Violet, too, preferred not to mingle
but remained smoking and drinking with her own set, who she
had known all her life, Alan apparently not with her.

Peg held out a hand. 'Let me take something.'

'You can take these sausage rolls, then. Sandy –' Mrs Capstick, also perspiring, spoke to an undergardener who was
doubling up as a waiter and holding out a silver tray – 'give
these to her ladyship and then go and fetch another tray.'

Peg grinned ruefully at Verity. Her ladyship. It was a hard
tradition for someone like Mrs Capstick to break.

Peg carried her laden tray along to the hall where the
servants' parties had always been held and she supposed they

would continue, though the family would be there from the start rather than arrive in a rather grand way to dispense largesse and make patronizing speeches – though it must be said that at the time she had not regarded them in this way. She too had felt deeply honoured to be singled out by Lord or Lady Ryland. There had been a lot in the tradition at Ryland that was good. There would always be workers on the estate and those who paid their wages and looked after them, but the mystique of the noble family as people apart would, she was sure, vanish with time.

In the crowded hall, where many of the estate workers had indeed forgathered by force of habit, she was surprised to see a lone figure standing by the partly opened window, looking out across the lawn, a cigarette between his fingers.

'Alan,' she said softly, 'are you all right?'

'Peg.' Taken by surprise, Alan turned. 'Sorry I was miles away.'

'No Violet?'

Alan looked irritated, 'Oh, Violet, is busy with her pals. I don't know any of them. Anyway I was just thinking . . . well . . .' he lowered his head,' I was thinking about you.'

'Oh, I see.' Peg felt lost for words.

'They were good days, weren't they, Peg?'

Peg looked puzzled.

'The agency. Red Lion Square. Remember?'

'Oh, yes.' She laughed, a little embarrassed. 'I see what you mean. When I was converted to Socialism.'

He looked at her gravely. 'Are you still a Socialist?'

'Of course I am.'

'Even though you're married to a lord?'

'I'm married to a man,' Peg said defensively, 'one who happens to have inherited a title he didn't want.'

'He could have given it up.'

'He couldn't.' Peg's tone became cold. 'He felt he had a duty and was carrying it out. But we've moved on, Alan. Times have changed. I've changed things here, but Violet may not approve.'

Alan nodded. 'I don't think she likes mixing too closely with the common people.' He added in a voice close to despair: 'I don't quite know what to do about Violet. I think I wanted to get near you.' Peg looked into his eyes and knew that for Alan times hadn't changed. That for him the Red Lion Square days were a most important part of his life.

'Maybe you shouldn't come again.' Peg felt a curious mixture of pity and anger. 'Maybe it's best to stay away.'

'Do you really feel that?'

Peg nodded. 'I think it's best all round. Yes.'

'I see.' Alan threw his cigarette out of the window and walked away, leaving Peg to try and cope with a mass of tangled and confused emotions.

'Are you all right?' Hubert, appearing as if from nowhere so that she didn't know how much of the conversation he'd heard, asked, looking at her with concern. 'Did Alan upset you?'

Peg shook her head. 'Not really, though I do wish he hadn't come. I think he upset himself, not me.'

'I think he still has a crush on you,' Hubert said, taking her hand.

'Perhaps. Let's forget it.' Peg shook her head as if wanting to rid herself of the memory. 'Are the children OK?'

'They're fine. I just went up to look.'

'Is your mother all right?'

'She's fine. Perhaps a little too much champagne . . .'

Hand in hand Peg and Hubert walked slowly through the crowd, stopping every now and then to chat to their guests. Soon the tables were pulled back against the walls and the floor cleared for dancing to a small band – a pianist, a cellist and a fiddler – who had been playing soft music in the background.

When they heard the change in music tempo people from upstairs began to drift down and soon everyone, following Hubert and Peg's example, started dancing and the floor was crowded. Among the dancers was Violet, who paused briefly to say that poor Alan had gone to bed with a headache, before stepping out with one of her contemporaries, perhaps one of those 'pals' who Alan did not know.

Nicola Thorne

Maisie, who had partners queuing up to dance with her, was a sensation with her flying blonde hair and flamenco-style dress, and several times the general dancing stopped for the revellers to admire her skill with a partner almost as talented as she was. This was not Ed, who performed numerous dances with relatives who would otherwise have been wallflowers. Among these was Stella but she didn't seem to mind because it was known she couldn't dance.

It had once been her passion and, watching the dancers, she had to control a moment of melancholy reflection until she reminded herself of the ring lying in the bottom of the lake and knew that that part of her life was over. Indeed she appeared almost happy sitting among old friends, men and women, people she'd been at school with, people she'd known all her life. Like Ed, Verity had the usual duty dances with elderly relations and then sat talking to their wives. After she and Hubert split, Peg danced with Admiral Mountjoy, with Frank, one or two cousins and several times with Ed. She disappeared for a long while in the middle of the evening to be sure the boys were safely tucked up in bed and to feed the baby, a precious half hour taken from a day that seemed one of non-stop activity. She returned to the ballroom in time for the last waltz with Hubert who folded her in his arms and nuzzled her hair as they danced very close.

The waltz finished, the lights which had been lowered were switched full on, there was a sudden air of bustle and activity as the tired helpers started to clear away the remnants of food: soggy sandwiches, bits of sausage rolls and crumbs of christening cake plus a mountain of bottles and empty or half-filled glasses.

It was nearly midnight and many people had already slipped away. Some of those who were staying in the castle congregated in the hall, finishing their drinks, smoking the last cigarette. Addie, Stella, Verity and a very tired Jenny put on their coats, said their goodnights and walked down the steps with Frank and the remaining stragglers. It was a bitterly cold night and it

214

had started to freeze. The myriad of tiny multi-coloured crystals twinkled in the light of the fluorescent moon, and the sky was full of stars.

After he had locked the great front door, Hubert went round turning out the lights and then he and Peg followed their guests up the stairs to bed just as the clock in the church below, where Catherine had been christened, struck one.

It has been a very long, very happy day.

Despite her tiredness, Peg couldn't sleep. Getting carefully out of bed so as not to disturb her sleeping husband, she put on her gown and crept along the corridor to the nursery and quietly opened the door.

Exhausted by the events of the day, Jude and Caspar lay fast asleep, their angelic faces illuminated by the light of that same full moon that had guided the departing guests home. For a long time Peg sat by their beds marvelling at their beauty, their sweet air of innocence. One day it would not be so; they would grow up and their lives would change in ways that could not be foretold. They would become men. Then she bent and kissed each one. Jude murmured, and for a moment she was afraid she'd woken him, and held her breath.

At last he grew quiet and she tip-toed across the room and opened a communicating door where Catherine slept in her cot next to Nelly's bed. Lying on her back, her tiny arms flung up on her pillow, the newly baptized infant was similarly asleep, but Peg didn't dare kiss her in case she woke her and in turn woke Nelly.

It seemed now as if not only the household but the whole earth slept while she, Peg, remained awake, but then came the hoot of an owl from the copse and she knew she was not alone. Peg returned to the boys' room and tip-toed over to the window to gaze out on the peaceful scene: the land with its light covering of frost, the moon that shone on the waters of the lake from its hiding place behind the trees that surrounded her home, her nest with all the love and joy within it.

In that instant she felt that she and her precious family were safe; cherished and protected from the rigours of a world that could be harsh, unjust and sometimes cruel.

And for that she was so grateful.